OF BLOOD SO RED

FOREVER AFTER: CRIMSON SNOW
BOOK TWO

SIERRA ROWAN

MOUNTAIN TREE PRESS

© Copyright 2023 - Sierra Rowan
Published by Mountain Tree Press

All rights reserved, including the right to reproduce this text and any portions thereof in any manner whatsoever.

This book is a work of fiction. All characters, names, places and incidents appearing in this work are products of the author's imagination or are used fictitiously and are not to be construed as real. Any resemblance to actual events, organizations, or persons, living or dead, is purely coincidental.

Proofreading: Happy Ever Author

eBook ISBN: 978-1-955991-07-0
Paperback ISBN: 978-1-955991-14-8
Hardcover ISBN: 978-1-955991-20-9

First published in 2023
Urbana, IL, USA

v.0.4

AUTHOR'S NOTE

If you would like content guidance, please see the author's website at sierrarowan.com.

1
GWYNEIRA

I'd survived a fight with a vampire. I'd *become* one too. By some miracle, none of the seven men who had saved my life by letting me stay with them at their magical cabin had been killed in the battle against my stepmother nor died when she commanded me to destroy them.

And now I stood on a snowy cliff, faced with a woman I'd never met who was acting like she knew *any* of this would happen.

"What do you mean you've been *waiting* for me?" I demanded.

The gray-haired woman smiled. It was the expression of a cat. Or of an enigmatic painting that could have been conveying any emotion from satisfaction to humor to pity, depending on how you looked at it, and nothing in her regal bearing hinted at which it was. An enormous ruby hung on a thick platinum chain at her neck, and the fur-lined white robe she wore set off her olive skin. Behind her, the two robed figures who accompanied her remained silent, their hoods disguising their faces and their hands folded before them, motionless.

"Exactly what I said," she replied evenly.

And that was no help at all.

My eyes flashed over our surroundings, taking in details and searching for threats at the same time, just in case she was delaying us for a trap. After all, mere moments ago, this place had been awash with magic and monsters. My stepmother, Melisandre, had been ripped from this world by the very creatures she'd summoned to feast upon me—ghostly, eel-like creatures of the empty realms who had disappeared when she did, vanishing back into the void beyond reality that was their home. And yes, this woman and her companions had fought them with us.

But that didn't mean they were on our side.

The night was still but for the snow swirling down from the pitch-black sky, obscuring the mountaintops all around. Glowing blue-white lights hung above us like stars trapped in globes of glass, unsupported by any rope or string. A pathway stretched back behind the figures before me, extending into a fissure in the mountain's sheer side and continuing on beyond where I could see.

And on the stone platform on which I found myself, my seven giants stood behind me like a wall of protection, watching our surroundings every bit as carefully as I was.

Not that the men *looked* like giants. While most Erenlians had skin like stone and towered easily ten or fifteen feet high, these men appeared human. Tall, yes. Easily six and a half feet or more, all of them. But not nearly the same as every other Erenlian I'd ever seen.

And for that, their people called them dwarves—and I'd gathered that was the nicest of the terms.

The gray-haired woman's smile remained unchanged when my gaze returned to her, as if she'd expected nothing more than for me to be cautious. "Come," she said. "We have much to discuss."

I didn't budge. In the past, I may have been tempted to acquiesce and engage in the intricate dance of bargaining and concessions I'd been trained for as the Princess of Aneira. But that was before my father was killed. Before Melisandre accused me of his murder. Before I learned she'd conspired all my life to poison me with her blood—the blood of a vampire, not that I'd known what she was until recently—and to turn me so that she could sacrifice me to those creatures of the empty realms to whom she'd sworn her soul.

Only my giants feeding me their blood had saved me from being nothing more than a rabid beast and my stepmother's puppet.

So there was no way in hell I would comply without more information. "Answer my question. How could you have been waiting for me?"

A thrum carried through my voice, making the sound strange in my throat, as if the energy of my words reverberated through more than just my body. The figures on either side of the woman flinched back, while all around them, a shimmer of light ghosted across the air and then faded.

Alarm shivered through me, and I fought to give no sign. What the hell had that been?

The woman's brow twitched up, but she didn't look angry or concerned. "Very well. I am Leontine, Second Matron of the Jeweled Coven, witch of rubies." Her smile grew. "I am also your godmother. And *you* are truly the daughter of Eira, witch of diamonds."

I stared at her. "My..."

How could I have a godmother, let alone one among these people?

I shoved the shock down. I didn't know where to begin with what she'd said, but showing how much her words had thrown me was a vulnerability I didn't want to risk, not when she could be lying for all I knew.

Before I could speak, Leontine continued on as if my shock was irrelevant. "You will need that power of command to survive what's to come. But for the moment, please, join us inside. You may be untouched by the cold, but it will be more comfortable for your men and for us to continue this conversation where there is a fire to keep us warm."

My eyes twitched to the giants. Their coats were gone and their sleeves were pushed up to their elbows despite the bitter wind swirling around the mountain peak upon which we stood. Each man bore a wound on his forearm: a cut surrounded by a bite. The former was what they'd done to draw me back to them when I first woke as a vampire. The latter was my work to drink their blood. Though the injuries were crusted with dried blood, they had somehow already mostly sealed up. But the wounds still looked remarkably painful.

Guilt and gratitude twisted in me at the sight. A few weeks back, these men hadn't even known me, and yet they each had sacrificed to save my sanity and my soul.

"We've got this," Dex told me softly, his dark gaze dropping to mine briefly with an encouraging glint before returning to the figures ahead of us with a far more cautious air. The former soldier took nothing for granted when it came to security, that much I knew. He and the others had also spent more time with this woman and her companions than I had, considering I'd technically been dead for the journey here. "If they wanted to hurt us, they would have tried it before they helped bring you back."

Uncertainty flickered through me. "They helped with that?"

He nodded once, a controlled motion. As reserved as he was right now, he was still breathtaking. From his dark eyes to his firm jaw, his powerful muscles and strong bearing, everything about him was always commanding—both in public and in the bedroom. The wound across his forearm was a dark gash of dried blood against his light brown skin, but he paid it no mind, his attention on the others as if he'd already assessed every threat around us and knew exactly how to respond.

Now as always, his solid presence comforted me.

"Come on, Princess," Clay added. "You think any of these folks want to mess with you after how you got rid of that queen for them?" Forever the joker, he waggled his blond brows, his sky-blue eyes glittering with excitement for taking on whatever challenge lay down the path beyond the hooded figures.

At his side, his twin brother Lars was more reserved, but he still gave me a smile. "We're with you, Princess. And honestly—" He twitched his head toward the wound on his forearm. "—the blood was their idea. They knew it'd help you."

"It's true." Niko nodded as my brow climbed. Only slightly older than me, the brown-haired guy with olive skin and deep, dark eyes was the shyest of the group, forever hanging back and letting the others take the lead. There was a core of iron in him, though. I had no question of that, given

5

how he'd stood with the others while I attacked them one after the other—to say nothing of how he'd saved me from my stepmother's spells before that.

But it wouldn't have saved him from me, not when I'd first woken as a vampire and been overcome with my stepmother's commands to kill. The men each offering me their blood had not only brought me back to myself, but likely spared whichever of them I would have attacked first in my crazed hunger. Had they not each tempted me away with the prospect of tasting them all, I would have drained the first of them I bit.

I looked back at Leontine and her companions. "How did you know they should do that?"

The woman tilted her head toward the path behind her. "I'll be more than happy to explain, but inside where it's warm."

My mouth tightened, but after a moment, I nodded. Continuing to insist on staying here would only freeze the men I cared so much for.

At my agreement, Dex moved ahead of me to descend the platform steps, Byron immediately accompanying him. Byron's head moved as if on a swivel, his curly red hair like a fire against the stark mountainside, and I had no doubt he was cataloguing everything he saw for analysis later.

The silent Ozias fell in behind them both, striding past to take the lead the moment they reached the base of the steps. The towering, bearded man rarely spoke, but he moved like a force of nature and a predator rolled into one.

Of course, the intense light to his dark eyes and the vicious scar on his face helped with that impression, as did the massive axe strapped to his back. The weapon was carved with runes and bore a blade edged in magical ore. In his hands, I doubted anyone in its path could hope to survive. I had no idea where he'd acquired it, nor what his life had been like to turn him into such a formidable warrior.

But it was doubtful I'd ever have the chance to learn more. No matter how much he intrigued me, Ozias had never shown the slightest interest in speaking to me, let alone in anything else.

And he wasn't alone in that. My eyes slid to Roan, who followed at the very back of our group as if reluctant to come too close to me. With pale skin and dark hair that made him look like a ghost or eerie spirit all on his own, Roan would barely even *look* at me.

But when I'd woken as a vampire, both he and Ozias had joined the others in saving me. And when it came to Roan, his whispered words as I drank his blood still lingered, filling me with curiosity.

Not you too.

"This way, Princess." Leontine's voice cut into my thoughts when I reached the base of the steps, and her calm smile never wavered as she gestured for us to follow the hooded figures toward the path leading away from the cliffside.

Snow swirled around us as we walked, and each flake prickled strangely on my skin when it landed. It wasn't cold. Nothing in me felt the chill at all. For that matter, even my lungs were motionless in my chest, untouched by the cold bite of the wintry air.

I'd spoken as easily as ever, yet I had no breath, and that fact sent anxious bees spinning up in my stomach.

It wasn't just my lack of breathing that set my nerves on edge, though. To walk made me more aware of my body, and with that awareness came a sense of *change* that made the bees go mad inside me.

I didn't feel like *myself*. Not really. I felt half wild inside, as if something about me no longer fit in my own body. Every joint was more limber and yet *wrong*, every muscle quivering like lightning thrummed inside. As we walked along the path, sounds began to make themselves known too, ones I should have had no business hearing.

Heartbeats. Hundreds of them. Truly, now that I listened, everything was becoming louder. The whisper of fur and fabric pricked at my consciousness, coming from the men's clothes and the robes of the figures ahead of me alike. The rush of blood in the veins of everyone around me was like a confluence of rivers surrounding me on all sides.

We rounded the turn of the path, and my feet slowed in spite of myself. A village waited ahead, tucked into a flat clearing between the side of the mountain and a forest of dark evergreen trees. Light glowed from the windows of cottages covered in snow. More lights dangled like stars from the tall trees surrounding the homes, while children ran between them all, laughing. Adults stood on porches, watching the kids or chatting with one another, and smoke rose from chimneys, drifting on a breeze that was so much gentler away from the cliffs.

"This is the Jeweled Coven?" I asked.

Leontine nodded.

"So many of you survived." Byron sounded taken aback.

A hint of sadness touched the woman's smile. "Only compared to annihilation. We lost countless witches in the war. But no, we are not all gone." The sadness faded. "Thanks to her mother."

With a pointed nod to me, she continued walking down the trail.

I hesitated. My mother saved all these people?

And I, her daughter, her legacy... was a vampire. Fangs hung past my lips. Nothing of life showed in the bloodless pallor of my skin. I could hear every heartbeat ahead of me, and my body quivered with the strength—and the distant urge—to chase them all down.

My mother was a savior.

I was a monster.

A new feeling joined the tangle of shame and predatory impulses inside. A tingling yet dark feeling like pure night sparkling in my veins. Suddenly, even the quivering of my muscles felt like only the beginning of my abilities, given what I'd now become. I wasn't sure gravity itself would be able to hold me back from lunging at these people if I so chose. After all, I'd flown when my stepmother attacked— though admittedly I'd mostly been yanked into the sky by her power and then fallen the moment it was gone. But the other vampires who were with her, the ones she'd bitten and turned over the years, had flown and even shifted from shadows into human form and back.

Nothing would stop me if I tried to attack these villagers. Nothing at all.

A hand took mine. I glanced over in alarm.

Niko gave me a tiny, encouraging smile. "It's okay. We're with you."

And just like that, the panic drained.

A shudder rolled through me to feel it go. I nodded at him, clinging to his words like the lifeline they were.

But when we started into the village, the effect of our

presence was immediate. Adults paused their tasks and children stopped their games. Wide eyes locked on us.

On me most of all.

I made myself keep walking despite how I felt torn between drawing myself up to avoid appearing vulnerable and the fact I didn't want to scare small children by looking like a terrifying monster.

A little girl shrieked and bolted back toward her home as we came closer.

Perhaps the latter was impossible.

At the center of the village, the woman and her companions turned, heading for a cabin much larger than the cottages around us. The sloped roof rose to a sharp point at least two stories high, and a broad porch stretched across the front, elevated several feet above the ground and accessible only by a wide stairway. Formed of thick wood logs so straight and even barely a trace of mortar was visible between them, the place radiated warmth and solidity.

And magic.

My skin prickled, as if the air was sparking like flint against it. The urge to take to the sky returned, and I clenched my hands into fists to resist it. My eyes darted over the windows flanking the broad door of the cabin, but besides the golden glow of a fire inside, I couldn't see anything of the interior.

Leontine ascended the wide steps.

My alarm grew. The air around her was warping ever so slightly, as if she wasn't walking through open space but through a nearly invisible veil. Meanwhile, the two hooded figures who'd accompanied her took up positions on either side of the stairs, facing away from the cabin and out at the village, as if nothing about what was happening on the steps bothered them at all.

My men came to a halt before they reached the stairway. "Is this safe for her?" Byron called from the base of the steps, his head twitching back toward me though he didn't take his eyes from the woman on the porch.

Leontine smiled. "None may harm us or our guests in this space."

Clay and Lars started forward cautiously, but Byron held out a hand, stopping them. "And are we your guests?"

She chuckled. "Clever man. Yes, the seven of you and the princess are all our guests here."

He paused another moment as if weighing the words and then lowered his hand. With a short nod to the others, he started up the stairs. Nervousness thrummed in my chest where a heartbeat should have been as I followed him.

Leontine opened the door and continued inside, and my nervousness grew at the sight of the enormous room beyond. Robed figures were everywhere—seated in a circle at the center of the room, gathering herbs from the vases of dried plants, or tending a fireplace large enough to stand inside. The walls and floor were all wood, but despite the height of the flames in the fireplace, the light didn't seem to reach all the way into the cavernous ceiling, leaving thick shadows at its heights.

A tingling sensation surged over my skin when I stepped into the doorway.

I recoiled instantly, an involuntary hiss leaving me like a startled cat. The feeling lessened, but didn't vanish entirely, like the pressure of a blade just at the edge of breaking skin.

"What's wrong?" Dex demanded, stepping protectively between me and the door as if to keep me back from it.

"Vampire," Byron murmured.

I looked over at him in shock. "What do you mean?"

"You may enter, Princess," Leontine called.

As if blown away by a breeze, the sensation faded.

Trembling with residual adrenaline, I fought the sudden urge to snarl at her like an animal. She knew what this was.

And at my first chance, I'd be discussing it with Byron. I'd had enough surprises to last me a lifetime.

Eyeing the doorframe warily, I stepped past Dex.

No trace of the strange resistance I'd encountered remained.

As if on some silent command, the robed figures seated at the center of the room rose to their feet and turned to face us. The others stopped what they were doing, and at a motion from one of the people in the circle, they retreated as one toward the walls, taking up positions with their hands folded and their heads bowed.

I stopped, eyeing them as if waiting for the trap to spring.

"Welcome, Princess." I couldn't tell who spoke, but it sounded like a woman, her voice cracked and weathered with age. "Welcome..." She paused, and when she continued, I could hear a calculating smile in her voice. "Dwarves."

Only years of royal training kept my face from giving my surprise away. She knew the term the giants had once called these men?

None of the men around me reacted. They'd known that fact already, I'd wager. But what they thought of it, I couldn't hope to guess.

A figure at the far edge of the circle lifted her hands and lowered her hood. She was older than Leontine with dark skin wrinkled so deeply it was hard to tell what she must have looked like when she was young. Her curly gray hair hovered like a storm cloud atop her head, but nothing about her seemed whimsical or flighty. Rather, her bearing reminded me of iron and stone. Of things unbowed or changed by time. She seemed like the mountain itself. Like all of creation could shift around her, and it would change nothing. She would crush any who thought to test her, and in the end, only she would remain standing.

"Thank you, Leontine," the woman said.

With a bow of her head, Leontine stepped to the side as if clearing the path for the woman before us.

"Welcome to the home of the Jeweled Coven," the woman continued. "I am Rufinia, First Matron of the Jeweled Coven and witch of diamonds. It's good you all have come." She turned to me. "Now we must make sure you don't die."

2
GWYNEIRA

"What the hell do you mean, *die?*" Clay demanded immediately.

Rufinia smiled. Just as with the smile Leontine had first given me, there was nothing in the expression, like a painting that could have portrayed a thousand emotions or none. "You're the daughter of a witch," she said to me. "A witch of diamonds, no less. And now you're... this. Turned into a creature"—the giants around me made angry noises at the word, but she carried on, ignoring them—"by the traitor responsible for the war that nearly destroyed us all. What that will mean for you and for us is the question we now face. If you can hold onto your humanity, if you can resist the pull of Melisandre's dark magic inside you, perhaps you'll survive. But if you don't..."

The First Matron's implication sank over me like a leaden blanket, and though she didn't finish her sentence, I didn't need her to. "You'll kill me."

My own words should have scared me, and so should

the acknowledgement I saw on Rufinia's face. But then, my stepmother had wanted me dead too.

She'd succeeded.

And I was still here. Cold inside. Cold *outside* too. I'd spent my whole life not knowing that the woman who'd raised me—the woman who was the closest thing I'd ever had to a mother—wanted me dead and sacrificed to monsters from beyond reality itself. And the idea that Rufinia might want me dead too?

Gods, some part of me wanted to tell her to take her place in line.

Because I'd never be ruled by fear again.

"Tell us what she needs to survive and be done with it," Byron ordered, his voice harder than I'd heard from him. His face was likewise set as stone.

For a long moment, the witch regarded us, but I refused to react to the infinite calculations I could see running in her eyes. Gods rest his soul, my father had trained me for this since I was a child, and so I did not tense. Did not let worry touch my expression. I was calm. Unconcerned. Under my own control down to the very marrow of my bones.

The new side of me, the vampire, noted the heart rates of the witches around me.

And how they sped up in the silence.

"Very well," Rufinia replied at last, inclining her head toward me. "To start, how much do you know about what she has become?"

The men glanced at each other.

"We know of vampires," Byron allowed, his tone cagier than before.

"Then you know what happens when they drink human blood."

I could feel the tension mount around me, but no one spoke. For my part, I kept the flurry of trepidation in my gut from touching my face or body, never mind that they were talking about me, and blood drinking, and human beings.

And that I had no idea what the First Matron meant.

When the others didn't respond, Rufinia nodded as if we'd confirmed something for her with our silence. "Vampires were created by the inhabitants of the empty realms—beings whom we know as the Voidborn, though what they call themselves, we've never learned. Their desire is for destruction, and vampires are one of their avenues for achieving that. But their creations have a weakness. In every realm where the Voidborn have made vampires, there is always a way for the ones they've turned to hold back the... shall we say, less *pleasant* aspects of what they've become. Some are saved by connections to ethereal creatures. Angels and the like. Others have different methods of survival. And one of those methods"—she smiled again—"requires giants."

"What does that mean?" Niko sounded alarmed. "I know we helped her earlier, but..." He trailed off with a nervous look to the others.

Nearby, Byron's eyes narrowed as he studied Rufinia.

"Most vampires care nothing for their victims," the First Matron said. "Indeed, they don't care about much at all. They enjoy inflicting pain and suffering. It's *entertainment* in their eyes. And it doesn't matter to them who their victims once were. Vampires view everyone from strangers to their own children as little more than walking entrees who scream most pleasantly when they die." The hatred in her voice was thick.

I wondered how many people she'd lost to my stepmother and others like her.

"But," Rufinia continued with a nod at me. "You'll note Gwyneira has not become like this, and the reason is simple. The only blood she's partaken of is yours."

I couldn't bring myself to look at the men around me. Rufinia wasn't wrong. I remembered the moments after I first woke as a vampire. I'd been barely more than an animal—one tethered to my stepmother's will. I'd heard her in my head, commanding me to kill everyone around me, and I could no more have disobeyed her than a puppet could break its own strings.

But when the men willingly offered me their blood, everything had changed. As I drank, I'd remembered them. Remembered my life and everything that mattered too.

"If you drink the blood of humans or witches, Gwyneira, all of this will change."

"But..." My voice was tight, and I cleared my throat. "My stepmother was never—"

"Melisandre and her fellow traitors were a case unto themselves. They bargained with the Voidborn. Gained their powers and completed the transformation to vampires but retained their own will—at least as long as they kept those beings appeased. But those they turned are slaves to their own feral impulses. Indeed, they are barely more than rabid predators chained by the commands of their makers."

"How do you know all this?" Byron asked.

The First Matron's gaze flicked to Leontine and the others, but I couldn't read her look. A resolute expression flashed across several of the witches' faces, but Leontine shook her head. "We should prepare her more first," she said as if protesting something.

Alarm shot through me. "Prepare me for what?"

Rufinia folded her hands in front of her. "Testing."

My men drew in closer to me as I tensed.

"What do you mean, testing?" Dex demanded.

"At the moment, Gwyneira has a hold upon herself. She is, for lack of a better term, still human. But what happens when that hold is put under stress? When her hunger returns or when any magic she may have inherited chooses to slip her control?"

I fought back a quiver. Setting aside the fact that I didn't want to reveal the slightest vulnerability if I didn't have to, I wasn't sure it would help my case to mention that—short of a few moments after being turned that had felt more like a dream than reality—I'd never knowingly used magic in my life.

"We need to know how tenuous your hold on your humanity is. How much of a danger you could present."

Clay made an incredulous noise, his blue eyes flashing with anger. "So you test her and if she fails, you'll kill her? Gee, what a tempting offer." He grabbed my arm. "Forget what I said earlier. Let's get the fuck out of here."

The door slammed behind us without anyone touching it. Magic prickled on the air all around.

"This isn't an offer only for *our* sakes," Rufinia said, her eyes locked on me as if nothing that just happened bothered her in the slightest. "This is for you. What happens if you lose control halfway down the mountain and kill every one of your companions? Or if you return home and can't maintain your humanity in the midst of all your infinitely *human* subjects?"

Shivers rolled from my gut at the intensity of her gaze.

"We *want* you to survive, Princess. Know that. Forces

are in motion beyond what we can easily explain. Your presence—even *their* presence"—she nodded toward my men—"is part of that. But unleashing the heir of a diamond witch *and* a vampire on this world would be a horrific choice unless we made absolutely certain you were safe first."

Dex shook his head immediately when I glanced at him and the others. "We'll find another way," he said. "One that doesn't have death as a possible outcome."

"Yeah," Clay agreed. "You're not a threat to us, baby. We don't need these people to know that."

A smile crossed my face at his words, but I knew he was wrong. Even before I'd been turned, when my stepmother's power started affecting me, I'd nearly attacked them.

And if I lost control now?

"What do I need to do?" I asked the witches.

"Princess," Niko protested.

I shook my head at him. "I have to protect you all too."

Rufinia straightened, ignoring the protesting men around me. "Come."

She started past us.

Dex made a motion to stop the rest of us from moving. "Where?"

"To meet Eliasora."

None of the stares had abated in the time we'd been inside the main cabin. If anything, more people had gathered, watching from their porches or from the sides of the path. And when they saw the direction we headed, murmurs started too.

"Told you they'd lock her away," a man commented from within the crowd.

Dex tensed beside me, his jaw muscles jumping.

"It's not her fault, you know," a woman replied. "If anyone deserves a chance, it's Eira's daughter."

"They should put her down entirely," someone else said. "She's Melisandre's creation too, I heard. Can't be trusted."

At the words, a snarl left Ozias, the sound half wild. Gasps came from the crowd.

No one spoke again.

I kept walking, trying to ignore them all. Grit and frost crunched beneath my feet, and the cold air passed over my cheeks without any need to enter my lungs. I could see from the corners of my eyes the steam that rose as the others breathed.

Had my stepmother never breathed? Surely I would have noticed that.

Gods, I had so many questions.

We rounded a turn and continued on toward the gate set between evergreen trees in the side of the mountain. Up ahead, Rufinia made a brief gesture, and quickly, the men guarding the gate moved to open it.

"What is in there?" Dex asked.

Rufinia didn't answer.

Dex motioned for us to stop. "That looks like a prison."

Glancing over her shoulder at us, Rufinia considered for a moment before speaking. "Not one for Gwyneira—assuming this goes well."

She didn't say another word as she continued through the dark opening, Leontine and several other witches from the cabin following her.

I started after them, and Dex caught my arm. "Princess..."

"I won't risk you," I said. "Any of you."

"What about yourself?" He shook his head. "Byron is highly skilled. He can determine if there's a threat another way."

"And if something goes wrong?" I glanced at Byron. "I trust you. I do. But I don't want to risk you getting hurt either."

The redheaded man blinked and looked away, discomfort on his face, though I wasn't sure why.

"You told me they helped," I continued to Dex. "They could have killed me the moment I set foot here, but they didn't."

"Unless they're after something else," Lars pointed out evenly, his blue eyes solemn.

I fought back a grimace. He wasn't wrong. I knew that. There were a million possibilities here, and plenty of them were bad.

Inside me, my new vampire side whispered of taking to the sky to leave this place.

I wasn't sure I wanted to know what it planned beyond that.

Drawing myself up, I met the men's eyes—those who would look at me anyway. Roan was glaring at the world in general, and Ozias was staring toward the cave opening as if to kill it.

"If my options are risking you all or this," I said. "I choose this."

I headed for the open gate.

Behind me, Dex sighed. "Stay sharp," he muttered to the others.

Heavy doors stood open on either side of the cave entrance. Thick metal bars covered the gate, almost as if reinforcing it, although their surfaces were brown and pocked by age. A massive lock dangled from one side, and heavy chains did too.

"What the fuck do they have in here?" Clay said, almost as if to himself.

As I came closer, angular symbols flared to life all across the bars, lock, and chains, the shapes glowing blue like a flash of lightning frozen in time. The air prickled on my skin, as if tiny needles suddenly surrounded me.

But nothing else happened.

"You're permitted passage, Princess," Leontine called from beyond the entrance.

A nervous quiver ran through me, and I drew myself up, continuing inside. Torches burned along the rough-hewn walls, driving back any trace of shadow. The ground beneath us was as uneven as the walls but worn smooth in the center as if from the passage of numerous feet over the years. The path led downward, sloping and curving as it wound deeper into the mountain. Every so often, more symbols would flare on the walls, glowing blue or green or white.

But they only did that when I walked by.

"Protection against vampires?" Byron's voice was only partially questioning, and his eyes were intent as he studied the witches ahead of us.

"Against all creatures of the Voidborn," Leontine called. "Whatever they might be."

That didn't make me feel better.

A door up ahead brought the path to an end. Like the one to the outside, thick bars covered it, sealing it shut with a heavy bolt across the middle. When I came closer, more symbols appeared, this time not only on the bars but also on the frame, the walls, even the ceiling and floor.

Gods, what the hell *were* they keeping in there?

"Once we are inside," Rufinia said, "you would do well to speak only as much as is necessary and guard your words—*especially* about the princess. And be cautious how close to her you come. She's always trying to find a way out."

Rufinia turned, gripping the handle.

"Who is in there?" Dex asked. "Who's Eliasora?"

"You'll see." Rufinia pulled the door open.

The room inside was formed of the same stone as everything else, the walls rough and uneven like they'd been carved by hand. Torches burned along three of the walls, revealing two cages at the far end, each separated by a space about ten feet wide. Midway between them, a square of metal embossed with a strange symbol was set into the wall.

My lips parted, and if I'd had any breath in my lungs, I would have gasped.

They had another vampire here. But that was hardly the end of it.

Inside the cage on the right, a chain extended from a manacle around the wrist of a vampire woman. Glowing blue symbols shone from the metal links, bright as lightning bolts. The chain extended beyond the bars into the ten feet of open space between one cage and the next, and its end was fastened to the metal plate inset in the wall. Another chain ran from the plate to the second cage, where it was looped loosely around the bars as if merely to give it a place to rest.

The vampire herself was seated on a bed in the first cage,

but at the sight of us, she rose to her feet with an ease like gravity only barely applied, her body moving through space as if ordinary physics were irrelevant. Her hair was dark orange-red like smoldering embers, so tightly curled it became a cloud like Rufinia's, and her skin was the color of amber. Her brown eyes flashed over all of us before returning squarely to me, and when the corners of her lips curled up, revealing even more of her fangs, her expression reminded me of a cat with a mouse at its mercy. "Melisandre did it, didn't she? She turned Eira's brat."

Hearing her speak my mother's name made my skin crawl, but I kept my face calm. "Who are you?" I stayed far back from the bars even as she walked closer, the chain clinking as it came with her. The metal bars separating us flared to life with more blue symbols.

The woman gave me a hurt look, the expression clearly theatrical. "Oh, come now. No one told you?"

Rufinia gestured to the cage. "This is Eliasora."

"You mean Eira's *beloved* servant. Her loyal and faithful maid, always ready to tend to the needs of a diamond witch. And you look just like her, at least in the eyes. And that bearing." She scoffed. "So proud."

Fangs peeked past her lips as she grinned. In spite of myself, I recoiled.

Her eyebrow twitched up, her smile remaining in place. "But then, how is Eira? Dead, I hope. Did you kill her? That would've been a treat to see. And how about Melisandre? Did she pull off her whole plan, feeding you her blood at your birth and all, or was that a recent thing?"

I held myself still, but the side of me that wasn't human any longer quivered in my chest. It wanted to attack this creature. Silence her incessant questions.

Destroy her completely.

"What is the meaning of this?" Byron demanded of the other witches.

Rufinia regarded the woman in the cage coldly. "Eliasora was an ally of Melisandre's. She and her fellow traitors sought to destroy the Jeweled Coven."

"You mean we *did* destroy it." Eliasora's tone was contemptuous. "How many of you are left these days? Fifty? Fewer? How many of your mates did you lose? And don't get me *started* on the children." She chuckled. "So tasty. I still daydream of how they screamed when they died."

I could practically feel the rage rolling off the witches around me as if it heated the air.

Still smiling, Eliasora leaned her head to one side, regarding me. "So did they bring you here for testing? What's the plan when you fail? I hope it's to lock you up in here with me. I'd love to have company. The guards are so boring. I haven't gotten to eat one in years."

Rufinia turned from her, pointedly addressing me as if the vampire wasn't in the room. "Eliasora's connection to the Voidborn provides the best method of testing your control that we have yet devised. If you can withstand her, you shouldn't present a threat to the innocent. If not..."

"I understand." I was grateful at least that my voice was steady, giving no sign of the nerves pounding their way through me.

The First Matron bowed her head briefly in acknowledgement. "Now, if you would please step inside?" She motioned toward the empty cage on the left.

Murmurs of protest rose from the men behind me, but I didn't turn. If this went wrong and if I couldn't control myself, I had to hope the cage would stop me from harming anyone.

Eliasora cackled as I walked toward the open gate.

"Place the manacle around your wrist," Rufinia said as the door swung shut behind me and the lock clicked, sealing me in. "The spells will do the rest."

I took up the metal, holding my expression still as blue light flared inside the symbols carved on it.

"Princess..." Niko murmured beyond the cage.

I tried for a smile. "I'll be fine."

Or I wouldn't have to live with the alternative.

The trepidation inside me spun higher, and if I'd had a heartbeat, it would have been thundering in my chest. The click of the manacle felt like a whip crack in the air, and the metal hung heavy from my wrist.

Rufinia walked into the open space between the two cages and placed her palm on the center of the symbol embossed on the plate inset into the wall. White light glowed from more symbols I hadn't even seen etched in the metal, edging out into the chains where it pulsed against the blue glow like the two were vying for prominence. "Ready?"

I nodded.

White light rushed through the chain right at me.

3
MELISANDRE

Murder had never been an issue for me, but this was becoming ridiculous.

If the creature before me wasn't devouring the shepherds wandering the hills or the cluster of insipid milkmaids who'd made the mistake of walking alone by their barn, he was eating the sheep and cows themselves—which, quite frankly, was disgusting. Feeding from humans was one thing. They were practically made to be killed. But animals?

One might as well eat mud.

But given how his razor-sharp teeth and narrow jaw were covered in feathers as well as blood, he clearly didn't share my opinion of feasting on grubby animals. Dropping a dead chicken onto the dried grass, he swiped his oddly protruding jaw clean and immediately turned his black eyes to scanning the rocky horizon. Meanwhile, the bird's body began disintegrating into dust the moment it hit the ground, drained of more than blood.

Drained of the very force that held it as *substance* in this world.

I kept my expression still. I'd seen this countless times now, with every victim this creature claimed, and though it still disturbed me, I didn't dare show any sign.

Lest the creature decide it would be entertaining to make me join them.

"Satisfied?" I asked in the politest tone I could muster.

The thing before me harrumphed. He barely appeared human, and that mostly applied to his shape alone. His skin was mottled gray with a green sheen that appeared at random moments either like the shimmering shell of a bug or else like rotting flesh. His face looked like an eel, strangely protruding to a point, and his eyes were dark slits with no eyebrows while his nostrils were narrow gashes with scarcely any definition at all. He had no hair on his head, and his fingers were elongated and pointed at the end, as if they'd been crafted by someone who understood the concept of hands but thought they should share traits with tentacles too.

But his teeth... oh, those were the clearest sign that I was dealing with a Voidborn, one of those creatures from beyond this realm who wanted nothing but destruction. A row of sharp points in his mouth, his teeth gleamed like polished metal every time he smiled. Even my fangs couldn't look that intimidating.

Which was annoying. I was accustomed to being the most terrifying creature walking the earth. He challenged that, and for it, I would have killed him.

If I could have.

"Hardly sufficient sustenance," the man replied, the words hissing and sibilant, as if his mouth couldn't quite form the shape of them. "Find another. I need more if I am to pass unnoticed in this world."

I highly doubted that thing would pass unnoticed even if he put his head in a sack.

Fastening a polite smile on my face, I turned away from the vile monster and the dust that had been a chicken. "Of course."

He chuckled with satisfaction behind me.

My skin crawled and a cold feeling coiled in my gut, one that I *wouldn't* name. Early on, I'd tried to escape him, but I'd scarcely made it five feet before a choking sensation gripped my throat and my insides writhed like cold fingers were digging into them. I'd fallen to the ground, convinced death was coming.

He'd just laughed.

I was his, the bastard explained once I could stand again. He'd tied me to him down to the very core of my being when I was thrown into the empty realms. I existed purely because he willed it now, and I could no more leave than I could walk in the sunshine without burning. This was the price of my vampire power finally come to pass.

It was nothing like what I expected.

I shuddered, burying the cold shiver in my gut as deep as I could, where I could ignore it. My sister witches and I had sworn ourselves to the Voidborn in exchange for the power to defeat those arrogant fools in the Jeweled Coven all those years ago. We'd known that the gifts came with a price, and that these creatures would collect eventually. We'd been led to believe they'd devour us, dragging us into the empty realms to feed on us for however long it took for us to finally die. And to be sure, I hadn't sat idly waiting for that day. I'd turned my stepdaughter Gwyneira into a vampire. As my creature, I'd intended to take command of her and force her to let the Voidborn devour her in my place.

Nothing had gone as I planned.

Gwyneira had escaped me. She'd fled to the mountains and somehow ended up in league with giants, one of the few creatures in all creation whose blood could loosen my hold on her.

And the Voidborn had taken me instead.

Except instead of feeding on me in endless torment, this creature had taken hold of me and used me to get back into this world.

And I had no idea why.

The wind whipped around me as I crossed the color-sapped terrain. Based on the layers of clothes that had covered the shepherds and milkmaids, I imagined it was cold, though I could scarcely feel it. The sky held the kind of chilly clarity often seen in the depths of winter, when every star was like a pinprick of ice in the black firmament. Beneath our feet, the rough grass shared more in common with rugged sprigs of tundra than soft blades. The only trees in sight were stunted, their bark darker than any I'd seen in Aneira.

Only the gods themselves knew where we'd ended up, or how long it would take to get back to Aneira. But get back I would, because somewhere in this damnable world Gwyneira still lived, and she'd want to claim the Aneiran throne.

I'd put up with nineteen years of insufferable humans in order to rule that kingdom, and my plan had always been to use it to wage war and annex every neighboring kingdom besides. By the time I was finished, everything this side of the Wild Lands would be mine.

Like hell I'd let that idiot child get in my way.

Or some creature from beyond this world.

At long last, the village came into view beyond the crest of a hill. Weak light glowed from the windows of the hovels clustered within the village proper, as if they barely had the supplies to build a fire. Even the rough log wall around the town limits was rundown.

And only half a dozen guards were posted outside it.

"How about this?" I asked, glancing back at the creature.

His lips pulled back in a cruel smile. If I hadn't loathed him for the hold he had upon me, I would have appreciated the promise of violence in it. "Delicious."

He started down the hillside, and I followed quickly, if only to keep my feet from being taken from beneath me by pain again.

"And after you finish here?" I asked.

His head turned toward me, his neck twisting around farther than it would have if he'd had a regular spine. Discomfort stirred within me at the sight. I squashed the reaction immediately.

I would never appear weak before this *thing*.

"You wish to know my thoughts?" he replied.

Only a fool would miss the threat behind that pleasant tone. But I'd survived for nearly two decades as the wife of a pathetic human king. I'd swayed his insipid daughter into believing I was her loving stepmother.

I knew how to appease those who thought themselves in power until I could get what I wanted.

"I only wish to know how I can be of assistance to you, my lord."

He stopped, regarding me for a moment with those

inhuman black eyes staring out from a face that gave nothing away. "My lord," he repeated flatly.

Wary confusion flickered through me. "If you do not like the term—"

"What is it?"

I blinked. "A term of respect."

"But your kind, they have names, do they not?"

I scrambled to regain my proverbial footing. This conversation was not going how I'd expected. "My kind?"

"Beings such as yourself."

Did he mean vampires or *all* beings beyond the empty realms?

I shoved the thought aside. It scarcely mattered.

Forcing a pleasant expression back onto my face, I softened my tone. He'd thrown me momentarily, to be sure, but I wouldn't let him continue to do so. For all I knew, he was only feigning this ignorance as some kind of game. "Yes."

"Hmm."

He started walking again, offering nothing more to explain himself. I bit back a snarl of frustration and strode after him.

The rotting wood of the village wall drew closer. In the darkness, the human guards finally spotted us.

"You there!" one of them called. "What's your business here?"

The creature chuckled, coming to a stop at the edge of the torchlight. The humans gasped at the sight of him.

"Very well," he said to me, ignoring them as several ran for the gates and the rest started toward us with swords. "You may call me Alaric. That's an intriguing name from another realm that will be ours. It means 'all-powerful ruler,' which is fitting. And as for what I intend…"

My insides lurched as he lunged forward, weaving around the chipped swords of the guards like lightning. The humans fell like toppled toys at the creature's hand, his tentacle fingers moving as if they were blades, cutting tendons and spines alike.

Until only one guard remained wriggling by his neck in Alaric's grasp.

The man's scream dwindled to nothing as the creature bit down and drained him, same as the animals and shepherds and milkmaids who came before.

"There are thousands of my kind beyond the barrier surrounding this reality," Alaric continued in the same conversational tone.

Shouts rose from the village. The humans were trying to mount a defense.

Alaric paid them no mind. "My brethren are hungry. They crave breaking the barrier as I have done. They dream of feeding on light and life. And you and I?" With a tongue too long to be human, he licked the blood of the other guards from his fingers and then grinned at me as the shouts from the villagers grew louder. "We are going to let them in."

4
GWYNEIRA

The white light hit the blue glowing symbols on the manacle around my wrist, and my eyes went wide. A cold sensation rushed over me—the first temperature I'd truly perceived ever since I'd woken as a vampire. It was sharp like a knife, biting like winter frost, and it made me tense as if my body was instinctively afraid of being cut open.

"Now," Rufinia said, her voice calm and controlled. "We shall begin."

Before I could even open my mouth to ask what this had been, if not beginning, Eliasora gasped and dropped onto the bed in her cage as her legs gave out beneath her. A tangle of dull amber light joined the flood of white emanating from the symbols etched on the chain and manacle. The force of it hit me like a wall, taking my legs from beneath me as well and sending me crashing to the floor.

Cries reached me, but they were distant and hard to understand. My mind was swirling, impulses pelting me faster than I could process them.

Hunger. No, *ravenous* craving like I needed to feed from anything and everything around me. I gritted my teeth, my fangs nearly piercing my lower lip as I struggled to resist the urge to fling myself at the bars to get past them to the delectable heartbeats on the other side.

Because they were pounding so hard. Racing with fear that I could taste like sugar on the air, and gods, it would be easy to bring them down... so *very* easy...

Deep in my mind, a strange impulse rose, like a predator rousing itself from slumber, shedding the weight of goodness and humanity that had held it down. It was dark and deadly, hungry as hell, and ready to leap to action. It craved that. The chase. The feeling of prey between its fangs.

It cared for nothing else.

My fingers curled into fists, my nails biting into my palm. Dark clouds of its desires hovered all around my mind, eroding my self-control, threatening to overwhelm it entirely. All the predator needed was for me to stop fighting. To give in to how amazing it would feel to lose my human form, race through the gaps in the bars, and tear down everyone around me.

Just like the other one wanted to do. That creature. The one in the opposite cage who was currently staring at me, her eyes practically glowing with anticipation and her lips parted around her fangs. She grinned, muttering something I couldn't hear over the growl of the predator stalking closer and closer in my mind.

But I knew what she wanted all the same. For me to lunge at the bars. To prove their paltry magics wrong by shifting form and killing the bitches currently holding us both captive, because wouldn't it be amazing to watch them die? We could share the feast together. She'd be in charge, of course. I could feel how she was somehow *more* of whatever we were than me. But I could obey her and get everything I wanted.

I only had to surrender to the predator I truly was... and attack.

Pressing my clenched fists to the hard stone floor, I ripped my gaze from her. Seven sets of eyes were locked on me. Watching. Waiting.

And if I just gave in...

Gods, they'd taste amazing. They already had. Like fire and ice and the darkness inside the earth itself, back when they let me bite them after I'd first been turned. The *power* that had come from them, it was...

Warmth and cold twisted through me, accompanied by darkness and light, stone and iron. The power of my giants still lingered, carried on a strangely cool breeze that coursed through my being, as light as gossamer and as crystalline as frost. It wasn't the vampire. It was something else.

A whisper of hope holding me back from a rabid need to feed.

I trembled, my vampire side clawing at that tenuous layer, determined to rip past it. I *could* bite them. Taste them again. Bathe in their blood and their magic just as the one in the other cage had done, years before with the witches here. She still relished that memory. I could have my own version of it too, and gods, it would be ecstasy.

Such ecstasy...

But then they'd be dead.

My head shook, my eyes squeezing shut as impulses warred inside my mind. Surely it was foolish to make the giants dead, though? I... I cared for them. I was fairly sure I could even love them. And to attack like the beast inside me wanted...

How *desperately* it wanted. The urge to do it was so strong. But if I listened...

The predator grew louder in my mind, stalking closer and closer, shredding my resistance with every step. I clamped my lips shut against a whimper, not letting a trace of the sound emerge as I struggled to hang onto the fact that, if I killed my giants, they'd be gone. The vampire and I... we wouldn't have them anymore, and... and we didn't want that.

I knew we didn't. I was so hungry, but I *knew* we...

The magic rolling through the chain faded, taking away the white light and the amber glow that had accompanied it, leaving only the blue radiance that had shone from it initially.

Shudders racked me. The outside impulse to attack faded like mist at dawn, leaving only the predator in my mind.

And it didn't care that the commands from the other vampire had faded.

But I wasn't fighting a war on two fronts any longer, and in my head, I shoved the predator back as hard as I could, silently commanding it to go.

Slowly, that side of me receded like a beast deciding a confrontation wasn't worth it—at least, not right now.

I braced myself on the floor and pushed to my feet. In the other cage, Eliasora lay on the bed, her eyes closed like she was exhausted.

Everyone else was watching me.

"Do I pass?" I asked Rufinia in as measured a tone as I could manage.

My giants looked at the witches, and every inch of the men's body language was guarded.

A hint of a smile crossed Rufinia's face. "Indeed. You resisted admirably, Princess."

"Let her out then," Clay demanded immediately.

She nodded to one of the witches, who unlocked the cage and then the manacle around my wrist before retreating quickly.

As if still concerned I'd attack.

"What happens now?" I asked as I walked from the cage. Clay and his brother Lars drew in close, protective, while Dex watched the witches as if weighing the odds they'd still do something to hurt me.

I held myself stiff. I wanted more than anything to hug my men and reassure myself of how we'd all survived, but I wouldn't let down my guard, not in front of these witches.

And especially not in front of Eliasora.

"Now, you are free to remain here, if you wish," Rufinia said. "We can show you to the cabin we prepared. It is located at the far edge of the encampment, for your privacy, and in the coming days, you can decide what you would like to do from there." She paused. "Your mother was a powerful witch. Since you have proven yourself able to resist the pull of the vampire within you, I would suggest you now prioritize learning about what magic you might have inherited from her."

A quiet giggle came from the other cage. "That's right. Train up your little diamond witch. Like that's going to save her."

"Quiet," Leontine snapped.

Eliasora ignored her, pushing to her feet. "You think you've won something? Fought back the big bad vampire they stirred up inside you?" She grinned at me. "These pathetic bitches can't hold a candle to the Voidborn, and when *they* find you and let that beast inside you out to play..."

Deep in my mind, the predator rumbled as if echoing her sentiment.

"She said *quiet*," Roan growled from where he stood at the rear of the group of giants. With his back pressed to the wall, I couldn't help but notice he was as far from me as he could get, but his eyes were locked on Eliasora like he'd gut her if it meant making her shut up.

"Oh, please. I haven't listened to these fools since even before I helped my sister witches summon the Voidborn. Why would I start now?" Eliasora turned a smirk on me. "Even if they let you leave this place, where are you going to go? Back to your kingdom?" She chuckled. "You think your people will accept you now, given what you've become? You think they'll welcome you back with open arms and hand you the throne?" Her fangs glinted in the light. "I remember Aneira, little girl. There's no happy ending for a vampire and her collection of Erenlian pets in that place."

"That's enough," Leontine said. She turned to Rufinia. "We should go. We've given this traitor enough of our attention."

Rufinia nodded and motioned for the other witches to leave.

I lingered, cold shivers spreading within me. The vampire side of me had been thwarted in attacking my men and the witches once, and it still seethed at that. But now it couldn't understand why I wasn't attacking this woman for her horrible words.

Especially since I feared she might be right about my people and my home.

My shivers grew worse.

"The Voidborn could solve all your problems, Princess," Eliasora said. "They could make everyone in your kingdom bow and offer themselves up for your bite. All you have to do is surrender and become their creature, and you can't *imagine* the power that will follow. Because you *are* theirs, no matter what you want to believe. Their power inside you will win in the end, and when they tighten their grip on you, well..." She chuckled. "Better to serve them willingly and survive."

I turned and strode out of the room.

5
BYRON

I understood the rationale behind keeping a prisoner such as the one we'd just seen. Information, testing other vampires, even research into weaknesses to exploit. I could see the practicality and the logic.

But the *risk* it presented...

"Are you okay, Princess?" Dex asked as we emerged from the tunnel.

Gwyneira nodded, though her expression looked perturbed.

But not afraid. At least, not like she had been when we found her in our cabin. No, there was a strength in her that had been refined by all she'd faced, a core of resolve that hadn't broken even after everything she'd been through.

She'd been beautiful from the moment I laid eyes on her.

Now she was breathtaking.

Clay shuddered as the witches closed the gate behind us, sealing the tunnel away. "What the fuck was that all about? Those creatures are coming for the princess?"

Rufinia's mouth tightened, but she didn't respond.

"Is it really safe to keep that woman in there?" Niko asked. "If she got free..."

"Of course it fucking isn't." Roan's voice was cold as he glared at the witches, his dark eyes practically glowing with rage. "That thing isn't a woman, it's a monster. You should have killed it, not kept it as a damned *pet*."

Gwyneira looked over at him sharply, alarmed, and Dex and several of the others did the same.

Roan tensed, a cascade of expressions flying across his face almost too fast to read. Embarrassment was there. Discomfort too. I suspected he'd forgotten himself for a moment.

And forgotten what the princess had become.

His jaw muscles jumping, Roan turned away, muttering something about needing air, though the gods knew we had enough of it here under the night sky. I caught a flash of shame in his dark eyes before he spun and strode off, as if he regretted upsetting her with his vehement words.

Yet, I wasn't sure he was entirely wrong—about the vampire in that cave, at least. "Is there any danger that Eliasora could contact her masters or others like her to summon them?" I asked.

Rufinia shook her head. "We have enough suppression spells on that cell that even the Voidborn will never be able to find her. And she knows it. Her only entertainment these days lies in needling whoever comes by."

"Was she always like that?" Gwyneira asked.

Her voice was thoughtful, and though I would theorize she was trying to hide it, there was the tiniest hint of caution on her face—and even if my specialty was reading books and not people, I could still guess at why.

She was concerned about what might happen if she lost the battle to hold onto herself.

Leontine frowned. "Yes and no. Eliasora was... jealous. They all were. Our powers are arranged in a hierarchy based upon the gemstones to which we have an affinity, and theirs..."

"Your mother was a diamond witch, as we've said," Rufinia stated, her voice hard. "The highest level of our powers. But Melisandre could only find an affinity with raw chunks of carbon. Eliasora was barely able to manipulate coal. The others were the same. They did not have the strength, skill, or affinity to sources of power that would have made them powerful witches. But rather than accept the hand they'd been dealt by the gods and fate, they concluded their best recourse was to steal power by becoming what you saw in there."

"What is important to know, however," Leontine said more gently. "Is that, while what the Voidborn did warped them, it did not introduce anything that was not already present, even if only as potential. Eliasora, Melisandre, and their allies willingly chose to sacrifice any trace of good in themselves for the pursuit of power. They knew what the cost would be, and they embraced it willingly, destroying any chance of fulfilling the purpose destiny had given them in the process."

The princess's eyes darted between the two witches. "Destiny?"

"We are all called to a purpose, Princess, and not all purposes are considered glamorous. Some choose to embrace that fact. To sacrifice momentary pleasure or gain for the sake of serving something bigger than themselves.

Others put what *they* desire ahead of all else—no matter what vows it breaks or who it may harm."

I held myself still despite how my gut twisted with discomfort. It was as if they were speaking to me. As a dwarf among giants, I'd spent my early childhood with the knowledge I would never amount to anything in Erenelle society.

Yet I'd still found my calling.

The Order of Berinlian, a fellowship of scholarly monks committed to the study of magic. They'd taken me in after my parents died when I was a young child, and the proudest day of my life had been the one upon which I'd taken my vows. As a scholar of the Order, I swore to live a life of celibacy and service, devoting my mind, body, and soul to the singular purpose of furthering our understanding of the mystical arts. I would have no family but the Order. No lovers, no children. My life's meaning would be found in the pursuit of knowledge, and with that, I was thoroughly satisfied.

But then Aneirans burned the monastery and all the tomes and relics within, brutally slaughtering every scholar they saw. I'd escaped with nothing but the clothes on my back, covered in the blood of those I'd tried and failed to save.

And I'd never found another one of my brethren since.

Yet even with the loss of the Order, I remained determined to live as I'd sworn I would that day I stood beneath the sacred dome in the Hall of Magic and took my vows. Even after joining up with Dex and the others, I kept to the hours of study ordained by Berinlian himself. I held to the commandments to expand knowledge while protecting the sanctity of life. When the others lamented their lack of romantic prospects and sought to soothe their carnal needs in taverns or villages we traveled past, I'd never felt the least compulsion to join them. I had my studies, my devotion to research. I would forever remain a celibate scholar of the Order, even if only in my heart. After all, it had been the only destiny I'd ever wanted.

My eyes crept toward Gwyneira.

Desire was such a destructive thing.

"Is there any way to undo what Eliasora and the others made themselves?" the princess asked, a thread of hope in her voice that I knew could be so easily snapped. "What they made me?"

I pulled my gaze from her, holding myself motionless against the compulsion to reach for her, comfort her. Gwyneira was oblivious to the conflict she caused me—as well she should have been. I worked hard to never give any sign of the war I waged with myself every time I was around her.

Because when I was near her, I couldn't discern what was true anymore. What was real. Was it the vows I'd sworn to the Order... or the howling of my soul that she was my treluria?

"We've never found a solution to that problem," Leontine said, and my attention snapped to her in alarm before I realized she was not answering my inner conflict—because of course she was not—but rather the princess's questions. "When Eliasora and the others became what they are now, their bodies died and then came back as this. Same as you. To undo it would invite only death."

Gwyneira looked away. I ached at the flicker of sadness in her eyes.

"What about her claims about the Voidborn?" Dex

asked. "Even if they can't detect Eliasora, could they target Gwyneira?"

Rufinia paused. "Not directly, no. They may try to find agents for their desires, much as they did with Melisandre and Eliasora, but the Voidborn themselves cannot exist beyond the empty realms. Reality itself repels them. We have no record of them ever successfully entering this world."

A modicum of tension drained from the men around me, but I found I couldn't react the same. Suspicion percolated in the back of my mind instead. There was a flaw in the First Matron's logic. I knew it.

Because the witches were assuming a static system. An unchanging status quo. But reality itself *was* change and if something as ravenous as the Voidborn ever found a way to exploit that...

Drawing herself up as if to set all of Eliasora's words behind her, Rufinia continued. "We have a cabin made up for all of you, as I said. It has been secured against daylight, so when the sun rises, you should be able to retire there without concern. Tomorrow after sunset, we can begin the testing." She gestured to the path. "Leontine, if you would show them the way?"

The others set out behind the witch, and when Gwyneira glanced back at me, my heart did the same flip-flop movement it had ever since she first opened her eyes at our own cabin all those weeks ago.

And just as I had back then, I struggled between the twin impulses to go to her or to run the other way.

I dropped my gaze, praying to the gods and the Order's patron Berinlian that they would somehow assuage the conflict inside me.

"Scholar?"

I froze, my eyes snapping to Rufinia with alarm. Why would she apply that title to me, when I'd said nothing of my former life since arriving here?

Her solemn face supplied no answers. "If you would, I have someone who would like to speak with you."

I threw a glance back at the others to find Dex watching. He gave me a look I knew well—the former soldier running a dozen scenarios through his head before settling on one—and then his head moved briefly. "Catch up to us in a bit," was all he said.

I nodded, hating how some part of me was grateful for the reprieve from the tension I felt whenever I was around the princess. It felt like a betrayal, being glad to escape that strange need I felt for her.

Except... knowledge would help her too.

My tension eased slightly, and I made myself focus as I always did on the task at hand. "Very well," I said to the witch. "Show me."

❄

The path back through the village felt different without the other men or the princess nearby. The stares lessened. The witches barely spared me a glance.

It was Gwyneira at whom they had been gawking.

On some level, I understood. These were people who had lost friends and family to vampires. Of us all, the princess walking free was most likely to draw their fear and attention.

But anxiety still made my stomach churn. If someone tried to hurt her and I wasn't there to help...

I drew a slow breath, forcing myself to concentrate on Rufinia as she led me through the small village. Gwyneira had been hurt over and over after we fled the cabin the seven of us had called home, and I was not unaware that my intervention had helped save her more than once. But the others had skills too. And whatever Rufinia wanted me to see, more information always was beneficial in making any decision.

Gods, don't let me fail the princess with my absence...

Rufinia never slowed as she strode onward, the path twisting past trees and a forest that *had* to be sustained with magic. This high in the mountains, it was a miracle we could survive, let alone that the trees and vines could. Foliage tangled into a dense tapestry on either side of the winding path. Rabbits hopped away at the sight of me, though not—I noted—from the witch, and little birds flitted through the branches. If not for the fact the stars appeared so much closer than they ever had before, I would have thought I was back in a forest of Erenelle.

We neared the slope of the mountainside again, and the First Matron slowed. Another gate blocked the end of the path, this one ornate and carved with runes and sigils but by no means as reinforced as the one that guarded the tunnel to Eliasora's cell. Striding toward the gate, Rufinia motioned with one hand and the door swung wide silently on well-oiled hinges, perfectly balanced. I followed her, only to pause as we entered. Unlike Eliasora's prison, the walls here were smooth, as if sheared back in a single stroke.

I recognized the work.

Giants.

The First Matron kept moving, walking quickly down the tunnel and not giving me a chance to ask the origins of the carving around me. Lights illuminated the length of the corridor, set back in the walls the way those in my homeland used to be.

At the end of the hall, she reached another double door, finally throwing me a glance, a weighing look in her eyes as if she was gauging how I might react to whatever lay beyond.

Trepidation swirled within me. What exactly was she planning?

The First Matron motioned at the door and it swung open of its own accord. Gold light spilled out into the corridor.

My eyes flashed over the space beyond, taking it in. Tall bookshelves lined every wall at least two stories high, while bookcases filled much of the rest of the space. Glass globes with golden light hung from the ceiling, their glow too steady to be mere candles. A voice carried from deeper within, and the sound of it froze me.

No. It wasn't possible. It *couldn't* be...

My feet sped up, carrying me past Rufinia and the bookcases alike. I rounded the end of the shelves, and then shock brought me to a halt. "*Dathan?*"

The large figure perusing a bookshelf turned. Books were spread across the long table near him, and he held another in his hands. He was easily ten feet tall, wizened with age, and his gray hair was like dried-up moss, gnarled and tangled around his face. He wore rumpled, stained robes just as he always had; a blot of ink here, a burn mark from a spell there. He'd never cared anything for personal appearance, not when there was work to be done.

And I hadn't seen him since the day the Order fell.

"Byron." A broad grin spread across my mentor's wrinkled face.

I strode toward him, still reeling from shock. "How are you here? I thought the Aneirans killed you!"

A rueful expression flashed across his face. "Well, they did try." He tilted his head to one side, and a long scar caught in the gold light, tracing a line from his temple to the base of his neck.

I exhaled, taken aback. "But how are you here?" My hand twitched toward the library as if to encompass the entire mountain. "Erenelle is hundreds of miles away."

"Gateways. After I survived what those Aneiran bastards tried to do, I made my way to the castle. I thought to find any survivors there. I gathered whoever was still among the living, and we took the royal gateway as far from Erenelle as we could." He shrugged. "Turns out, the other end of that magic portal was here. The royal family was aware that some of their kind had survived." He nodded toward where Rufinia stood several yards behind us, watching us both. "The remnants of the Jeweled Coven took us in. We've been here ever since."

I looked from the First Matron to Dathan and back. At whatever she saw on my face, Rufinia gave me a small smile and then headed for the exit.

Ignoring her, I turned back to my mentor. "How many survivors? Is the royal family here?"

Dathan's expression fell. He looked down at the book in his hands as if collecting his thoughts. "I was only able to save some of the servants. The Aneirans killed the royals. Every last damn one of them, far as I know. We've gleaned rumors over the years that some of the Order might have been taken prisoner, but I've never been able to confirm it. There are about twenty of us here now."

I looked away, reeling. Only twenty giants. Out of all Erenelle... only twenty.

A shuddering breath left me. Maybe more of my people were alive elsewhere, besides those in the Aneiran mines. And if any others from the Order had survived, even in the mines, it would be a miracle. And no, when it came to the royals, I'd never known them. I'd *hoped* they weren't dead, of course, and I'd mourned them as souls lost to the war, but in truth, I'd suspected they were gone. After all, by now they surely would have mounted *some* sort of effort to save those imprisoned in Aneira if they'd survived.

Instead of their deaths being just one more way Erenelle had been shattered.

"But what about you?" Dathan continued. "I hear you're traveling with an Aneiran princess?"

I froze. Answering yes would be simple enough, except there was so much behind the simple word.

Like a craving for a princess I couldn't have and should not want.

I cleared my throat, aware he was waiting for an answer. "Along with several other survivors, yes."

It was an evasion, but he didn't seem to detect it.

"I hear she's a vampire," he stated.

"Against her will, yes."

He didn't respond.

My unease grew. "I'm aware of what the other vampires are like, but I assure you, she is not in *any* way similar to them. Indeed, if she could be cured of her condition, I know she would welcome it in a heartbeat."

"Huh." Dathan set the book down. "What are her thoughts on our people?"

Here, at least, was safer ground. "She is committed to freeing them as soon as possible. We have only to return her to Aneira."

"And you trust her?"

A lot more than that.

I nodded, a controlled and measured motion.

Dathan harrumphed. "About time an Aneiran had their head on straight."

A breath left me.

"I've read everything here about vampires," he continued. "*Curing* her isn't really an option. Not if she doesn't want to simply return to being dead. But as for helping her travel back to Aneira... well, there's the issue of the sun to consider."

A sickened feeling spread through me. From the moment she'd woken as a vampire, my analytical training had me turning that very problem over and over in my mind, seeking a solution. If a spell could aid her, or a charmed object, or something else entirely, surely I could find it or craft it.

But as yet, I'd come up with nothing.

I didn't want to admit that, though, and thus I confined myself to merely saying, "Indeed."

Dathan gave me a smile I knew well. The one that said the secrets of the world were nothing compared to a determined mind. "Don't worry, my boy. I might just have a solution."

6

MELISANDRE

The pathetic excuse for a carriage that we stole from the village had originally belonged to a fat and ugly man who'd fancied himself the ruler of that tiny town. He'd blustered quite impressively when Alaric broke down his door, and he'd wet himself as the creature drank his life away. The transport would work effectively to keep the sun off us once daylight arrived, though the seats were threadbare and the cushions had molded themselves to the uneven wood planks beneath.

To make matters worse, the horses were not remotely comfortable with whom they hauled, jerking and jolting us every time the wind shifted and they caught our scent again. But one of the man's stablehands had been more than willing to drive us, barely raising a fuss when Alaric shoved him toward the carriage.

I got the impression the young man had hated the old fool, though of course money and the fact the creature spared his life had been his true motivation for obeying the order to drive.

Not that we would spare him forever, I hoped.

I swallowed hard, my mouth dry and my insides twisting. Normally, I could go for some time without feeding—magic was useful like that—but being thrown into the empty realms and becoming tied to this creature had taken a toll. Not to mention how the creature never deigned to share a meal.

Much more of this and I'd starve.

From the corner of my eye, I watched him. After feeding upon the entire village, his appearance had started to change. The effect had been subtle at first—a shift of skin tone here, a slight increase in the definition of his features there—but by the time he finished, his mottled gray-green skin was gone, replaced by a neutral tone of beige, and his hairless head now bore a crop of amber-colored hair. The strange shape of his face had receded, becoming a strong jaw and a sharply pointed nose.

Those dark eyes, though... they hadn't followed suit. Their shape was more human now, but there were no whites, no defined irises. Just a dark abyss with a slit of gold that never quite let on where he was looking.

Or what he saw.

His head began to turn in my direction. I looked back at the window.

From what I'd seen outside, I suspected we were heading south. The shadows cast by the moonlight were at the right angle for it, and the road was becoming hillier as we headed toward the distant shapes of mountains. Before those peaks, though, a darker smudge lay on the horizon. A forest, I suspected. One that stretched as far as I could see in either direction.

It might have been the woods in the north of Gentresqua

or it might have been somewhere else entirely, but throughout every second of this rickety carriage digging into my spine and rocking over the rough road, Alaric had not told me where we were going nor why it required traveling to accomplish his goals.

I had patience. I'd played a long game for nineteen years with that idiot princess and her father. But back then, I'd never had this coil of ice in my gut, one that it had taken me all this time to finally admit had a name.

Fear.

I was tethered to a creature who would torture me if I tried to stray too far from him, and who could starve me merely by not allowing me to leave his side to capture prey upon which to feed.

I hadn't been this powerless in longer than I cared to remember, and the feeling was as unwelcome now as it had been then.

The carriage lurched. A grunt came from the driver, followed by cajoling calls to the horses to keep them moving as the wheels trundled over the rough terrain.

A delicious scent carried back to me on the breeze. Blood. He'd cut himself. Not badly, from the thready nature of the smell, but enough that I could still detect it.

My insides twisted tighter, hunger making my teeth ache with the urge to let my fangs descend.

"Trouble?"

It took me a moment to realize Alaric spoke to me and not the driver. With effort, I held some measure of calm on my face and looked over at him. "Of course not."

Never show weakness. Never if you want to survive.

I forced a pleasant smile onto my face, holding tight to the personal rule that had gotten me through all my decades of life and my first encounter with the Voidborn alike.

His eyes narrowed, becoming nothing but a black line with a hint of gold in the middle. "You think I intend to starve you."

Alarm ricocheted through me. Surely he could not read my thoughts?

I drew myself up. "Have I said anything of the sort?"

He chuckled. "We made your kind. I can smell the fear of my own creature."

Rage joined the coil of ice—because how dare he think I was *his*—but the feeling couldn't sustain as another whiff of blood reached me past the carriage curtains.

Alaric leaned closer, and his teeth were as unchanged from his original form as his eyes. Metal points glinted at me in the shadows as he smiled. "Just make him last, pet. A sip here and there to tie him to you as your thrall, and the boy might even sustain you until we reach our goal."

My eyes darted over to meet his fully, and I refused to let myself recoil from him. His appearance wasn't the only thing that had changed since the village. Where once he'd been unfamiliar with the simple term "my lord," now he was using nicknames to describe me.

And insulting ones at that.

But as much as the shift alarmed me, his words still rang in my mind, and gods, I hated him for how much they made me want to shudder with relief. The boy was to be my meal. I would not starve. However... "And where is this goal we share? A day's ride? Two?"

Alaric only smiled as he sat back again.

My teeth clenched. I forced them to relax. I would feed first, if only because wisdom dictated I should maintain my strength for killing Alaric. But I would most certainly see him dead.

I was no one's *creature*.

❄

By the time Alaric called for the carriage to stop, the trees were all around us, though the moon still hung heavy in the sky. In the forest, small animals scurried away, their frantic heartbeats fading into the distance as they fled until only the panicked drumming of the horses' hearts remained. As the young man climbed from the carriage driver's seat, my teeth ached and my body quivered with ravenous craving.

And when he opened the door, I had him in my fangs in less time than it took for him to gasp.

Blood filled my mouth. I gulped it down, absently pinning him as the boy tried to struggle.

"Pace yourself, pet."

My hand clenched on the young man's wrist, rage driving my fangs deeper into his throat. How was Alaric learning these words, these concepts? And that he *dared* to call me *pet*...

Oh, to be draining him instead of this boy.

With effort, I made myself draw back and seal the wound on the stablehand's throat. The young man's eyes were dazed, his skin drained of color. But he wasn't dead and likely wouldn't die.

He reached for me, a delirious expression on his face.

No, he was exactly what I wanted. A blood thrall to feed me when I needed it and do my bidding in the meantime.

I rose to my feet, wiping a trace of blood from my lips.

Ordinarily, I was no child to spill my food around my mouth as I drank. But sometimes hunger got the best of me.

"Better?" Alaric asked with a glinting metal smile.

"Where is this goal?"

He chuckled. Everything about me seemed to amuse him.

It was infuriating.

Behind me, the young man stumbled to his feet and staggered toward me. "Again... please..."

I shoved him away. "Be patient."

The stablehand whimpered, but he remained where he was.

He'd do anything if I would only bite him again, I knew.

"Good advice, that." Alaric's smile was unchanged.

Images of flaying the bastard alive and watching him scream flitted through my mind, pleasantly calming. I forced myself to smile back. "Indeed. But I have been quite patient, you'll note."

"Only on the petty scale of time as you know it. My kind have waited beyond the length of time itself."

My eyes narrowed. "You're immortal, then."

He chuckled and turned away, walking deeper into the moonlit forest.

I followed immediately, wary of the hold he had on me. I'd only regained my strength and wouldn't waste it letting his power cause me pain.

Like a puppet, the stablehand tottered after me.

A scowl twisted my face. I didn't care for that image. After all, at the moment I could no more leave Alaric than my thrall could leave me.

But the thought this creature couldn't be killed was intolerable. And surely, it had to be a lie. I knew about the Voidborn. Reality repelled them. Only with my help had Alaric made it into this world anyway. That couldn't have come from being invulnerable or else he wouldn't have needed me to begin with.

The bastard had to possess a weakness. Something I could exploit.

He stopped walking. I tensed.

"There." Alaric pointed.

Cautiously circling wide of him, I looked in the direction he indicated.

The tiny hovel was nearly lost amid the trees and undergrowth. Barely more than a shack that had nearly collapsed under its own weight, the place was formed of rotting wood beams with a slab of tree bark for a front door. I would have thought it abandoned completely, except for the tangles of twigs and stones dangling by frayed threads from tree branches all around it.

My eyes narrowed. I recognized those arrangements. "Stelaruna?"

The forest fell silent, even the wind dying all around. Beside me, Alaric made a soft sound of amusement.

A creak broke the quiet. My brow climbed.

Stelaruna was like me, a vampire witch who'd overthrown the Jeweled Coven. She should have been unchanged after all these years, the same raven-haired beauty who *would* have made the other witches swoon if not for the fact that—like all of us—her lack of innate power had relegated her to the lowest rungs of the coven.

But now her hair was grey and though her pale skin only bore a few lines, she walked with a limp that *any* amount of blood should have healed. The dress of purple velvet for which she'd been known was ragged and threadbare, its rich color faded with time.

At the sight of us, she drew herself up, lifting her pointed chin as if to stare us down. "Of all of us, I never thought *you* would be the one to become their lapdog, Melisandre."

My temper flared. I'd never liked Stelaruna. She was stubborn and arrogant, digging in her heels about the little things. But now... "How dare you speak to me that way?" My magic swelled, ready to strike her down.

But an instant later, a lurch rolled through me, as if my power had hit a wall inside me and could go no farther.

Stelaruna scoffed contemptuously and then turned her attention to Alaric as if I wasn't even there. "You cannot have it."

Incredulous, I looked between them. "Exactly what do you—"

"Silence, pet." Alaric waved his hand and my throat closed, choking off my words.

Shock drove my hand to my neck, though there was nothing there.

"You think to stand against me?" he continued to Stelaruna, ignoring me. "When my brethren and I made you what you are?"

Her expression turned disgusted. "You made us puppets, nothing more. Creatures with power only so long as we saw fit to be a force of destruction for your ends." She looked at me. "Think on it, Melisandre. You were a lowly carbon witch. Shackled to serve the higher powers of the coven, and with no abilities beyond lighting candles and frightening that father of yours when he tried to trade you for a cow. But what did this give us? Just another leash!"

Alaric smirked at me. "Oh, do tell her, pet. Explain the bargain your fellow vampire has forgotten."

At a wave of his hand, my throat suddenly cleared.

I seethed, balking at the prospect of speaking on command like a trained dog but raging at being forced into silence as well. "Yes, I was that. And you were Rufinia's daughter's maid, Stelaruna," I snarled. "You could barely channel magic through *sand*, let alone a gemstone. But with this bargain you so clearly despise, we washed the mountains with the coven's blood." I trembled with rage. "Or have you forgotten how your ripped the heart from Rufinia's girl?"

Cold disdain tightened Stelaruna's face. "I remember. And I *also* remember the first time the Voidborn tried to break through and claim me. Or do you think I chose to age this way?"

Confusion drove me to glance at Alaric.

"Yes, yes." He rolled his black eyes. "But before you think the fact you're not dead means you can stand against me now, have you considered we were only testing methods of using your kind that day?" A derisive chuckle left him. "We've created vampires in *countless* realms, you stubborn pest. We've seen worlds beyond what your petty mind can imagine. Places with metal towers rising thousands of feet in the air and horseless carriages that travel dozens of miles in a single hour, and we will claim them all. You are nothing compared to our power."

Stelaruna regarded him coldly. "I am a guardian. I know why you've come to the middle of this gods-forsaken forest, and I won't let you take it."

I glanced between them. Nothing stood around us but

old trees and a cabin that would have been better used as firewood. What was here that I couldn't perceive?

Alaric only scoffed at her words.

Contempt grew stronger on Stelaruna's face. "You mock, but it won't matter. If you truly try to shatter this realm, you'll only face the Nine."

My eyes narrowed, the title familiar but I couldn't place it immediately.

She turned to me. "I don't care how many die, Melisandre. I don't care if you take this whole world just as you always planned. But the Voidborn are going to leave *nothing*. Not nations or people or even piles of corpses to rule. We thought they would feed on us. That they'd drag us into the empty realms for however long it took for us to die. But we're their *key*. The way into this world, not to rule it but to devour it." She jerked her chin toward Alaric, still watching me. "Fight him with me. Stop this now before the Nine are awakened and destroy us too."

I kept silent as the memory surfaced, though I only vaguely remembered the Nine she spoke of. Some old prophecy of warriors at the end of the world, and thus nothing I'd bothered with. Prophecy existed for only two purposes: for fools to explain away events already in motion or for them to cling to some grand vision of the future so they didn't have to lift a finger to change the present.

It meant nothing to me.

Except now, a chill crept over my skin and I didn't know why. Maybe it wasn't even the Prophecy of the Nine that disturbed me.

It was the concern Stelaruna might be right. I knew what the Voidborn were. What they craved. Alaric had even admitted as much, back before we reached the village. And his presence, let alone that of his brethren, clearly wasn't to my benefit, regardless.

But if they were to destroy this world, taking with it anything I might have ruled, any power I obtained...

The icy coil in my gut quivered with shades of a fear I hadn't felt in decades. A fear that was the reason for everything.

A fear that had given rise to the promise I would never, *ever* let anyone remain stronger than me for long.

My hand curled into a fist as my eyes slid back to Alaric.

"We can still rule, Melisandre," Stelaruna said. "But if there's going to be an *ash heap* to conquer after this, we must—"

"Enough," Alaric snapped.

He flung out an arm. The sensation of fingers digging into my insides suddenly returned, icy and horrifying. The air warped ahead of him, rolling toward Stelaruna. She threw her hands up, shouting a spell in defense.

The air between them erupted in a flash of light and then jarring dark, as if a lightning blast had inverted itself in an instant. All around it, the trees and grass turned to dust.

Stelaruna didn't wait. Dropping one hand palm down toward the earth, she chanted in the old tongue of the witches, her eyes locked on Alaric.

The hairs on my skin stood on end. In the clearing, the twig-and-stone baubles began spinning rhythmically, one after the other, round and round while dust rose around us, glittering with rainbow colors like gemstones.

Alaric just smiled.

The dust rushed in toward us.

In my gut, the twisting sensation of hands inside me wrenched tighter.

Sparks lit the air as the dust slammed into an invisible barrier all around.

Alaric's metal teeth glinted in the moonlight. "My turn."

I caught myself on the rough ground as my legs gave out beneath me. Every part of my body felt like the energy was being dragged straight from me into him. Alaric didn't even glance my way as he lifted his hand, his fingers elongating and curling as if he was holding an invisible ball of air.

And then he flipped his hand downward, propelling the invisible sphere into the earth.

The ground shuddered. Stelaruna shouted another spell, more dust swirling around the unseen barrier surrounding us.

I barely noticed. He was draining me into him, and I couldn't even shout a curse at him. My vision swirled, splitting and blurring like my mind had suddenly become fragments of dirty stained glass scattered in the air, some in me, some... elsewhere.

Like staring at Stelaruna. Or sinking into the earth, falling through the darkness toward something bright. A confluence of veins of light, like a place where glowing rivers met before rushing onward.

Oh gods. I knew where we were. What she had been guarding.

A nexus of ley lines.

"Melisandre!" Stelaruna cried.

I wrenched my head up, trying to focus my scattered vision. Her back was pressed to the door of the shack. She gripped the frame as if it was the only thing keeping her upright.

"Don't let them do this!" A wave of magic slammed into

her, throwing her harder against the door. "This world is ours, not theirs!"

Alaric scoffed. "That's enough from you."

A stronger wave crashed into her, and she screamed. Her defenses failed, burning in the air like fire around her. Against her skull, her skin pulled in tight while her gray hair fell from her head. Pinned by magic, she didn't fall, but instead shriveled against the wood shack, her muscles and tendons drawing in to contort her body, warping her screams until her throat couldn't form sound any longer.

Gristle and bone crumbled to the ground.

My mouth moved. I had to get free. I couldn't let that happen to me.

Deep within the earth, something cracked.

Terror shot through me. I ripped my gaze from her remains and looked down. My eyes saw dirt. My splintered mind saw the vein of light deep in the earth bucking and twisting like something alive trying to escape a snare.

And failing.

Alaric whispered words in a language made of nothing but hisses and snarls, utter satisfaction in the sound.

The light shattered.

Darkness rolled out from the nexus, spreading through the veins and smothering the magic that flowed through the earth. All around us, the forest withered and died, the trees crumbling and turning to ash.

Instinct drove me to try shifting to smoke to escape the dying earth around me.

Pain radiated through my body like knives were stabbing me from all sides. I choked on a cry and gave up shifting, scrambling backward instead and shoving to my feet while the horses reared in their harnesses, causing the carriage to lurch and making the stablehand leap from the seat.

He didn't make it far. As his feet hit the dying earth, he froze, gasping with his eyes going wide. The color drained from his face as his body began turning to ash and crumbling in a wave from his feet, up his legs, and through his torso.

"Help me..." His cry turned to a rasp as the erosion chewed through his throat and up through his skull. Behind him, the horses panicked, frantically trying to flee.

Before the destruction took them too.

I spun, searching for a way out.

The grass beneath me turned to gray ash.

Nothing else happened. The destruction simply rolled past me, crumbling trees and bushes and leaving me untouched. The warped sensation of my vision being fractured between multiple places receded, but in a way that felt like part of my mind was pulling away from me.

Sinking back into Alaric.

Between panicked glances at the dying earth, I threw a look at him.

That hold he had on me *felt* different. Tighter. Like the hooks of his grip had sunk farther into me, even though I would have sworn there was no deeper for them to go. And now my mind was here with me, but... not.

He paid me no attention, surveying his handiwork with a satisfied expression like a cat watching a mouse die beneath its paws. Mounds of ash and dust surrounded us, and bright moonlight beamed down on them, unfettered by anything now that there was only an empty space where the forest had been. In the distance, the destruction continued rolling onward like it was setting fire to a rope and burning the length to ash.

"How…" My voice was weak with shock, and I hated the sound. I cleared my throat with effort, grasping after the last shreds of dignity I could. Yes, I'd just scrambled across the ground like a frightened child. Yes, my heart was racing like I was a rabbit who'd narrowly escaped a wolf. But none of that mattered. I was a queen, dammit.

As long as there was still a world left to rule, anyway.

I suppressed a shudder. I'd never liked Stelaruna, true. And I'd only allied myself with her all those years ago because we shared the interest of taking power over the coven and the world.

But if she was right…

I swallowed dryly. "What was that?" I continued in a more controlled tone. "What did you do?"

He arched an eyebrow at me. "You couldn't feel it?"

I didn't respond.

Alaric's smile broadened, his inhuman eyes glinting with enjoyment. "I simply unleashed the opening salvo. Created a crack in the armor of this world, if you will." He started toward where the remnants of the carriage lay. "Come along, pet. We have much to do to make this world fall."

7
GWYNEIRA

The cabin was quiet and as far from the rest of the settlement as Rufinia had said. After so many weeks at the giants' home in the mountains, I'd become used to the silence.

But this was different, and not just because the house around me was not fashioned by the men with whom I shared it.

I *was* the silence, and in a way I suspected no one alive had ever experienced. There was no thrum of blood in my veins. No whisper of breath in my lungs.

Just... nothing.

And all I could think about was how no one in my homeland would ever accept that.

They'd see me as a monster. They'd view my men as a threat.

Was I a fool for thinking I could go home now?

In an overstuffed chair in the corner of the main room, I shifted position beneath a woven blanket. My hair was still damp from the bath I'd taken earlier—alone, sadly. It seemed the men had decided to give me space tonight, perhaps in deference to how I hadn't slowed down to grapple with all the changes that had befallen us since I'd died and come back to life.

At least, I hoped that was the reason, rather than the possibility they were now afraid to be with me too.

I couldn't ask, though. Most of them were asleep in the various beds throughout the cabin's other rooms, the exhaustion of the past few days pulling them straight into slumber. Ozias had remained outside, though where he was now, only the gods knew. Roan was crouched by the fireplace, his attention on the flames. He hadn't looked at me once since declaring the witches should have killed Eliasora.

I wasn't sure what to make of him. When I'd woken after the fight with my stepmother, each of the men had called to me. I'd heard them all, from Clay's light cajoling to Ozias's order to get up.

But Roan, he'd said something else. Something I couldn't understand.

I watched him in the light of the fire. "Roan?"

He tensed, everything about him going as still as a statue. But he didn't respond.

"When I woke up on the cliff," I continued into the silence. "You said *not you too*. What did you mean?"

For a long moment, he stayed still, so motionless I'd swear that, like me, he had no heartbeat or need to breathe. And then he replied, "There are enough dead, that's all."

His voice was as even as a frozen lake. He made no move to leave his crouched position by the flames, nor to take his eyes from the blaze.

But nothing in me could believe his words. "Really?"

Slowly, he turned to me. His pitch-black eyes gleamed in

the firelight, eerie. *Alien*, though I couldn't have put my finger on why.

Like Roan wasn't the only one looking back at me.

I fought back a shiver. Whatever I was now, it was reacting to that strange gaze, like the vampire inside me was stretching beneath my skin in response to him.

It made trepidation swirl in my gut and heat fill my core, and the combination was confusing as hell.

Slowly, he rose to his feet in a smooth, liquid motion. "You shouldn't want to know more about me, Princess. You should stay the hell away."

The combination within me grew stronger. "Why is that?"

"Because I don't protect people. I make them burn."

Chills rolled through me at the way he said the words. At his certainty and the irrational way it still stirred heat within me.

I swallowed dryly. "You saved me."

A cruel smile twisted his lips, cold and scathing enough to slice flesh from bone. "Only for now."

I trembled, torn between trepidation and how the thing I'd become wanted to lunge at him, accept the challenge, and see which of us would come out on top in the end.

Knowing I'd enjoy it either way.

"Princess?"

I flinched at the sound of Niko's voice. Drawing a sharp breath, Roan turned away, returning to the fire and sinking back down beside the flames as if he was one of them.

Still shivering, I glanced over. Niko stood in the doorway to one of the bedrooms, his dark hair and eyes making him appear like a ghost in the darkness. With a brief look at where Roan crouched by the fire, Niko walked over to my side. "Are you okay?"

I nodded.

His brow furrowed despite my reassurance. He glanced again at Roan and then motioned to the door. "Would you like to take a walk?"

I hesitated. "You need sleep."

He shrugged, a gentle smile crossing his face. "Doesn't seem right just leaving you sitting here all night."

My awkwardness grew. That was pointed. I couldn't miss it. By the fire, Roan's shoulders shifted slightly, but he didn't turn around at the words.

Was Niko trying to *protect* me from Roan?

Unsure what to say, I rose to my feet and followed as he led me from the room. But my eyes skirted back to Roan, questions pressing at me. Each of the men seemed to trust him. They'd never given me any reason to question that until now.

So what had that been with Niko? And why had Roan warned me to stay away?

❈

In silence, Niko led me around the side of the cabin, heading for the forest behind it. Despite our altitude, the forest looked like a mix of evergreens and trees almost like ones I would have found in Aneira—towering trunks topped with thick branches and leaves that blocked out the moonlight, casting the bushes and fallen logs beneath them in darkness.

At least, it *should* have been darkness.

My eyes darted over the undergrowth, my curiosity

about Roan momentarily forgotten. The closer we came to the trees and the darkness, the more the moonlight seemed to give way. But where there should have been shadows, instead, something else was happening to my eyes.

Each branch, leaf, and log was gradually becoming outlined in a shimmering silver glow on the barest edge of color, though it never quite landed on any specific shade.

Was this magic? I'd never seen it before.

Or was it some side effect of what I'd become?

I pulled my gaze back to Niko. With a surefooted certainty that made him seem like a woodland creature himself, he walked into the forest, weaving beneath the trees and stepping over fallen logs without pausing, almost as if he could spot them as clearly as I could. "Are you seeing this?"

He glanced back at me, his brow twitching up questioningly.

My hand flinched toward the forest in a tight gesture.

He paused. "What are you seeing, Princess?"

"What do *you* see?"

Again, he was silent for a heartbeat, watching me. "The forest tells me where to step and what's around us. I see some things, but it's mostly dark."

My chest quivered. "It's glowing."

He nodded like somehow that didn't surprise him.

"What *is* this?" I pressed.

Niko shrugged. "Night vision. Most night-dwelling predators have it."

He made it sound so simple, like this was to be expected, rather than the description of a monster. And when he extended a hand to me, there was no trace of worry in his expression.

I couldn't move to take it. "Doesn't that worry you?"

His head shook.

"Why not?"

"Because I trust you. And I trust the forest. It would tell me if I was in danger."

I stared at him. He'd always been the quiet one among the seven giants. The shy one too, seemingly content to let the others take the lead, which made his behavior with Roan all the more disconcerting.

But then, when I'd originally arrived at the cabin all those weeks ago, he'd also been the one to stand up for me and insist the others let me stay. Even when he'd learned I was the Princess of Aneira, he hadn't wavered, instead welcoming me to their home with a bouquet he grew before my eyes using his magic.

And now he was all alone with me even though I was a vampire, and he seemed utterly unconcerned.

If I'd had breath in my body, his courage would have stolen it away. "Are you sure?"

He smiled and nodded.

Swallowing dryly, I took his hand. His skin felt so warm it was almost hot against mine.

Alive where I was not.

And yet he didn't show a trace of fear or disgust for that fact, nor for how much colder my skin was than his own.

Unbidden, an ache spread through my chest, not of grief but gratitude. Though my eyes didn't gather any tears, somewhere inside I just wanted to cry for how he made the fact I was a vampire seem so simple. So ordinary. Something to understand and not fear.

It simply *was*, and for that, I loved him.

Without a word, he brought me with him beneath the trees, his hand never leaving my own.

Seconds slipped past in the quiet night around us. A rabbit bolted at the sight of me, while from a nearby tree, an owl stared down at me, tracking me with its unblinking eyes and not making a sound.

It reminded me of Roan somehow.

The thought brought me back to what had transpired earlier. "What was that about, back at the cabin?"

"What do you mean?" Now he sounded tense, at least a bit, and like he was trying to hide it too.

"With Roan. It seemed like..." I wasn't sure how to ask. "Is there something I should know about him?"

He didn't respond.

I stopped walking, taking my hand from his. "Niko?"

When he glanced back, his normally gentle expression twisted momentarily with frustration, though it seemed more aimed at himself or something else, not me. "It's probably nothing."

I fought back a frustrated expression of my own. Didn't he know that was exactly what people said when their concern actually *was* something, and they were just foolishly talking themselves out of it?

Gods, I had too much experience with that. Too many weird occurrences back home in Aneira I made myself believe were nothing.

Then my stepmother turned out to be a vampire who wanted to kill me.

And who'd succeeded.

"*What* is?" I pressed.

He was quiet for a moment. "The forest has been...

uncertain of Roan lately. It's always said he's different than the rest of us. He and Ozias both, but... not in the same way."

Wariness prickled through me. "Different how?"

Niko shook his head. "I don't know. Neither of them has ever said anything. And they don't really spend time with each other or talk to each other, so maybe they don't even know..." The frustration on his face grew. "I shouldn't be talking about them like this. They're both loyal and I know their hearts are good, and whatever's going on with Roan... I trust him with my life. He wouldn't hurt us."

I wasn't sure what to think. I didn't doubt his belief in them—he knew both men better than I did—but Roan had also warned me about himself.

And I had no idea what to think about Ozias.

But they *were* different than the others. Any fool could see that. And different from one another too. Ozias was like a force of nature. There was an inevitability to him like the crushing power of the mountains themselves but paired with a stealth like a silent predator in the woods stalking its prey.

And Roan felt like a blade, cold and lethal but with a twist at its core—one that would either be its strength or the thing that cracked it through.

I shivered, the impressions overwhelming, and I pushed them aside as I focused back on Niko. "Then why ask me to come out here?"

In the strange silvery night vision I now possessed, I saw his cheeks darken, and he ducked his head a bit as if embarrassed. "Would you believe I just wanted some time with you?"

I blinked, flattered. But I knew that wasn't all of it. Even if he trusted Roan, I could still tell he was worried about the man.

Looking a tad embarrassed, and more than a little shy, Niko turned and continued into the woods.

"Where are we going, then?" I asked, following him.

"There's a clearing up ahead."

More questions pressed at me, but I trailed after him all the same. The darkness thinned, the silvery edges to everything turning to actual moonlight as glimpses of the sky became visible between the branches overhead. The traces of snow on the ground lessened, revealing more patches of rocks and dirt amid fallen branches. Wisps of mist curled up from between the stones, but at my startled look, Niko explained, "Steam vents. They keep it warmer here than elsewhere."

In a patch of moonlight barely large enough for the two of us, he slowed. A stillness hung around us, like we were the only two people on the mountain. Maybe in the world.

"I wanted to ask you something," he continued, his voice quiet.

Suddenly nervous, I gave a tiny nod for him to go on.

"I don't know much about vampires." He took my hand again, his fingers intertwining with mine. "But I do know about nature. There are some creatures who—when they don't have access to enough food—they shut down. They're not dead, but they're not exactly alive either. They wait out the winter or whatever natural phenomenon is going on, and when sustenance is available again, they sort of come back to life."

Alarm prickled through me. "What are you saying?"

He took a step closer to me, his dark eyes tracing over my face. Even with our coats and winter gear separating us, his body heat reached me, warming the air as much as the steam vents nearby. "Feeding helped you. It brought you back to us when she tried to make you into her creature."

I tensed at the memory.

"But," he continued, "you would have noticed if your stepmother didn't breathe, right? When you were growing up, I mean. You would have noticed if she was"—his brow twitched down as if he was searching for a term—"pale as snow."

I tried to find words to ask him what he was getting at, except I had a sneaking suspicion, and it made fear twist through me. But not just at the knowledge of what he meant.

At the way his words made the creature in the back of my mind rouse like a starving predator, growling and hungry and ready to test any theory with its teeth.

He bobbed his head thoughtfully. "My guess is she fed more than you have. So now you need to do the same. And I..." One of his hands rose, brushing back a strand of my hair. "I'm here for you."

I trembled, and in spite of myself, my eyes flicked down, taking in his lips, his throat. With the strange night vision I now possessed, I could pick out the twitch of his vein, and my insides rioted with hunger at the sight.

"It's okay."

At the simple words, my eyes snapped back up to his. There was no fear in his gaze. Nothing but kindness, same as ever, and it made the hunger tangle with how I *never* wanted to hurt him, until my insides were an inextricable mess.

"I care for you, Princess. I... I meant what I said back before this happened. If there's such a thing as treluria, I know you're it, so this..." He smiled. "It's okay."

My head shook. "No, it's not."

"Princess—"

I took a step back, pain rising at the dark, hungry feeling that was only growing stronger with every passing second. I *couldn't* risk hurting him. Hurting any of them, really, but Niko was so kind and gentle and if I lost control...

It wouldn't be a question of forgiving myself. That would never happen. It would only be a question of surviving the horror of what I'd done. I'd barely held on when Rufinia and the witches tested me. If I failed now...

He dropped his gaze from mine, a flicker of hurt passing over his face. "I know I'm not like the others," he said quietly as if answering something he thought he saw in my eyes. "Not built like them. Not a fighter quite like they are. I was never a soldier, or scholar, or anything. I lived in the forest, and that's what I know."

My motionless heart ached. "It's not that."

"Then what?"

I trembled, at a loss for a way to explain how, of all of them, he was the one who felt the most... familiar. Sure, he was closer to the size of a human man than most of the other "dwarves"—closer than Ozias or Dex, especially—but he would still tower over some of the people back at the castle. But that wasn't the most important thing.

There was a *peace* to him. The other men had an edge to them, probably from everything they'd been through. Like, if pushed to it, they wouldn't have an issue with unleashing violence. It wouldn't faze them. And true, I didn't fault them for it, but it wasn't what I'd known in my life before. My father tried to keep the war away from me. My closest companions had been people far removed from violence. And although I suspected Niko had seen as much suffering as the rest of the men, it had never quite hardened him in the same way.

Niko let me feel like the person I used to be, just by virtue of being himself. And even now, with my deathly cold skin and fangs peeking out from between my lips, he was still looking at me like I was the most cherished and beautiful thing he'd ever seen.

If I destroyed him... "I don't want to hurt you."

His eyes flicked to my mouth, lingering there without a trace of fear. "You won't."

Even seeing him glance toward my lips and fangs fueled the hunger stirring inside me. In the night and the forest and the silence, the vampire inside me was emerging, spreading through my limbs like a wild creature stretching after being kept bound for too long.

With effort, I made myself retreat, but there was a tree behind me, and I bumped into it. Had it been here the whole time? I couldn't recall. Rough bark grated against my leather coat, and something moved against my hip. I looked down sharply, afraid it was a snake.

A single vine twisted against me languidly. For a heartbeat, I feared it was attacking me like vines imbued with my stepmother's dark magic had days before. But then I looked up to see a hint of self-consciousness flash over Niko's face.

"They do what I wish I could," he murmured.

My eyes dropped back to the tendril gently stroking my leg, the tiny movement somehow erotic and yet comforting all at the same time. He wished to touch me this way?

"Is that okay?" he asked softly.

My insides quivered with need and heat as my gaze rose to him again. "Yes."

A grateful smile crossed his face. He stepped closer, and

none of my silent, half-hearted pleas for my body to move away reached my muscles. I could feel the warmth radiating from his skin, the slight contact of the vine, and I could hear his pulse in my ears like a distant drum urging me onward. It made me want to launch across the space to him.

It made me ache inside.

"It's okay, Princess."

He was so close that his pulse in my ears was all I could hear. Slowly, carefully, he reached up, brushing a hand along my cheek and leaving a trail of heat in his wake. He leaned his head to the side, exposing his throat. "I trust you."

I wanted to tell him he shouldn't. I wanted to tell him to run and leave me be. But his words snapped the last thread of my restraint.

Like I was the snake I'd thought the vine to be, I struck, sinking my fangs into his neck. Pure fire flowed down my throat to flood my body as I swallowed his blood down.

He'd been right.

Everything in me surged to life. My heart raced hard like it'd never stopped. My lungs breathed deep, drawing in his delicious scent.

The flesh between my legs throbbed with need.

I moaned against his neck, hot desire rolling through me, like my body could finally express the *other* hunger for him that I'd possessed all along. His hands took my sides, holding me tightly, but after a moment, the contact sent alarm clanging through me.

Oh, gods, what if I was hurting him?

I pulled back swiftly, but blood was still pumping from the bites on his neck. Instinct drove me to lick at it hungrily, claiming every drop.

My alarm returned. Beneath my ministrations, the wound vanished as his skin healed.

I looked up at him. "Did you do…"

The desire in his eyes made my words trail off. My renewed breath stopped completely, hot arousal pooling low inside me. Turning his head slightly, he moved toward my lips, not closing the distance, waiting for me to meet him halfway.

Gods, yes, please.

All my thoughts fragmented as my lips collided with his. A strange sensation moved through my mouth, and with shock I realized my fangs had slid away, retracting so as not to hurt him as his tongue plundered me.

A thrill went through me at the realization I didn't have to remain looking like a monster, but it scattered as Niko's hand slid into my hair, holding me to him. His other hand moved down my side, pulling me against his body. Through our clothes, I could feel his hard cock against my stomach, and I pushed tighter to him, need clamoring in me and making me so desperately wet. My fumbling fingers tugged at his breeches while I prayed he wanted this as much as I did.

His lips broke from mine, and worry shot through me. Maybe he didn't. Maybe I was getting so far ahead of myself, it was shameful.

Dark hunger filled his gaze, bringing all my fears to a halt. "May I taste you too, Princess?" he whispered.

Breathless, I twitched my head in a small nod. "Yes."

His hands pushed my coat away from my shoulders, and I let it fall. His fingers traced around my side, finding the ribbon at the back of my vest and tugging the bow undone. Sliding up my spine, he loosened the crisscrossed ties until his fingertips ghosted over my shoulders. Delicious shivers ran through me to pool lower in my body, making me wetter still.

Gently, he drew my blouse and vest away, exposing my breasts to the night air. Even with my heartbeat and breathing restored, the cold barely touched my skin, like I was more resilient to it than I'd been before.

For a long moment, his eyes lingered on me, and then his fingers moved to my leather pants. Tingles ran through my body as his skin brushed mine while he pulled them down, undid my boots, and then kneeled, lifting one of my feet and then the other, removing my clothes completely.

Naked in the dark forest, I didn't move. My nipples tightened, unaffected by the cool air but *entirely* affected by the way his eyes rose to mine and the desire pounding through my veins. I reached down to draw him up to me, but he stilled my motions with one hand.

A smile pulled at the corners of his lips, the expression gentle as ever but now with a wicked edge, like honey mixed with pepper, sweet and spicy. The sight sent my renewed heartbeat flying higher. Releasing my hand, he eased my legs wider, and my lips parted with anticipation.

He bent closer to me and traced his tongue along my slit. My head fell back against the tree behind me, a raw sound escaping my lips. With a noise of appreciation, he returned, his tongue delving into me, working at my opening before he shifted position, his fingers moving to take over stroking me from within as he sucked and licked at my clit.

Something slipped around my side, drawing my eyes back downward. Narrow vines were twisting up from behind me, undulating across my skin. Some thicker ones slid down my legs, holding them wide for him and moving over me as if massaging my thighs, while delicate others ghosted up to tease around my breasts, my nipples, looping around the hardened nubs and then tightening like tiny bindings.

I gasped, fighting to hold myself still as the vines twisted over me, brushing gently in places, scraping over my skin in others, and tightening deliciously on still more. I'd never imagined something like this, but the pinpricks of pain mingling with the pulse of pleasure from his tongue on my clit was dizzying. I needed this. Wanted it. I loved the times I'd spent with several of the other men. They were all marvelous. But the illusion of restraints and the inexorable mix of pain and pleasure stirred something new inside me. The predator in me relished the delicate balance of dominance and submission, even at the barest hints of it here. And all the while, Niko worked me with his tongue and fingers, licking up my arousal like he could never get enough.

My breath grew ragged. Pleasure pulsed through me as if on a direct line from my nipples to my clit as more vines twisted over my breasts, making my hips lurch against him. The pressure built higher and hotter at the combination of his tongue and fingers and the countless vines tangling around as if he had infinite hands with which to touch me.

The tendrils around my nipples tightened sharply, and I gasped, the sharp bite throwing me over the edge into my release. I came in a rush, my knees going weak as a surge of pleasure rolled through me.

His hands and the vines both kept me upright as the waves of my orgasm eased. With a satisfied smile, he rose to his feet.

"More?" he asked.

Breathless, I nodded. I'd never deny him his pleasure as well. And I needed him.

Desperately.

"Be in me," I whispered. "Please."

His beautiful gaze filled with joy and heat as he smiled. Pulling me away from the tree, he lowered me to the ground.

The forest floor was soft.

My eyes flashed around. Gone were the snow, branches, and rocks I'd seen earlier. Now a carpet of tiny plants and thick moss had grown beneath me, just large enough to provide us a place to lie down, while steam still rose from the vents beyond it, warming the air.

I looked back up at Niko. Never taking his attention from me, he tugged his shirt and pants away.

My lips parted as my eyes roamed over him, my night vision painting his olive skin in tones of silver. He was lean, but far from weak. Shadows traced the cords of muscles on his arms and torso, leading to the dark thatch of hair around his erect cock. As he lowered himself over me, my legs fell to either side, my core aching to have him in me now.

His mouth curved into a smile, and he laid a kiss on my lips before angling himself over me. "Were the vines okay?" he whispered. "If you didn't—"

I rocked my hips toward him. "Make me yours, Niko."

Desire lit his eyes, and vines erupted from the earth around me as he slid his cock into my slick channel. As he drew out and then entered me again, the tendrils wrapped my breasts and nipples, while others held my legs wide for him. Still more played along my ass, getting slick with my arousal, and then returning to my rear opening.

My eyes flew wide. With what I was, infection or any other concerns were almost certainly nonexistent. Which was good, because I could barely think to care about them anyway. "Gods, Niko. Please. Yes."

I felt him smile against my throat, his kisses pausing briefly and then resuming, leaving a hot line down the column of my neck. He never stopped driving himself into me, even as his vines teased around my other opening and then pushed into me.

I gasped. Still more tendrils tightened around one of my breasts again, pinching and massaging while his hand worked my other breast and his cock thrust into me harder and harder.

Ragged noises escaped me, full of pleasure and pleading all at the same time. His vines undulated inside and around me while his cock hit me so deep, all of it like he was doing exactly what I asked.

Making me his.

"Yes," I breathed. "Niko, yes."

Movement in the forest beyond us drew my attention, but before I could panic, my night vision picked out the details.

Ozias.

He stood mostly hidden by a tree amid the forest, his thick beard and dark hair only part of what made him nearly vanish into the woods behind him. He was as still as any wild animal, frozen in place, and his eyes were fastened on us while Niko thrust into me. I couldn't even see him blink.

But the fact he was watching didn't send a shred of anger or embarrassment through me. No, it was hotter than fire itself, somehow making me even more aroused than I was already. In a rush, my orgasm overtook me like an unstoppable force quaking from deep inside. I cried out, the world vanishing in a surge of pleasure as I squeezed my eyes shut, rocking with the waves of ecstasy.

Niko's motions became faster and more ragged. He groaned as he came hard too, and my channel pulsed around him with the aftershocks of my orgasm, milking out his passion that spilled hot inside me. Breathless, he stopped moving while the vines retreated from me, slipping back into the earth like they'd never existed.

I opened my eyes as he gently kissed me.

"Thank you," he whispered as he drew back again.

I smiled. "Thank you too."

He returned the smile and pulled out of me, rolling to the side on the bed of moss. I nestled closer to him, relishing his warmth and the peace settling over me from all we'd done. My fingers strayed across his chest, tracing the lines of his muscles and feeling the pump of his heart.

My gaze drifted back to the woods again. Greedy as it may have seemed, I wanted all of them, including the man who'd been watching us from the woods.

But Ozias was already gone.

8

OZIAS

I was a fool.

With my cock aching and my mind spewing insults at myself, I retreated through the forest, everything in me clamoring to claim that black-haired beauty currently being fucked to pieces behind me. Even the cold air of the mountaintop couldn't wipe her scent from my memory, not when my heightened senses could have tracked her across half the mountain range itself.

Gods, to feel her legs wrapped around me as I drove myself into her... to feel her come apart around my cock, crying out from the orgasms I'd wrung from her beautiful body...

Everything about this place was wrong, from the magic that muffled the voice of the earth to the way the witches stared wherever we went. But that was why I'd followed the princess. To protect her. To help Niko defend her if the eerie silence of the earth proved to be more than just a byproduct of the defensive magic wrapped around it.

But what I'd seen...

Shivers rolled over my skin, my senses rioting with the urge to let the animal inside me come out to play. From the moment I'd laid eyes on her in our cabin weeks ago, that part of me had growled she was mine. Let the others call it treluria. Let them think it was some ancient fairytale of destiny and binding by the gods. My innermost nature howled she was my mate. That part of me wanted to shift and show her all that I could be, as if to impress her. To sink my fangs into her, marking her so all would know she was mine.

It wanted to believe there was a chance in hell a beautiful woman like that would survive something like me.

I ground my teeth, fighting the way that side of me snarled and thrashed inside, desperate to return to her. But I couldn't let it out, not as long as I was anywhere near where another living soul might see.

Especially not Gwyneira.

I stumbled over a rock and cursed myself harder. The earth itself was taunting me, trying to pull me from my thoughts of her. But it was a losing game. The mere *idea* of her made my beast clamor to bring her to the ground and pin her there, rutting with her supple body until every inch of her unquestionably submitted to being mine.

And the fact my idea of sex was anything but gentle didn't matter to that creature. That I was more animal than man was irrelevant too. The wilder part of me pelted the rest with imagined sensations, from the taste of the sweat on her skin to the scent of her desire surrounding me while her body writhed beneath my own. My ears rang with the moans I'd heard her make only moments ago, while the damned beast inside me dreamed those cries could be for me.

And what cries they'd been...

I bit back a groan, one hand catching me against a tree while the other shoved beneath my waistband to yank my cock free. A few strokes was all it took, and I was coming, empty pleasure erupting from me to spill onto the dirt.

My heartbeat slowed as my fingers dug into the rough bark of the tree. The cold air twisted around my loosened breeches, cooling me back to sanity. Gods, what a fool I was, craving the impossible. Craving a princess who could never—

A branch cracked behind me. Tucking my cock away quickly, I turned.

Gwyneira stood several yards back, frozen beside the fallen log that must have betrayed her footsteps. Her dark eyes were wide, her beautiful red lips parted, shaped like a tiny *O* in her surprise. The black strands of her hair were mussed by sex and the forest floor, and her thick locks were pulled around one shoulder as if she'd been trying to finger-comb them back into order when she'd come upon me. I'd heard nothing but the small crack of the branch to warn me of her arrival, proving how much of a predator she was now.

Deep inside, my beast growled low, torn between approval for how silently my mate could move and incredulity that the boy had let her go off alone in this forest where anything could have happened to her.

"Why did you leave Niko?" I snarled.

She blinked as if thrown that those were the first words from my mouth. "I-I told him I needed a minute."

That mollified the beast inside me—*slightly*. Though heavily muffled by the magic here, a whisper of the earth's voice informed me he was only a short distance from us, outside of earshot for regular conversations but close enough to hear her if she screamed. And yes, it was still reckless of him to let her walk alone in these woods, but respecting her needs mattered too. Niko was young, but it was good he understood that.

Except it only left her standing here, staring at me while my beast dragged my eyes over her form, the impulse to take her growing stronger with every second. Never mind that I'd just spilled my seed on the ground. The beast would find other ways to bring her pleasure until I was ready to fill her.

My teeth clenched as I pushed the animal within me to the dark recesses of my mind. She was a predator, true, though I wondered if she realized how much of one she'd become. But regardless, she could never be mine. Forget how much my beast wanted to show her its true form, something I hadn't *willingly* shown a soul in years. No matter how I looked right now, I wasn't human inside. Wasn't even Erenlian, not at my core.

No, I was too rough, too violent, and my desires were too dark for anything as beautiful as her. My true nature would only drive her away in terror. Hell, from her expression, she'd seen what I'd just done, and that alone had shocked her.

And if she dared to risk being with me, I would only break her.

I stayed still, waiting, my body like stone. But as the seconds ticked past and she didn't say another word, the pressure to fill the void between us with speech bore down on me, the sensation foreign after a lifetime of near silence. Speech was never needed in the forest, only action or stillness. But suddenly, I wished I had words like the scholarly Byron or even that clown Clay to fix this moment.

She wetted her lips. My eyes tracked the motion in spite

of myself. My nose twitched, picking up the scent of her arousal—though of course that was just left over from her tryst with Niko, nothing more. "My apologies," she continued. "I shouldn't have—"

My beast propelled me a single step closer to her, but the slightest hint of a flinch from her brought me up short. Gods, had I *frightened* her by getting myself off like this? Or by watching her with Niko?

Most likely both.

I didn't know what to do. I could track anything, hunt anything, but in this moment, I was as lost as an orphaned fawn.

"I saw you." Her words were stronger, as if she'd settled something in herself. "Earlier." She took a step toward me, and this time *I* was the one who wasn't sure whether to retreat.

I didn't move a muscle.

"You were watching, and..." Her small white teeth slipped over her lip briefly, no hint of fangs to be seen. She was like me, then. Two forms, and I was relieved for her sake that she could change back if she wished, much like I did.

Except I couldn't tell her that.

She walked closer, her delicious scent coming with her. Frost and apples, sugar and cinnamon. It made me want to lick and bite her, to taste that sweetness between her legs and mingle my scent with hers until everyone knew she was my mate.

"When I saw you there..." Her hand came up as if to touch me.

My heart thundered in my ears, and my beast stretched beneath my skin, straining to feel her, fuck her, take her so deeply she could never question for a moment whether she

91

was mine. I'd mark her as my mate and she'd bond with me more closely than she could even imagine, and then nothing would ever steal her from me again.

An ache spread through my bones, the urgency to change forms growing intolerable. Gods, I wanted that so badly. I had only to shift and claim her for that dream to come true.

Shuddering, I shoved the beast back harder and turned away. "Sorry. Won't happen again."

I strode off quickly, stalking toward the gods knew where. My beast was thrashing inside, desperate to break free and make her mine, and I didn't need to see the look of horror and disgust on her face if I lost control of this form. I hadn't shifted involuntarily in years, but with her...

The *last* thing my beast wanted was to stay in control.

But I'd horrified enough people when I was a child to last me a lifetime. I'd been only four years old the first time I was abandoned. My own mother dragged me out into the forest and tossed me into a river, hoping I'd drown. If not for the wolves who found me, I would've died.

My first memory was that day.

I'd learned a hard lesson, one that was reinforced each time I came near civilization. Whenever I lost control or stayed too long and the "good" people of Erenelle saw my other form, the result was always the same. Some tried to kill me, either as a trophy or out of their own fear. Others tried to cage me as a carnival attraction.

I had scars from them all.

"Ozias."

Gwyneira's voice brought me up short as if it was a leash, and a shiver ran through me to hear her say my name. The gods knew I wanted her screaming it beneath me as I pounded into her. I wanted her moaning it as I knotted her and claimed her for always. Yet even that soft tone wrapped its bindings around my heart, like she could reach in and touch the deepest parts of me with only a word.

But then the hairs on the back of my neck rose.

Quickly, I spun, every instinct I had suddenly clamoring with alarm.

"It's just I—" She cut off, whatever she saw on my face making her scent spike with worry.

I noted her heightened fear, *hated* it had something to do with me, but I forced my attention to scanning the terrain around us and the earth below. Something was off, more than just the silence. Whispers reached my mind through the muffling power of the magic around me, like far-off cries carried on a wind beneath the earth.

Impressions and knowledge came with them. I'd always been able to find my way anywhere, because until we'd come to this place, the earth had always spoken clearly to me, telling me precisely where I was located.

But here was different. This mountaintop wasn't where I'd thought. Where it *should* have been, given how far we'd walked and what territory we'd crossed. And the mountain's voice had been so smothered by the magic here, it was only now that I could hear the truth.

The cries within the earth grew louder, wailing that something was wrong. Something had broken, yet I couldn't tell what.

But that *something* was a threat to my mate, and I damn well would see it dead before I—

A rumble came from deep within the mountain, so faint that it couldn't be felt by anyone on the surface yet.

Except me.

The princess gasped as I lunged toward her. "What are you—"

My hand closed around her wrist just as the trembling spread through the soil beneath our feet. The trees began to sway, spruce needles raining down.

And then the rumbling grew stronger.

"What's happening?" she cried.

I didn't waste time responding. I had no clue what this was, but I could feel the earth protesting, the shaking so deep it felt like the soul of the world was in rebellion. It hadn't started here, though. It was radiating from somewhere far to the north, growing stronger with every second.

And it wasn't an earthquake. Not exactly. More like a reaction to something, but I had no clue *what*.

Pulling Gwyneira behind me, I raced toward the nearest break in the forest. Earthquakes on a snow-covered mountain were bad news on a good day, and the earth beneath me made clear this was anything but *good*. If an avalanche was going to come at us from the mountain slopes nearby, I wanted her away from this forest and tucked into the safest place I could find.

Light flared across the magical shield surrounding the coven's hideout. A boom shook the air like a deafening blast of thunder, and the night sky glowed like day for a moment.

The trembling stopped.

I didn't dare stop moving.

Stumbling along behind me, Gwyneira gasped out, "Ozias, where are we going?"

I burst past the edge of the forest. The witches' cottages still stood, though hanging pots had fallen from their porch eaves and cascades of snow had slid from their rooftops to pile around their bases in mounds of white. The witches themselves were outside, staring around at the mountains and terrain.

None of them looked like they had a clue what was going on.

But they weren't moving to set up a defense, and I snarled curses under my breath at the sight. None of these people were predators. Even with all their power, they still waited like sheep for someone in charge to tell them what to do.

Footsteps crunched on gravel and snow, and my head whipped toward the sound. Dex, Roan, and the twins came running around a bend of the path, and relief filled their faces when they spotted us both.

"Are you okay?" Dex demanded immediately. My beast approved of how his eyes locked on Gwyneira. Even if she was my mate, the beast within me listened enough to my Erenlian side to know Dex had a claim on her too. It pleased the beast that Dex worried about her safety.

And that he didn't question whether I could take care of my own.

Gwyneira nodded. "Yes, you?" At their noises of confirmation, she continued. "What was that?"

Dex glanced at me, his eyebrow twitching up in silent repetition of the question. "Shaking came from the north," I answered. "Deep in the earth."

Roan scowled at the terrain like he was waiting for it to attack us. "That didn't feel like that tremor we had back beneath the cabin, though."

"It wasn't," Niko said, coming up behind us. "After the shaking started, the forest went berserk here in a way I've never felt before. Like... like it was afraid it was going to die."

He cast a quick glance to Gwyneira, continuing in a murmur. "Are you okay?"

She nodded. "You?"

Reaching out to clasp her hand briefly, he nodded back. A blush touched her cheeks at the contact, and they both ducked their faces away, smiling bashfully.

My heart ached. She'd never look that way at me.

I made myself shove the pain down. Protecting her would be my only contribution to her life, and it would have to be enough.

"So if it wasn't like what happened that day, what the hell was it?" Clay asked.

I forced my attention to the mountainside, surveying the open clearing wreathed by the dark forest, all of it cast in silver by the moonlight. I recalled the day the others spoke of. We'd been mining, same as ever, when suddenly the earth shook around us. In only moments, it somehow had moved the ore we sought through the rocks, gathering more of it together in one place than I'd ever seen.

And not just any place. In a cave directly beneath our cabin, as if the earth itself had been preparing for the princess to arrive—and to keep her safe.

But Niko was right. This time was different.

"Maybe the difference is just because the witches are here?" Lars suggested, and I could see the hope in his blue eyes. "Some fluke caused by their magic?"

I shook my head before the others could respond. "Something's wrong."

Before they could ask for more, Leontine rounded a turn of the path, coming to a stop at the sight of us. Her eyes were like ice and iron, but my beast detected traces of fear in her scent for the first time.

My beast growled inside my mind. This couldn't be good.

Drawing herself up, she motioned swiftly for us to follow her back the way she'd come. "Rufinia insists you join her. *Now.*"

9
GWYNEIRA

If I thought things were tense the *last* time we were here, I had been grossly mistaken.

Within the main cabin, witches raced around, their hoods thrown back and their robes disheveled, as if they hadn't bothered to take time straightening them after being knocked down. Frantically, people were gathering everything from herbs to crystals to silver knives from where the items had fallen. Other people were centered around maps spread across tables in the center of the room, their hands interlinked as they chanted in quick, low voices.

The moment we entered, Rufinia looked away from her survey of the chaos.

She did not appear pleased.

"What the hell was that?" Clay demanded immediately. "It felt like the damn mountain shook."

"An attack on the earth itself."

I blinked.

"Come." Rufinia gestured sharply for us to follow her

before whipping around and stalking toward a narrow door at the far end of the large room.

Warily, I followed, Leontine and my giants coming after me. Past the door, a room lined with shelves waited. The shelving itself was not for books, but instead held tiny cubbyholes with scrolls tucked inside.

There were hundreds, and the shaking had jostled them all, making rolls of paper extend erratically from their cubbyholes like the legs of a spider sticking through from the other side. A heavy oak table stood at the center of the room, several scrolls still unfurled atop it, and dim light came from the tightly enclosed candles in lanterns above, a few of which still swung gently from the earthquake. All around us, the scent of spice and old parchment was heavy on the air, and I breathed it in, distantly grateful to be smelling anything now that my lungs functioned once again.

Leontine shut the door behind us all, her hands clasped over the handle at her back and dark eyes trained on Rufinia as if waiting for her to speak first.

Dex didn't bother doing the same. "What did you mean, an attack on the earth itself?"

Rufinia's lips tightened. "This mountain is on a ley line —one of the many currents of power that run through the earth. And something just fractured a nexus of those lines."

I had no idea what that meant, but it sounded like it should have been impossible.

"The defenses here seem to have stopped the progress of the destruction," Rufinia said.

"We hope," Leontine added in a low voice.

Rufinia threw her a dark look.

"What the hell could do something like that?" Dex demanded. "Vampires?"

Leontine shook her head. "Even the vampires never had power like this."

My eyes darted between the two witches. "What about the others? The Voidborn?"

Chills rolled over me even to say that word, like maybe it would draw the attention of those beings to me. The only time I'd ever caught a glimpse of them was when my stepmother managed to tear a gash in the world when she attacked here... or in a mirror.

In spite of myself, I glanced around the room, but there were no mirrors in sight.

Not that I could be sure it mattered.

"Could one have gotten into this world?" Clay asked the witches, and something about his tense expression made me think he was as disturbed by this as I was. "Doesn't reality repel them?"

Rufinia nodded. "To tap into the ley lines themselves is possible, but to *damage* one like this would take a catastrophic level of power. The ley lines are the very embodiment of the energy of this world. The Voidborn never should have been able to come close to one, let alone use their strength to harm a nexus of them."

A horrible thought occurred to me. "Maybe... that's why they made vampires."

The First Matron's eyes met mine.

My core felt like it was freezing, and not because my heart had stopped or my lungs no longer worked. Niko's blood still strengthened me, making me practically human.

But fear was a force of its own.

"I know you said vampires didn't have that kind of

power, but if those creatures have a way to..." My chills strengthened, but worse was the fact a strange certainty was coming with them. "To *use* us. To tap into what they made us, like Eliasora kind of suggested they did, or maybe channel their own power through us..."

Rufinia's expression was unreadable. "Indeed."

The muffled voices of the witches beyond the door became the only sound in this tiny room. They seemed scared.

I suspected they had good reason.

"Could it be my stepmother? Could she have survived?"

Rufinia and Leontine shared a glance.

"The void between worlds," Rufinia said, "has always been understood as something that would destroy life."

The horrible flaw in that logic was so clear to me. "But... we aren't really alive, right?"

Leontine made a negating noise. "You're still animate."

My skin crawled at the memory of the Voidborn I'd seen in my stepmother's mirror, slithering around like eels hungry to break into this world. "So are they."

For a moment, the two women studied me, and I couldn't hope to guess at what they were thinking. I wasn't a witch. I didn't know much about magic, while they'd probably both been studying it since before my mother was a child. Moreover, now I was this *thing* and any wrong word still felt like it might land me in a cage like Eliasora.

But I also knew I wasn't wrong.

Rufinia's jaw tightened, and she twitched her chin at Leontine. "Have the seers search for signs of Melisandre."

Leontine stared at her for a moment like she was trying to wrap her mind around what Rufinia just said, but then she gave a short nod and pulled open the door behind her.

The noise of the other room rose and then fell as the door closed again.

"What about us?" Niko asked, his hands gripped tightly together. "What do we do?"

"You need to return to Aneira." The First Matron's tone brooked no argument. "Quickly. If something is attacking ley lines, then you—"

The door opened again behind us. Byron gave us a solemn look as he entered. "I take it you felt that up here too."

Rufinia continued as if he hadn't spoken. "The Aneiran capital of Lumilia is *also* on a nexus. That is why Eira went there years ago. If Melisandre survived—or, goddess forbid, if the Voidborn have broken into this world—the capital is certain to be a target. Sitting unclaimed as it is right now, that nexus will be ripe for the picking." Her gaze landed on me. "The power of that nexus will have imbued everything, from the castle down to the cobblestones, and you have stronger ties to that place than Melisandre or the Voidborn ever could. It will listen to you. You only have to make it to Lumilia before whoever is behind this gets there first."

I stared at her. "But I barely know magic. How will I—"

Rufinia whipped the diamond pendant over her head and then extended it to me. I blinked, my hand moving to take it automatically.

The stone was warm in my palm, warmer than it felt like it should have been. Within the core of the diamond, a light flared, glowing like a star.

Deep inside, I could feel the vampire part of me smile, as if this was something it wanted too.

Worry swelled in me. Quickly, I extended the diamond to give it back to her.

Rufinia shook her head. "The stone recognizes you. You *are* a diamond witch, even if you haven't accepted that. Your people and your home need you. The whole world does."

I swallowed dryly. "What if this gives *other things* an advantage too?"

"Then you must master them. The nexus at Lumilia could help you. That magic is tied to your father's blood, and your mother's blood will aid you in controlling it." She met my eyes. "Do not underestimate yourself, Princess, or the power of your mother's legacy in you. Doubt will only give our enemies the advantage."

I trembled, looking down at the gemstone in my hand. With a steadying breath and a quiet prayer to whatever gods would listen, I looped the chain over my head.

The diamond glinted between my breasts, and a quiver of energy moved through my chest, like a thread of power extended between me and the gemstone.

"So which way to that bridge thing?" Clay asked, the attempted humor in his voice ruined by tension. "Aneira's only a couple days' walk from where it—"

Rufinia made a negating sound. "The Moonlight Bridge is not an option. Nothing touched by the Voidborn may access it—and that means Gwyneira too. The princess was only able to cross before because she was technically dead at the time. Had she been resurrected before you were across, the result for all of you would have been... unfortunate."

Clay gave her an irritated look. "Okay, then we'll climb down the mountain. It'll just add a day or so to the—"

"You are several weeks' journey from Aneira."

I blinked. "What?"

"Nah." Clay shook his head. "There's no way that little bridge crossed weeks' worth of—"

"She's right," Ozias said, his deep voice quiet. He wouldn't meet my eyes when I looked at him, but the memory of what I'd seen in the woods suddenly flashed through my mind, making heat rise in my cheeks. Had he needed release like that because he wanted me? Or because he *didn't* actually want me, but had still been aroused by the sight of what Niko and I had shared?

I knew what I hoped, but I had no idea how to ask... or what I'd do if it turned out my attraction to him was not mutual.

Ozias jerked his bearded chin at the witch, still giving no sign he noticed my gaze, and I made myself focus again. "Their magic guards the mountain," he said. "It muffled the earth's voice. But the stones aren't Aneiran."

"Fantastic." Clay scoffed. "So where the hell are we?"

"The Wild Lands," Niko replied in a quiet voice.

My heart hit my throat. All around me, various shades of nausea or dread crossed the men's faces.

"I couldn't feel it before," Niko continued, his hands tightening on each other as if to hold in his nervousness. "But Ozias is right. The coven's magic muffled everything, but when the earthquake hit, there were cracks in that power and..." He drew a steadying breath. "Wild magic is out there."

"That..." Clay raked a hand through his blond hair. "Shit."

Dex watched Rufinia. "So when you say 'several weeks from Aneira'..."

She tilted her head briefly as if in acknowledgement. "If the mountains allow it."

I trembled. "How bad is it out there?"

"Paths change," she said. "They warp. Even time itself

becomes... variable. If the mountains cooperate, it could take a week or so. If they do not..."

"I don't suppose you ever developed any tricks to help folks get through that?" Lars asked the witch, hope in his voice.

Rufinia tilted her head in mild acknowledgement. "A few, but the magic in that territory is unpredictable and very nearly sentient. It adapts. What works to protect you from it now may not later, which is what makes travel so perilous. On our first attempt at a supply run using the path through the mountains, our people returned having traveled hundreds of miles in only a few days. They brought back tales of ravenous beasts and wailing spirits in the woods. But another group came back having aged a decade, despite only having been gone a week. The last two never returned. There is no way to predict how it will go or what the forest will do. As such, we have not used anything but the Moonlight Bridge to leave this place in years, nor have we had contact with whatever inhabitants may still live in the so-called Wild Lands—if there even are any people left there at all." She drew a breath, a hint of tension flashing through her expression. "But that is not the only issue at hand."

Before anyone could ask, Dex spoke up in a grave voice. "Sunlight."

Unease gripped me while Clay turned, staring at me as if just now remembering I was a vampire.

And I didn't know what to say. The sun would be rising within the hour—though the gods only knew how I could tell that, considering there wasn't a clock or window in sight. The knowledge simply sat in my head like I could hear the sky ticking the minutes of darkness away. And once the light returned, what would happen to me? My stepmother had always conspired to keep both me and herself from the sun—protecting our complexions, she claimed—but I'd never felt like I might *die* in it.

But that was then. Now...

"You got anything for *that*?" Clay asked Rufinia.

My heart sank as Rufinia shook her head. "We never sought to create such a thing, as it would have only given the vampires more power to harm us."

"So then how the hell are we supposed to help her get back to Aneira if we can't—"

Byron cleared his throat, cutting Clay off. I looked over to find his green eyes trained on me. "Before we give up hope, I may have another solution." Tension flickered through his expression. "But I'll need you to keep an open mind."

10
LARS

I always tried to look on the bright side, even after everything my brother and I had been through. No matter how dark things seemed, I had faith there was something positive to find, even if it was only that you were still alive.

But this might be pushing it.

I followed Byron down the long stone tunnel into the mountain. He hadn't said much to explain himself yet. Just that Dathan, his mentor from the Order of Berinlian, was somehow still alive, and that together, they had formed a plan to help Gwyneira deal with the sunlight and chaotic magic of the Wild Lands. Under ordinary conditions, this would *absolutely* have been a bright side.

But not when this was an Erenlian we were discussing, one whose good will would be all that stood between our Aneiran princess and death. Or when whatever Byron was about to propose we let that Erenlian do made my friend look as nervous as I'd ever seen him. His green gaze bounced around, avoiding Gwyneira whenever she looked at him, only to fasten on her when she turned away.

How could anything be a good plan if it had him so on edge?

"It's not a conventional solution," he repeated for the third time as he reached the door. "But Dathan is fairly certain it will work."

"*Fairly* certain?" Clay repeated.

Byron winced. "Please just try to keep an open mind."

I could tell the others weren't reassured by his words. I just wasn't quite sure why he thought they would be. After all, what if Dathan was lying? What if he wanted revenge on Gwyneira, even if it wasn't her fault her father and step-mother had waged war against our people?

Yes, I wanted to be optimistic, but there wasn't enough reassurance in the world for this. Not until I saw whatever this plan was for myself.

Byron opened the door. Beyond lay a veritable library, complete with books stretching up at least two stories on all the walls. More bookcases filled the center of the space, and he wove through them like he knew exactly where he was going.

I followed, only to pause as I rounded the last turn.

It wasn't that I'd thought Byron was lying. It was just a shock to see a "true" giant after all these years. I could scarcely remember the last time I'd been within fifty miles of an Erenlian who looked the way our people were "supposed" to, let alone laid eyes on one of them. Dathan's skin was gray and vaguely stone-like, his hair gnarled. He was a massive figure, towering over us with hands that could crush the bookcases around him and feet that could crush us too.

Discomfort stirred in me, bringing a swirl of fire in my gut as old memories rose of their own accord. Clay and I had been born to a family in high society, and simply because we didn't look like they thought we should, they'd made our childhoods a living hell every day until they cast us out. From there, we'd scraped and scrambled to survive, hiding from society caretakers determined to send us to school and bullies who wanted to beat up on the "humans." Barring the few street kids we'd stayed with before the war, we'd never had a positive encounter with our own kind.

And now the life of the woman I cared about rested in the hands of one of them.

Byron cleared his throat. "Everyone, this is my mentor, Dathan." He took a breath. "Dathan, this is… everyone."

Did the giant hear how tight Byron's voice was? Years of living with my friend, and I'd never quite heard that tone from him.

His green eyes were still going anywhere but toward Gwyneira.

Dathan smiled. "A pleasure to meet you." He paused, studying the princess for a moment.

Tension kicked higher in the room all around me. Fire spread in my veins, whispering like a breath of hot wind, waiting for me to summon it into being to protect her.

"Thank you for anything you can do to assist me," Gwyneira said, her voice carefully controlled.

Dathan nodded. "Can't be an easy thing, what happened to you."

She was silent for a moment. "No. But I claim no monopoly on difficulties."

I braced myself for what he might do or say.

A dry chuckle left him and he nodded once. "True

enough." Without another word, he turned and gestured toward something beyond the table. "I know a bit about what you're dealing with. After the other giants and I reached the coven's hideout, I made the subject of vampires something of a study. I understand that you have need of a way to travel safely through sunlight, but given our location and what you are, this presents something of a difficulty."

Gwyneira's face gave nothing away. I could so easily picture her sitting on a throne, beautiful and regal while she heard arguments from both sides and weighed them carefully, offering no hint of her opinion until she was ready to give her decree. She listened to Dathan without a single sign her life was at stake, and when she spoke, she could have been commenting on the weather. "Byron said you had information to offer in that regard?"

A hint of a smile pulled at Dathan's lips all the same. "I do. But, as Byron may have *also* told you, it is... unconventional. It could be rather alarming."

Now Byron wouldn't meet *any* of our eyes.

"What exactly are you talking about?" Dex asked.

Dathan cast a quick glance to Byron, his brow rising.

Byron grimaced. "Over here." He walked around the table, and we followed him.

My eyes widened at the sight of what lay beyond.

Clay scoffed. "Oh, you have got to be fucking kidding." My brother's voice was scathing, because while I had the power of fire, he'd always had the stronger temper.

Still... gods help us, I agreed.

An open rectangular box lay on the floor, large enough to fit a human. Gold and brass fitted its edges, while more metal braced it along the sides.

It was also made entirely of glass.

"You said open mind, Byron," Clay said, turning to the scholar. "You didn't say open fucking *box*. And how the hell is this a solution for protecting her from the sun? Have you forgotten how glass works?"

Roan made a growling sound. "It's not a box." His voice could have carved flesh from bone. His dark eyes snapped to Dathan and Byron alike. "It's a fucking *coffin*."

Dathan appeared unperturbed. "It is not a coffin. It is simply a way to transport her."

"That's the same thing as a gods-damned coffin, you ossified fool!" Roan turned away, squeezing his eyes shut and shaking his head sharply while his hands curled into fists. Nearby, Niko stared at him.

"Why this... box?" Gwyneira asked, the even tone of her voice starting to crack as she carefully avoided the description Roan had used.

"Because it is enchanted glass," Dathan said. "And because for your comfort and safety, it will make you rest while you are in it, allowing for easier carrying and less chance of knocking it open from the inside by accident."

"It'll make me sleep?" She gave Byron and Dathan a confused look.

My friend hadn't taken his green eyes from the ground. "Not exactly." Byron paused, but her silence seemed to pressure him to continue. "It'll... stop you. Keep you still. Totally still. You have to be able to remain motionless throughout the whole day, for safety's sake, and the easiest way to do that is... magic."

"Y-you mean... like I'm dead," she filled in, her voice shaking slightly.

Dathan made a placating gesture. "You won't stay that way. It will simply hold you motionless while you're in it, and you'll wake again when the lid is opened. But during the day, the glass will reflect back all the sunlight that might otherwise harm you."

Gwyneira nodded, but she didn't look remotely comforted. And why should she be?

Gods, they were talking about basically *killing* her, at least during the daylight hours.

Dex worked his jaw around. "You couldn't come up with *any* other option?" He directed the question solely at Byron.

The other man shook his head. "Carriages can't make it down the mountain. We have to go by foot. The path is treacherous, and if the princess moved—even by accident—it could unbalance us and get her killed."

"Why not stone, then?" my brother demanded.

"Because," Dathan filled in, "if the walls were stone and a sliver of light managed to get inside, the princess could be burning before any of you knew what was happening. I can enchant the glass. I cannot enchant the air itself. This means you can keep an eye on her and act before she becomes too injured to survive."

My stomach rolled, my treacherous mind throwing out images of that scenario faster than I could shy from the thought.

Gods, we couldn't let that happen to her. I didn't care what it took.

But I also hated this solution. Hated it more because now Gwyneira was staring at the box with an expression of someone heading for the grave.

"And if anything does go wrong?" Her voice was quiet.

"I'll be there," Byron replied. "I'll protect you."

She looked up at him. He was the first to turn away.

Dathan folded his hands as if something was settled.

"Given the path you need to travel, this is the best way to ensure you all can still make progress during daylight. When you get to lower elevations, hopefully you can find a carriage, though I would recommend keeping the box with you in case something goes wrong." His brow rose at Gwyneira. "Losing one of the Aneiran royals has caused this world enough problems."

A low growl left Ozias. Nearby, Clay stepped a little bit closer to Gwyneira's side.

But the princess just nodded. "I understand. If this is what it takes to get back and help your people and mine, then... very well." Closing her eyes briefly, she drew a breath, a tightness flashing over her face like she was fighting back fear. "Let's do it."

11
GWYNEIRA

I didn't want to die again.

But gods help me, this felt close.

While the others picked up the box, I turned and walked calmly back through the library and out the door, hanging onto my resolve by my fingernails and trying to ignore the way blue symbols flared to life on the walls as I passed. There were fewer of them here than around Eliasora's prison, but even this place had wards against vampires.

A number of the witches had gathered in the time we'd been inside the library, though, and as I left the tunnel, their conversations fell quiet and countless eyes turned to stare.

None of them were friendly.

I made myself keep walking, though gratitude flickered through me at the sound of the others coming out of the tunnel at my back. But then murmurs spread as the witches saw what the men carried, growing louder with every alarmed comment from the crowd.

"Is that a *coffin*?"

"Oh my gods, who's dead?"

The crowd started to draw in around us.

"She's going to kill someone. I told you she would. Why isn't the First Matron doing something about this?"

"Where *is* the First Matron?"

"That's enough." Rufinia's voice cut through the noise, bringing the rising tension to a halt. On the path ahead, she walked toward me, Leontine at her side.

At Leontine's sharp look, the crowd pulled back. I started to breathe again.

"This way." Rufinia motioned for me to join her.

Holding myself with as much dignity as I could muster, I walked past the glares and distrustful faces and continued down the path past the First Matron, the men following me.

"Apologies," Rufinia said as we left the crowd behind. "We had a few matters to attend to before we could meet you here."

"Of course," I replied politely, my eyes on the path ahead. My vampire hearing could still pick up fragments of angry murmurs from the crowd behind us, but now that Rufinia was here, they thankfully didn't seem inclined to follow. "It's no trouble."

She didn't respond.

We continued along the path, winding our way through the village and past the turn of the trail toward the cliffs where I'd first woken up as a vampire. The night was still dark all around us, though glass lanterns with glowing blue-white lights inside dotted the pathway at intervals like earthbound stars. Spruce trees stood like silent sentinels beyond the trail, their towering forms dark shadows against the stark mountainsides around us.

"Did my mother ever see this place?" I asked suddenly.

Leontine spoke up from behind me. "When we first came here, yes. She stayed for a time, but this life didn't suit her. She felt called to go back out into the world and defend others from Melisandre's kind."

An ache moved through me, and my eyes drifted over the path and the trees again. It was a beautiful place, in its way. A pocket of beauty on the sheer mountainside. And if my mother had stayed here, if she'd been even just a tiny bit selfish and chosen to hide, I wouldn't exist but maybe she'd still be alive.

It hurt to think about. More so because—if she had been anything like me—I could understand why she hadn't.

I couldn't have hidden away. Not while knowing the entire time that others were out there, suffering, and that I could do something to stop it.

But it still hurt.

Up ahead, a gap between two slopes of the mountainside came into view, the edges of either side jagged like the mountain itself had ruptured to allow the Jeweled Coven's sanctuary access to the rest of the world. In the opening, the air shimmered like glistening fabric, affording no view of what lay beyond. But the closer we came to it, the more a strange feeling permeated the air, as if infinitesimally small sparks skittered over my cheeks and every bit of exposed skin.

Six other witches were waiting near the opening, all with bags on their shoulders and rolled cloaks in their hands. One cradled a leather scroll case like it was made of glass more delicate than the box behind me.

To a person, they didn't look pleased to see us.

Or maybe just to see me.

"What's this?" I asked Rufinia and Leontine.

"Supplies." Rufinia gestured to the witches.

Quickly, each of them shed the bags and coats, laying them on the ground and then backing away.

"There is a map as well," she continued. "Though, sadly, it will be only partially reliable."

Behind me, the men lowered the box to the ground and then came closer. The twins hefted the bags, checking inside and then murmuring with approval at whatever they saw. Eyeing the witches, Byron took the case, opening it and pulling out a scroll a moment later.

In spite of myself, I drew closer, curious, as he unrolled the paper. A watercolor map covered it, detailing the mountain range.

And then it moved.

I tensed, alarmed, and my eyes snapped up to Rufinia.

"It's bewitched," she said calmly. "It will work best to show pathways and places close to wherever you stand, while attempting to reveal locations farther away. The magic in the Wild Lands will fight you at every turn, however. Be careful how much you trust anything, including the path before you."

"Awesome," Clay murmured.

I closed my eyes briefly, my nerves jangling again at the reminder of what we were about to do. I would not lose hold of my resolve, though.

Not when all this trouble existed purely because of what I'd become.

A pang went through me. That was the problem, wasn't it? If not for what I was, we could take this Moonlight

Bridge, whatever that might be. If not for what I was, the others could travel safely.

But I was a vampire and so the men I cared about—the men I *loved*—had to risk their lives.

While I did nothing but lie in a box praying I didn't die in my sleep.

A shudder ran through me, driven as much by rage as nervousness, and I locked my gaze on the witches again. I would not provide them a single reason to doubt me now.

In case that put my men at risk too.

Giving no sign she noticed anything amiss, Rufinia turned and nodded shortly to the witches who'd held the packs. From beneath the outer layers of their cloaks, they withdrew several swords.

"These blades will help defend against the creatures that you may find out there," the First Matron explained. "They are enchanted and lined with what ore Dathan and the others brought with them from Erenelle. Use them cautiously. Anything unnatural will not fare well against the edges of these blades."

Her gaze swept the men with a warning air, and I couldn't tell if it was my imagination that her cautioning look grew stronger when it touched on Roan.

"Be well," she finished with a nod to all of us. "We will watch for signs from the gems and the earth to tell us the outcome of your journey. For all our sakes, I pray you will not fail."

Without another word, she turned and walked away.

"Comforting," Clay muttered under his breath.

Lars' brow rose and fell as if in agreement.

The other witches ignored them. One by one, they followed Rufinia up the path, until only Leontine remained.

Her expression softened as she walked closer to me, and I tensed, not sure what to expect.

"If you should need help once you make it through to Lumilia or anywhere another nexus resides, use this to send me a message." She pressed a small ruby into my hand.

My mouth moved for a moment. "But I don't know how."

"Just send a bit of your power into it. The spell on the stone will do the rest." She closed my fingers over the gem and gave me a smile, the friendliest one I'd seen from her in the short while we'd been here. "I wish we could have had more time to talk while you were here, but regardless, I hope we can get to know one another better after this is done. Your mother meant a great deal to me, Gwyneira, and I was deeply honored the day she asked me to be your godmother. If I can aid you in any way, I will."

I blinked and swallowed hard, my throat suddenly tight. My father never really talked about my mother. It always seemed too painful for him—though perhaps Melisandre's spells had something to do with that too. Suppressing his ability to speak of her or some such thing. But between his silence and his death at my stepmother's hand, I'd been left without any family—or even anyone who knew them well besides servants or politicians.

"I'd like that." I pushed the words past the lump in my throat.

She patted my hand. "Be safe."

I nodded. She echoed the motion before turning away and striding back up the path.

And then it was just us, Dathan, and a glass box I had to admit truly was a coffin.

Awkward silence settled over us.

"I would like to check the enchantments once more before we go," Byron said tightly into the quiet. Without waiting for anyone's response, he walked over to where the others had set the coffin carefully on the snow.

My eyes skipped away from the box only to land on the horizon. The sky was still dark, but somehow, I could just *tell* it wouldn't stay that way for long.

Sunrise was coming. And with it, everything I feared.

Footsteps crunched on the path behind me, close enough that I suspected their owner had made the noise deliberately. "Are you okay, Princess?" Niko asked softly.

I glanced back to find him and Dex watching me. Beyond them, Clay, Lars, and Dathan were hovering near Byron, all of them watching as he checked over the coffin. Ozias had crossed to the glistening barrier that filled the fissure, pacing back and forth along its length like a wild animal surveying its cage. Standing far away from them all, Roan watched everything with a closed-off expression.

But... would they all be here when next I woke?

My stomach twisted as panic rose inside me, making me want to fight or flee. Gods, it made me want to stop time itself, if only to keep anything bad from happening.

But in this moment, I could do none of those things.

"Princess?" Niko bent slightly as if to catch my eye and check on me.

"I'm fine."

Dex's head twisted slightly to the side as he eyed me askance, clearly not quite believing my words. "We won't let anything happen to you, Princess. You have my word."

I closed my eyes, aching inside. "It's not that."

Their silence pressed at me.

"I'll be useless to you," I whispered.

They shared an alarmed look. "What?" Dex replied.

"Out there. You're going up against cursed forests and mountains and the gods know what else. Any bit of that could kill you." My chest ached worse. "And I'll be in a *box*."

On the horizon, deep blue tinged the black night sky. I wanted to scream at it.

"It won't be forever," Niko said.

I looked back at him. "How so? I..." Futile rage twisted in me. "This isn't going away. What I am. What the sun could do to me now. It's—"

"We'll come up with something," Dex said with a nod to Niko as if agreeing with his sentiment. "Just give us time." A smile pulled at his lips. "We're nothing if not stubborn."

Niko took my hand. "And so are you. Or have you forgotten how death itself couldn't stop you, and neither could your stepmother?"

I faltered, an unexpected blush burning my cheeks at his words. "Only thanks to you all."

Dex scoffed. "Hardly. You fought her off, inside your mind and on that cliff too." He put an arm around me, moving carefully so that I could keep hold of Niko's hand as well. "We're a team, Princess. You. All of us. We'll find a way to fix this. So your only job now is to trust that. Understood?"

Taking my chin, Dex tilted my head up so that my eyes had to meet his. His brow rose, waiting for my answer.

I nodded. "Understood."

His smile grew and his thumb moved, straying over my lower lip in a way that made my insides melt. "Good girl."

He bent down low, kissing me as if to brand his words

into my body. I melted into him, relishing his calm strength and the way it urged me to believe everything would be all right.

"Princess?"

Dex broke away from me with a sigh at the sound of Byron's voice. I glanced over to see the red-haired man and the others beside the coffin. Nearby, Dathan straightened, clearly done with his preparations.

Tightening his arm on me carefully, Dex murmured. "Trust us, remember?"

I nodded.

Clay gave me a smile as I came closer, though the expression couldn't fully hide his tension. "You save one of those for me, baby?"

Before I could answer, he pulled me to him, kissing me like he'd keep me with him by willpower alone. Lars followed suit, more gently but equally determined, and my heart was racing by the time they both let me go.

Dex took my hand, squeezing it lightly before nodding toward the coffin. My stomach roiled like it was full of bees, but I stepped over the sides, one foot after the other, praying I didn't crack the glass with my weight alone. A thick blanket lay on the bottom as a cushion, and when I sat down on it, air puffed around me.

I hesitated. It smelled good, like soap and fresh air, but amidst it all, there was a scent I hadn't realized I knew until just now.

A faint hint of the spice-and-earth scent of Ozias.

My eyes flashed toward him, questions swirling in my head. When had he given them a blanket to put in here? It must have come from the cabin, though I didn't remember him resting in there earlier tonight. And why would he volunteer one anyway?

Surrounding me with him.

My lips parted, driven by the urge to find something to say. But nervousness rose swiftly, stilling my tongue. What if I was reading too much into this? Maybe it meant nothing to him. Perhaps he'd simply decided to contribute a blanket when the others wanted me to be more comfortable in this box, and if I spoke up now, I'd only make a fool of myself.

At the far edge of the group, Ozias watched the fissure and never once looked my way.

"Sunrise is coming, baby," Clay murmured.

Shivers rolled through me, his words bringing me back to the reality of what was happening here. Moving carefully so as not to crack the glass by accident, I lay back. The gods only knew why Ozias had put this blanket in here, but even though the flesh between my legs pulsed with desire for him, that wasn't the strongest reaction.

Comfort was. Like even in this place, even with what was about to happen, somehow this made me feel safe.

I only wished I could thank him... if we survived.

Byron lifted the glass lid, and tension lined the faces of every man above me. Gently, he crouched down and set it into the groove of metal that lined one side of the box, until the lid was open only on one side.

Even though the coffin was made of glass, what little light had been around us from the coven's hideout dimmed. A heaviness spread through me, like my body was turning to dull and motionless clay. I fought to keep my eyes open, but the weight of them was increasing with every passing moment, all while my heartbeat thudded slower and slower, fading into the distance.

Holding open one side of the coffin, Byron looked down at me. Tension on his freckled face, he bent close. "Rest well..." His eyes skirted toward where Dathan stood some distance off, and his voice dropped lower. "Treluria."

His face was the last thing I saw before he lowered the lid and darkness claimed me.

12
ROAN

Byron lowered the lid over her. Inside the coffin, she lay there for a moment, and then a shudder rolled through her body. Her eyes closed and her chest stilled.

"Now what?" My heart pounded as if it could keep both me and Gwyneira alive. "How do we know she's okay in there?"

"Princess?" Niko called.

She didn't respond.

I looked at the others, my brow raised in silent repetition of the question.

Most of them glanced between Dathan and Byron as if waiting for the answer, while Lars just looked to the horizon. Behind the mountains, the sky was growing lighter by the second.

"We wait," Byron said tightly. "If the enchantments don't work..." His jaw muscles clenched, and his copper curls shivered from the tense way he held his body. "Dathan and I will save her."

Inside me, my demon writhed, not accepting the words even though I couldn't think what other answer the man could have given.

But gods damn us all, he didn't sound *half* as confident as I would have liked. This was Gwyneira's life at stake, dammit.

On the horizon, the deep blue of the sky grew lighter and lighter still, taking on hues of pink and lavender.

The first rays of dawn stretched past the mountains.

My eyes snapped to the princess. An iridescent shimmer like light upon a blackbird's feathers rolled over the glass, making it appear as if rainbows danced around her briefly before fading away.

And nothing else happened.

A shaky breath of relief escaped me, and I wasn't the only one. Lars closed his eyes for a moment as if thanking the gods, while Clay raked a hand through his blond hair and Niko gave us all a nervous smile.

"Okay," Dex said, sounding equally relieved. With brief motions, he gestured to the others. "Two of us to a side at all times. That way if one falls, the other three can keep her steady. The others, take the front and rear. Stand guard."

Ozias strode forward immediately, taking the lead like he fully intended to kill anything that dared to block our path, even the fissure in the mountainside itself. Inside me, the creature grumbled in its sleep, vague impressions rising of its wish to do the same to protect her.

I made myself take a step back instead, letting the others lift her and ignoring the questioning look Dathan gave me. The old giant's curiosity didn't matter. Better that he didn't know the truth anyway. Because being that close to her... it wouldn't be smart. Not when I could only too easily imagine what would happen if something went wrong.

"*You'd never hurt me, Roan.*" Arlo grinned. "*I trust you.*"

Fire all around, bubbling and charring his skin, and yet still my little brother screamed...

I flinched, pulling myself from the memories while the monster inside rolled in its slumber as if disturbed by the images of that day. It was growing more and more restless lately, nearly rousing completely at times.

All the more reason to stay away from Gwyneira. I wouldn't leave her—*couldn't*, given that the mere thought made the demon within me stir even more. But the thought of her dying like that...

"Roan, you coming?" Clay asked, throwing a glance back from where he stood with the others, Gwyneira's glass coffin already hoisted on their shoulders.

"Yeah." I trailed them, silently snarling curses at the monster to stay asleep, stay still.

Stay locked away until the day we both finally died and no one would be in danger from us anymore.

The sensation of the air prickling across my skin grew stronger as I came nearer to the fissure.

"Be safe," Dathan said to us.

Byron nodded. "See you soon, I hope."

His mentor smiled.

"Deep breath," Dex said to the others.

Ozias gave a low growl, but I saw his chest move as he did as Dex instructed. Stalking forward, the large man strode through the gap.

Light danced in the air around him, blue-white like tiny crackles of lightning the size of stars. They rolled out around

Ozias like he was a pebble dropped into a vertical pond, increasing as he continued through the fissure.

And then suddenly, they faded, taking any view of him with them.

Clay craned his neck as if to get a better view. "Hey, Oz? You good?"

A heartbeat passed. "Good," the man called back, succinct as always.

Clay exhaled in a rush like he'd been holding his breath.

Dex's jaw muscles clenched. "Come on."

They walked forward. The lightning was stronger this time, dancing across the air ahead like cracks in a frozen lake inlaid by light. The energy made the hairs on my arms stand on end even through my coat, and inside my mind, the demon stirred, rumbling its displeasure.

I slowed. If I crossed that, would the monster inside me wake?

The others vanished through the gap. I didn't move.

"You okay, son?" Dathan asked beside me.

"Fine."

"Roan," Dex called. "We're through."

I let out a breath, my eyes darting over the fissure, but there was no other option. Either I stayed behind, abandoned Gwyneira and the others, and dealt with the witches' and the giant's questions as to why I didn't follow... or I risked whatever effect this barrier would have on one of the secrets I held most tightly in my life.

"Your friends are waiting," Dathan pressed, cautious curiosity in his voice. From the corner of my eye, I saw the way he was studying me.

Dammit.

I started forward, only to freeze again as the creature

rolled inside me, pressing at my skin, snarling in its slumber at the magic in the air.

"What's up, man?" Clay called. "We need to go!"

My teeth ground. "Fucking stay asleep," I muttered under my breath, praying to the gods who'd never meant to make a thing like me that the demon would do as I begged.

I walked into the fissure.

Magic bit at my skin, snarling through the layers of my coat down to prick and tear into my body like needles. My form was Erenlian, but I'd long ago learned that was only a mask. A thin disguise over my true self. And the magic here was ripping into it, determined to reveal the monster I truly was inside.

Nothing like me should be in this place. I wasn't of this world, not fully, and the magic here knew it.

And the demon did too.

My lips pulled back into a snarl as I fought the way that side of me wanted to wake, wanted to fight and kill. I squeezed my eyelids shut as heat built behind my eyes and rolled off my skin. My scalp burned. My back and hands too. I clenched my teeth so tightly, I was sure they were going to crack.

I stumbled past the barrier.

The pain faded with every step I took away from the magic, and swiftly, I shoved the demon down, not opening my eyes until the heat in my eyeballs had dissipated. Swiftly, I glanced over my body, but my winter gear was still in place, and when I ran a hand over my head, my hair and neck were the same.

A shuddering breath entered my lungs, smelling faintly of charcoal and ash, but the stench was fading quickly on the mountain breeze.

When I finally looked around, the others were staring at me.

Fuck me. What had they seen?

"Damn," Clay commented. "Pretty sure that thing hated you most of all."

I faltered for a heartbeat, relieved and yet uncertain if I should be. I made myself shrug, attempting to act as if I had no idea what he was talking about. Scoffing, he turned back to the path ahead.

Niko's gaze lingered on me. I couldn't interpret the look on his face.

"Let's get going," Dex said grimly, his attention returning to the mountains.

Noises of agreement came from most of the others. Silent, Niko turned, helping the others hold the coffin stable as they started off.

I let out a breath, focusing for the first time on our surroundings.

I almost wished I hadn't.

The path beneath our feet was barely wide enough to be a goat track carving an uneven line over rocks and ice. To our right, what little ground we stood upon came to an end in a rocky drop, and an ocean of empty air waited there, separating us from sheer, stony peaks wreathed in clouds and snowy slopes that looked deceptively close in the thin air. Only a miracle had kept me from stumbling over the edge when I left the fissure, and even now, my legs locked against the sudden sensation the ground beneath me could vanish at any time.

I'd never really considered whether I hated heights. But then again, this went beyond the definition of "heights" straight into the territory of madness.

The creature rumbled within me again, stronger, and my skin prickled from the way the monster wanted to do something about the threat we now faced. And it could. I knew it could. Even this place wouldn't destroy me.

It was everyone else who would die.

"Roan!" Clay called. "Come on, man!"

Battening down the demon as tightly as I could, I braced one hand on the rocky wall beside me. "Fucking witches and their fucking hideouts," I muttered as I started down the nightmarish excuse for a trail.

13
NIKO

I would not fail my princess. And when this was over, I would explore more ways for my nature magic to bring her pleasure.

This was nothing but an admittedly terrifying interlude before we could be together again.

Gripping the base of the glass box I *refused* to call a coffin, I held onto the thought as I picked my way along the narrow track of rock and ice, careful to move at the same speed as Dex, Lars, and Clay. My three friends were taller than me, and the effort of holding her box aloft at a level even with them put a strain on my shoulders, but I refused to be the weak link.

I would not endanger my princess. Not now, not *ever*. I'd dreamed my whole life of meeting my treluria, no matter how much of a fantasy some might have considered the prospect to be. I'd believed she was out there.

I had only to trust nature to guide us both to each other.

But while I waited, I'd put my time to good use. Whenever we found one another, I wanted to be worthy of her. To do what I could to be a good match, because the gods knew she'd deserve that. In the years my friends and I spent on the run from Aneira, I'd gone with the others to taverns, but not to find companionship like they did. I'd watched my friends with women, making note of the countless ways they brought those women pleasure. I'd lingered at the bars, listening to the women around me as they spoke. At first, most of them had considered me less desirable than my massive, broadly muscled friends, if they didn't just ignore me entirely. But when I did pay for their time only to want to talk with them instead, they began to see me as appealing.

So few people saw those women as living beings, every bit as valuable and fascinating as any other part of nature. I enjoyed the fact my attention, my desire to hear their wishes and dreams, their concerns and fears seemed as pleasurable to them as it was educational for me.

I paid them well, but I never slept with them. *That* I would share with my treluria, no one else. But I learned all the same.

And when this mountain was behind us, and the Wild Lands were too, I'd put those skills—*all* my skills—to good use for the one who'd found me as I always dreamed she would.

An icy wind swept across the path, blasting the mountainside and tugging at my coat and boots, threatening my balance as if to taunt my thoughts.

I gritted my teeth, fighting to control the way my magic instinctively tried to compensate to keep me steady. My awareness of nature was a constant background noise in my mind. I didn't have to try in order to hear it, let alone use it. At least, not until I'd experienced the suppressing power of the Jeweled Coven's protections on their hideout.

But like taking a muffle from your ears made every ordinary sound suddenly seem loud, now the voice of nature felt like a shout inside my head.

One that was... odd. Wrong, somehow, like a faint tinge of pollution on the wind that could be dangerous if you came too close.

And it wasn't the only thing that was becoming increasingly strange.

My attention flicked back toward Roan before I could force it forward again. I'd told the truth when I spoke to Gwyneira in the forest. Even at the coven's hideout, nature hadn't said he was a danger to us, no matter how strangely he'd behaved since she arrived among us. But something *was* changing. Roan had always kept his secrets, and I didn't fault him for it.

But now, nature wasn't sure what to make of him anymore, and for the first time, I began to wonder if the friend I'd trusted for years could be hiding something worse than the horrors of war and his own fears.

And true, it could have been the strangeness of this place reacting to him. But nature wasn't the only thing responding to my friend like there was something different about him compared to the rest of us. I'd seen the defenses around the Jeweled Coven. They'd been strong when we crossed them.

They'd looked like they intended to *kill* Roan when he passed through.

A rock bobbled beneath my boot, and I snapped my focus back to the pathway, cursing silently at myself. Yes, the voice of nature was odd. It was getting odder by the moment, but idle speculation was a waste of time because in that regard, at least, I knew why.

We were walking into the Wild Lands.

And if Roan was acting strangely too, well, we'd all been through a lot in the past few weeks.

The unease stirring in my gut didn't buy my explanation.

But maybe that was caused by the Wild Lands too.

Gradually, the track began to widen and curve away from the cliff. Trees appeared, at first just scraggly things clinging to the mountainside. But as our path continued between them and the trees gained safety in numbers from the sheer winds on the mountain, the trunks became straighter and the foliage denser. Sighs of relief came from the twins as we continued farther from the cliff's edge, but ahead of me, Dex just cast a sharp look around, nothing in his bearing relaxing in the slightest.

"Keep your eyes peeled," he ordered. "This isn't over."

I could practically feel the way the relief drained from my friends on the other side of the glass box.

Warily, I studied our surroundings as we headed deeper into the forest. My eyes felt scorched from so many hours in the glare of sunlight on snow, but while the forest was a reprieve from the blinding light, it presented its own problem.

The trail was starting to disappear. No longer blasted clean by the brutal wind, what little path we'd had was now being steadily swallowed by trees, bushes, and snow.

Cautiously, I eased my grip on my magic, testing the earth. Whether or not it was overgrown, I should still be able to feel where the path had been. The undergrowth would be different there.

A slithering feeling rolled over my skin, like snakes made of oil were brushing past me.

I pulled back, tensing to keep from jostling Gwyneira. What the hell?

My eyes darted over a forest that no longer felt like a forest, but rather like the thin skin of an illusion over top a pit of dark vipers. And one misstep would prick the surface and set them free.

"Hey, uh, we're losing the trail here," Clay called. "Niko, Oz. Either of you feel a way through this?"

I couldn't see Ozias past where Dex held the glass box ahead of me, but no answer came from the large man.

"Um... no." I hesitated and then added. "Something is really wrong here."

"Wild Lands," Byron murmured as if that explained it.

Which... I supposed it did.

"What's the map say?" Clay asked. "Is there a trail?"

I heard the crinkle of paper as Byron unfurled the scroll. "Sort of. Enough, I think."

Oh, gods help us. I glanced around again, desperate to do something to aid him. But the feeling of danger remained, as if anything I did might draw the ire of whatever magic permeated this place.

Dex twitched his chin up ahead. "Follow what you can. Just be careful."

More paper crinkling, and then the sound of a bag. Byron putting the map away, then. A moment later, we all started moving again.

I held the glass box tightly, focusing hard on not letting my own power disturb the magic of this place. It felt like a losing battle. Like just by being here, being *alive*, this place was becoming more and more aware of us.

Not that I could have explained why I felt that.

But maybe it was in the silence.

Truth was, I'd grown up in a forest. Someone had abandoned me there as an infant, but a healer woman found me. She had little use for village life or other people, preferring to make her home where only the wild plants and creatures could keep her company, but she'd taken mercy on me. She raised me as her own, teaching me how to read the forest and listen to what it had to say, even before the full extent of my magical affinity for nature became apparent.

I was familiar with the way a forest could go silent. How every animal would go still when they detected a predator in their midst.

This wasn't that.

This was a place where every shadow had teeth.

The trees became even denser, their trunks closer. Any hope of identifying a path by finding the largest gap between the evergreens vanished. Every direction looked the same, barring the rifts in the snow formed by our boots forging along.

A choked sound came from where Roan walked behind us all. I tried to look back without jostling Gwyneira or tripping over Dex.

"Guys?" Roan called, wary alarm filling his voice.

I came to a stop as Dex and the twins did the same. Carefully, we lowered the box enough that we could look back without risking dropping her.

"What is it?" Dex asked.

Roan pointed upward. "That's not…" A breathless noise escaped him. "It was midday when we got here."

Clay sputtered, but I didn't take my eyes from the sky, a chill settling over me that had nothing to do with the winter around us. Even if I couldn't stare directly at it for fear of blinding myself, I didn't need to look right at the sun to know that somehow it had jumped position.

And in the wrong direction.

"Just keep going," Dex said. "Ignore it."

Roan made an incredulous sound. "Ignore...? The *sun* moved *backwards.*"

Dex's face was grim. "It's the magic here. It's fucking with us. We just need to—"

An ear-piercing shriek rang out from the woods.

I threw a frantic look around, adrenaline racing through me, but the sound died as quickly as it came.

And nothing in the forest moved. There were only trees and shadows and a sun I'd swear was rewinding itself through the sky even as we stood here.

"What do you see?" Dex hissed at us in the echoing silence.

From the corner of my eye, I saw the others shrug, wariness radiating from them.

"Niko?" he continued. "Ozias? Anything?"

My mouth moved. How did I explain what I was feeling from this forest? And was I putting us in more danger by *not* using my magic or by risking it agitating this place further?

The scream came again, closer, like a woman's sheer wail of terror. Roan moved fast, putting himself between Gwyneira's box and the direction of the cries.

But then suddenly the sound wasn't coming from that direction but behind, racing closer like its owner was barreling through the woods straight at us.

Ozias snarled and stormed back from his position in the lead, putting himself before the other side of the glass box, his axe drawn and ready.

"What the hell *is* that?" Clay demanded over the sound of the cries.

The wailing switched back, charging toward us from the original direction again. It sounded like a woman being tortured, like she was racing at us with her dying breath. Yet I couldn't see *anyone*, even as the cries sped closer and closer.

The sound hit like a wall.

Suddenly, the screaming was all around me. I dug my feet into the leaves and dirt, fighting not to retreat for fear of tripping over Gwyneira's box and breaking it.

But gods, the *sound*... the way the forest was *howling* with it like even the ground was screaming in my mind...

Like a blast of wind, the cries whipped onward and raced away through the woods.

Silence fell.

A shuddering breath left me, and I glanced back at my friends. They were all there. Alive. Unharmed.

But gods, we all looked shaken.

"What... the fuck... was that?" Clay gasped.

I shook my head, unable to form words to answer.

Not that I knew what to say.

Clearing his throat and bearing an expression like he was holding himself together by willpower alone, Byron stretched the scroll out again. "The path is the same," he said, his voice tightly controlled. "Whatever that was, it didn't interfere with the map."

"Assuming we can trust that thing," Clay pointed out.

Byron frowned. "Niko, Ozias. Can either of you tell if—"

Another scream came from my left.

I whirled toward the noise. The figure of a woman in a cloak and shawl tore through the woods alongside us, throwing frantic looks over her shoulder as if she was being chased. Her brown hair streamed behind her. A jeweled pendant bounced on her chest as she ran. She never looked our way.

"Help me!" she screamed, still looking back and running for all she was worth between the trees. "Oh, gods, please!"

Byron took a step toward her.

"Don't," Dex snapped.

Byron froze, throwing a baffled glance at him.

"Her feet."

My own confused worry turned to ice.

Her footsteps weren't leaving a trace in the snow.

"Gods, please!" she screamed. "Please, please, plea—"

She fell, her body turning to smoke that blew away as if being erased by a breeze.

Chills rolled through me. Illusions. All of it. I'd labored this whole time under the belief that I could keep from provoking the magic here, and gods, what a fool I'd been.

It was already watching us. Playing with us. Even as I gingerly let my power out, I could feel how the thin veneer of a shield between us and the writhing magic of this place was fading.

If it had ever been there at all.

"Did you see her necklace?" Roan murmured.

"Jeweled Coven," Clay said, his normally joking tone utterly devoid of emotion, like he'd been shocked too badly to even react at all.

Lars nodded. "One of their lost expeditions, maybe."

The others made tense noises of agreement. I said nothing, taking slow breaths to stay calm, praying that maybe—oh gods, somehow, maybe—I was wrong.

We weren't already in the belly of the beast. We weren't

trapped with no choice but to keep going, because how else would we get the princess home?

"Niko?"

I jumped, looking over sharply to find Dex watching me.

His eyebrow rose. "I asked if your magic could pick up anything about what we saw?"

My mouth moved again, and I swallowed hard before I could find my voice to speak. "Just that we need to be careful. *So* careful. This forest..." I glanced around and then froze, shock hitting me all over again.

The shadows around the trees weren't where they should have been. Not based on the position of the sun, anyway.

"The light." I shivered. "It's *wrong*. It..."

"Yeah." Dex's voice was flat. "I noticed that."

"What the fuck *is* this place?" Clay muttered.

Dex shook his head. "Doesn't matter. We keep going. We watch each other's backs, and we stick together. Got it?"

Nods came from the others. I looked back at the forest. Everything was silent again, but I didn't for one second let myself believe the woods weren't watching us. Everything here was a predator, just waiting for the right moment to strike. And meanwhile, when I glanced overhead, I would have sworn the sun had moved even farther back in the sky.

I swallowed hard and hefted the glass box with the others, being so careful to keep Gwyneira steady. We shouldn't have come here, though I knew we'd never had another option.

But gods help us all, this was starting to feel like it might have been suicide.

14
ROAN

After a while, I stopped checking the sun. There wasn't any point. It jumped backward and forward at a whim, and all while the shadows it *should* have cast never changed a bit. I couldn't tell what time it was, nor when this day should have been coming to an end.

Because it sure as hell never did.

Dull pain throbbed through my feet with every step. My spine ached from my pack jostling against it, never mind that the bag hadn't felt heavy when I started out. How long had we been traveling now? Surely more than a few hours. I was a miner and I had spent years on the run from Aneiran forces. For mere *walking* to feel this exhausting...

Gods, we could have been out here for days already, for all I knew. Nothing in the forest offered the least sense of time or distance. Every tree looked the same, and from the worry I saw on Niko's face each time he glanced back, I suspected even his gifts with nature weren't aiding him in knowing where the hell we were. By now, the only thing that *was* clear was that the forest was doing more than fucking with us.

I suspected it was enjoying this.

Wails came in the distance over and over, sometimes filled with pleading, other times nothing but blood-curdling screams. Every so often, figures raced past, sometimes crying or pleading or else making no sound.

And through it all, I could feel the demon inside me, watching. Pushing at my control, but not out of terror, no matter how my Erenlian side felt about its reaction. No, as the hours passed, a horrifying new realization came to me. The side of myself that I'd hidden for so long wasn't *scared* of the nightmare playing out around me.

No, slowly but surely, it was becoming angry—and in a way I couldn't understand.

Screams only irritated the demon. Cries stirred nothing but disgust. As we continued on, the voices in the forest were joined by others—babbling ones who pleaded in animal-like grunts and whines. From time to time, those noises were joined by silent figures who stared at us from between the trees, their empty gazes locked on horrors we couldn't see.

But then came the laughing ones. The ones holding weapons who charged around the woods as if to attack someone, crazed looks in their eyes. Sometimes they vanished with a sudden expression of horror. Or else their faces would change, blood suddenly splattering them while they smiled. They'd been driven mad by this place. Of that, I was certain. And why wouldn't they have been?

We were in the forest of the damned, and I was starting to fear there was no way out.

I shuddered as another shrieking laugh came from the

trees to my right. I made myself glance toward the sound no matter how little I wanted to see another horror. I wouldn't let my guard down against anything that might be a threat.

Inside me, the demon's anger grew.

I clenched my teeth. Bodies hung from the trees again. Soldiers this time, though I didn't recognize the insignia on their uniforms. So many kingdoms had been devoured by this place that it almost didn't matter. But the trees had changed now. Sometime in the past eternity, they'd started to be joined by oak and others of the like.

I wished I could trust that meant we were actually descending the mountain, rather than them simply being another game played by this nightmarish place.

The bodies swayed from the branches, rocking back and forth like ornaments in hell despite the fact there was no wind around us. Beneath them, another soldier laughed and cackled.

The demon muttered wordlessly in the depths of my mind.

My heart stuttered in my chest. Damn me, I had to get away from here. Away from this place, these men. With every passing moment, the monster within me only grew more incensed by this place, and the gods only knew what would happen if I lost my grip on it. I should just run to save myself and my friends alike.

Irritation rose from the demon. To run would mean leaving her.

I was many things, but for her, I would not be a coward.

"Gods have mercy," Lars muttered. "Where is the way out of this nightmare?"

In the lead with Ozias, Byron didn't say a word.

"Dammit, did you hear him?" Clay snapped. "Where the fuck is the way out of this?"

Byron shook his head, still not answering.

"You ignoring us?"

"Stay calm," Dex ordered.

Clay gaped in his direction, though his view of the other man was blocked by Gwyneira's coffin. "Seriously? You're telling me to stay *calm* in this shit?"

"Please," Niko begged in a tight voice. "Don't... don't fight. It likes it when you—"

"You know something about what this place wants?" Clay demanded, half turning toward the younger man. Between them, Gwyneira's coffin rocked slightly.

My heart hit my throat, but the other men gave no sign of noticing the jostling.

"Please," Niko begged, and the coffin bobbled to one side as he shrank in on himself as if to retreat. "It's so loud. It—"

"We keep moving," Dex interrupted, starting forward even though the others weren't moving as fast.

The coffin rocked again. No one else reacted, and inside me, the creature rumbled, rage rising higher. She was going to get hurt. They didn't care. They *should*.

But before I could panic at its rage, something within me twisted, as if the demon was suddenly looking out at the forest around us, and more impressions hit me. We knew these men. They'd offered their own lives just to bring Gwyneira back from the madness of her stepmother's curse. They would never risk her. Except...

A growl echoed from deep within my mind.

"What the hell do *you* know, anyway?" Clay snapped at Dex. "You got us into this, and now it feels like we've been walking for a gods-damned year." He started to reach for his weapon, sending the coffin tilting wildly. "Why should we listen to you any—"

"*Enough!*" I shouted. The demon's voice thundered through mine, thick and hot in my throat like the monster shouted with me.

Everyone froze.

All around us, the strangest feeling of something oily and bleak slithered away, retreating like a predator suddenly unsure it wanted this prey any longer.

Clay blinked hard, and Dex shook his head as if dislodging sleep. Niko's brow twitched down, alarm on his face—for me or himself, I couldn't tell.

"What..." Clay quickly shifted closer to the coffin, bracing it as if suddenly remembering it was there.

Dex repositioned himself too, helping keep the princess stable.

The rage inside me turned to cold contempt, but not aimed at them.

At the forest. Because the Wild Lands had been doing this, and the demon had known.

Like hell this place would fuck with anything that was ours.

I shuddered, torn between shock, relief, and horror while the monster inside me sank back like a satisfied king on its throne.

"Everyone okay?" Dex asked, sounding much more cautious than before.

Nods and murmurs of acknowledgment came from the others.

Dex cast a glance at me, and I tensed at the question in his gaze. But he didn't ask me anything as he turned back, saying instead, "Let's get going."

I trailed after the others. No one could know what I was. It had to stay that way, because no one who knew the truth would dare keep me around, and as selfish as it was, I didn't want to be alone.

But until this moment, I'd never felt like *this* much of a bastard for lying to them all these years. Because this forest was a monster. A hungry, ravenous beast that meant to eat us all alive.

And in the face of its power, I'd still scared it into submission.

Which only meant I was something worse.

15
DEX

Roan had saved us. I was sure of it.
 I just didn't know how.
 Gripping the slick sides of the coffin carefully, I kept myself from looking back at the man as we forged through the snow. The cobwebs of whatever had overwhelmed us earlier still clung to me, like residual traces of the hangover from hell. And I didn't for one moment let myself believe the threat was gone.

The forest still felt like it was watching us.

I adjusted my hold on the coffin, thanking the gods I hadn't dropped it. Now that I was thinking clearer, I knew I'd tried to start off without the others. A moment more, and the glass would have fallen, taking Gwyneira with it.

I could have killed her, and all because of whatever this forest tried to do to us. For that, I wanted to tell Lars to burn this place to the ground.

Shrieks echoed from deeper in the woods, almost as if in answer to my thoughts. The shouts weren't filled with fear. Not like the ones early on. These were the cries of madmen.

Like the forest was taunting us.

Up ahead, Byron glanced back at me. His eyes narrowed and he slowed.

My wariness grew tenfold. "What is it?"

"The magic here is still trying to grab hold of us." My teeth ground as I glared out at the trees.

"The rage on your face isn't like you, my friend." My eyes flashed over to Byron. But his words still penetrated.

Some of my rage retreated, like a wave uncertain whether to roll away from shore.

It only left irritation in its wake. "This place..."

He nodded. "It's stirring up emotions in an effort to make us destroy ourselves."

When he put it like that...

I let out a breath. "Does the map tell you how much longer we'll be in this hell?"

His mouth tightened. "It's... confusing. Every time I think it shows where we are, the terrain changes."

"So we really are trapped." Clay's voice carried from the other side of Gwyneira's coffin, filled with a cold gallows humor I hadn't heard from him since we fled the destruction of Erenelle.

"Is that true, Ozias?" Lars called up to the man in the lead.

Ozias was silent for a moment. "Not sure." He glanced over his shoulder, looking past me to Niko.

"It's like the forest isn't really the forest," Niko said. "It's... only sort of here. Like a dream."

Clay scoffed. "Nightmare, you mean."

"We're moving over the earth," Ozias interjected gruffly. "The sun isn't there."

I didn't know how to respond to that, and from the silence of the others around me, they didn't either. Yes, the sun was appearing here and there like a child playing peek-a-boo, but it was still providing light. So it had to be up there.

Except my body ached like I hadn't felt since my latter days in the war when I was still serving with the human soldiers. We'd hike for days and nights on end to reach the next place the Aneiran king had ordered us to attack.

But surely we all hadn't been here for days and nights on end already? And if we had... what happened to the night, because I sure as hell hadn't seen a shred of darkness since we set foot in here.

"If the sun's not there," Clay asked. "Where the hell is it?"

Ozias grunted, glaring around at the forest.

"Lars?" Clay pressed. "You know what the hell he's—"

The light suddenly shifted, growing dimmer and turning golden like the last shreds of day. Through the trees, I could just make out the last fiery glow of the sun only a short distance from the horizon and sinking fast.

"Oh, fuck," Clay said. "We pissed it off, didn't we?"

Cold dread sank over me. If daylight in this place was bad, what would night be like?

Fuck everything. We needed shelter. Defensive positions. A vantage point to see the threats coming... if such a thing was possible.

"Move *now*," I ordered, watching the forest. "Ozias, find us a secure spot. Best you can do. A cave, anything."

The man took off immediately, and the others followed. With both hands on the princess's coffin, I went with them, wishing I trusted my grip enough to let one hand drop to my sword.

"Faster," I urged.

The others didn't need the encouragement. Our boots forged through the snow, which thankfully wasn't as deep as it had been. Maybe we really were at a lower elevation.

It was meager comfort out here.

The light continued to fade. Long shadows stretched from the trees.

But suddenly, the forest wasn't the only thing around us anymore. Now, crumbling buildings came into view. Gray and weathered with gaps where their roofs had collapsed, the structures were pierced by trees that had grown straight through them.

Every instinct I had screamed that we shouldn't go anywhere near them. It was in the way the empty windows didn't *feel* empty, like the bloody specters from the forest lurked in there too. It was how the dying light played strangely across the graying boards, like a child plucking at the keys of a musical instrument, trying to decide what tune to play.

It was how I knew—just *knew*—that whatever had tormented us all the way here was old friends with whatever waited inside there.

And both were hungry.

My eyes darted around. The structures were on either side of us now, and I could see a few more farther ahead. There was no way to avoid them without going back.

No way in hell was I telling these men to retreat toward the nightmare behind us.

"You think it was a village?" Niko whispered as if afraid something might hear.

"*Was* being the operative word," Clay muttered. "We need to get the fuck out of here."

"Just keep going," I said. "We'll get past it."

The others didn't respond, but they also didn't stop moving.

More details appeared between the trees; more houses in various states of decay. Here a bucket sat beside our path. There a cart sagged into the underbrush, two of its four wheels gone. A doll in a stained blue dress sat amid the broken glass of a window, its empty eyes staring out at us as we passed.

I shuddered. I couldn't see any bones or marks of fire, nor any sign of what must've driven the villagers away from this place.

But given our location, I could fucking guess.

How many lives had the rabid magic of these lands claimed? A thousand? Ten thousand?

We wouldn't be next. Not if I had a damn thing to say about it.

Behind me, Niko gasped.

I craned my neck, trying to check on him without dropping the coffin. "What is it?"

"Something—"

Howls rose all around us. Pitch-black smoke poured through the gaps between the decaying buildings.

"Fuck!" Clay cried.

Even though there was no wind, the clouds of smoke twisted, writhing impossibly like something alive. In moments, the twists had gathered together, transforming like cloud shapes come to life.

Suddenly, snarling wolves surrounded us. The black twists of smoke poured off their fur. Their mouths steamed.

Each of them was nearly the size of a horse, with enormous fangs dripping with slobber that hissed like acid when it hit the ground. With a sound like a pickaxe being dragged over rock, their claws scraped across the cobblestones as they paced around us. Their eyes glowed green like a vicious aurora, every gaze locked on us from all sides.

"Hold."

My eyes snapped toward the source of the cold voice. A man stood between two of the creatures, a gloved hand resting on one of them, as if he was a horse master with his prize stallion. A black cloak covered him and a deep hood cast his face in shadow, leaving only a suggestion of dark skin and intense eyes that were fixed on us.

And on the princess.

"I understand if this won't make sense to you," he said calmly. "And unfortunately, I don't have time to explain. But the woman you're carrying? For all your sakes, she needs to come with me."

Metal whispered around me as Ozias and Byron drew their weapons.

Roan stepped up beside me, his eyes locked on the stranger. "You touch her—" His voice was like ice. "—you die."

Ozias let out a low growl that could have rivaled any of the beasts around us, and several of the creatures shifted their weight as if hearing the challenge in the sound.

The stranger's teeth were a slash of white in the shadows as he smiled.

Revealing long fangs.

"Very well, then." He dropped his hand from his beast's side. "Take them."

The wolves charged.

16
MELISANDRE

It had been years since I was forced to travel by foot. Decades, really. I'd taken to shifting form and flying with such natural ease, it only served as further proof I'd made the right decision to become a vampire.

Instead of plodding along the ground like some peasant too poor to afford a horse.

Let alone a queen whose carriage and driver had been reduced to ash.

Alaric's power tugged on me as he changed direction, veering along a path of his own choosing. There was nothing actually resembling a trail through this godsforsaken wilderness, yet that hadn't stopped him for the countless nights we'd been traveling.

No, this was worse than being a peasant. This was like being a dog on a leash, tied to its master with no choice of its direction.

My feet ached. My back as well. I would have thought being a vampire would spare me mundanities like this, providing me endurance enough that my physical form wouldn't feel such pain.

Even vampires had their limits, apparently.

And this bastard didn't give a damn about them. Ever since Alaric killed Stelaruna and destroyed our only means of transportation, I'd been reduced to endlessly trudging through the woods by night and sheltering in caves and beneath overhangs by day. I couldn't even feed decently, having to choke down the blood of whatever grubby forest animals I could scrounge instead.

It was intolerable.

I muttered a curse under my breath as I tripped again over a tangled root lost in the underbrush. My night vision was excellent—better than any of my sister vampires, really—but this forest was trying even my skills. We'd crossed some sort of barrier and entered this quiet wood nestled in the lee of a sheer mountain range several hours ago, and barely a cluster of minutes had passed before I realized where we were.

The Wild Lands. Or the edge of them, I surmised, if only for the fact we were still alive. Whispers came from the trees, and from the corners of my eyes, I could see vines and roots moving through the brush. Nothing came close, barring the damnable roots, and even then, they only seemed to target me.

The sound of a little girl sobbing came from my left. My gaze snapped over to it.

Nothing was there.

"Scared, pet?"

My teeth ground at Alaric's voice, but I stilled them immediately, fighting to keep my expression calm. "And why would you assume anything here causes me fear?"

"Because we are at the edge of cursed territory. The energy here is unlike anything I've felt thus far in your world. It carries ghosts."

I drew myself up straighter. "The Wild Lands, yes, I know. They have nothing in them I would fear."

The words weren't exactly a lie, more of an omission considering that I scarcely knew what fully occupied this territory. No one did. The Wild Lands were vast. A swath of magic-warped territory that spanned the length and width of several countries—though they'd all been swallowed in its creation, their people never heard from again. Expeditions into this cursed place would either return after only weeks having aged years... or years later having only aged a few days.

If they came back at all.

But survivors told mad stories of the sun moving in the wrong direction, nights that never came or never ended, and whole seasons that passed in an hour, wheeling past like a child playing with a spinning wheel.

"Are you truly unafraid, pet?" Alaric smirked at me. "I think you mistake my power for your own."

"And what power would that be?"

"I marvel that you haven't figured it out."

"Or perhaps I've simply kept my findings to myself."

He chuckled as if the very idea amused him. "You realize there is nothing you can fully keep to yourself, pet. I told the truth when I said you gave me a ride into this world. Your energy is tied to mine, to be drawn on when and how I choose. Without you, I would merely find another, but for the time being, tying you to me offers a window into that precious little head of yours."

Rage boiled up inside me, and it took effort to hold my

face still. I would not take his word for this, of course. I trusted no one's assertions but my own. And though, yes, I had felt his magic gripping me in a chokehold like a collar attached to a chain, that scarcely meant he had a window into my mind.

The thin line of his nascent eyebrow arched. "You don't believe me."

"It is hardly proof that you are a mind reader. Rather, I only hear that you need me... perhaps more than I need you."

I was poking the bear. I knew that. But my irritation was too great.

That he had come from the empty realms was bad enough. But beyond even his physical form, he'd become something I hated—an arrogant man who believed his mere presence entitled him to control me...

Like hell I'd take his word for anything.

"Very well." His razor teeth glinted in the moonlight. "Allow me to *prove* to you what power I have."

I held my disdainful expression, but a cold tendril of apprehension suddenly twisted deep in my gut at his words. Perhaps I'd been foolish to allow my temper to make me push him this much.

Turning, he continued deeper into the forest, leaving me no choice but to follow.

The whispers grew louder around us. From the corners of my eyes, I'd swear the trees were crowding in closer as if to trap us, though whenever I looked toward them, I couldn't tell if any of them had actually moved. Up ahead, I could hear traces of wildlife: a deer somewhere in the distance, its heartbeat steady but on the edge of speeding into motion if it sensed a threat. Closer by, I caught sight of wolves moving through the underbrush, keeping pace as if they planned to attack.

They'd die with my fangs in their throat if they tried to harm me.

Alaric stopped. Turning briefly, he flashed me a smile of glinting metal teeth and then looked back at the forest.

A chill slid across my skin and turned clammy, as if a frigid oil slick had crawled across my flesh, coating me from head to toe.

And then it sank deeper, moving through me until it reached my gut, wrapping around my insides like a snake and then squeezing tighter. Heaviness spread through me, as if something was drawing my energy away.

Alaric extended his hands towards the forest. "Humans would tell you this was a kingdom once. That all its people are now gone, eaten by the trees, much as every other kingdom that once inhabited this place." He chuckled. "They'd only be partially correct."

Magic thudded into the ground like the earth was a drum. The energy rushed out and my guts twisted as if trying to follow it. I could feel it surge through the ground, all of it pouring from me into him and then outward. It raced into the tree roots and up into the trees themselves.

Trunks and branches warped like hot wax, contorting and turning black. Nearby, the wolves took off, tearing away from us in terror, but they were too slow. The magic caught them, throwing them to the earth where they howled as their bodies warped and twisted, as overcome as the trees. Their bodies contorted, some merging together, others decaying into nothing.

But suddenly, they weren't the only things howling.

Clawed hands shoved up through the soil to grasp at the

air. Shrieks and growls filled the forest, and all around us, figures dragged themselves from the soil.

"Others lived here long ago," Alaric said. "When humans came to this place, their witches and sorcerers thought they'd locked these creatures away so profoundly, none would ever return." He made a scornful sound. "They were wrong."

One by one, the creatures emerged from the earth, shoving away from the dirt to drag their bodies upright. Gnarled faces snarled in the night. Tusks flashed in the moonlight.

Orcs. I'd read of them when I was a child apprenticed to the Jeweled Coven. Ancient witches had bound them away in a nether realm because nothing could exist when they were around. They were creatures without reason, and they had no moral code that anyone had ever been able to see. Every attempt to make peace with them had failed before it even began, and no person who attempted to do so ever survived. Monsters to the core, they'd butchered whole communities and decorated themselves with the bones of their victims.

I'd always admired them. Not their appearance, of course. The history books had hardly done their hideousness justice. But the brutal efficiency of removing those weaker than themselves so as to expand their own interests... I approved of that thoroughly.

Not that admitting such a thing had gone over well when I'd been part of the Jeweled Coven. Those fools wanted peace between kingdoms.

They never understood how *peaceful* people could be when they were terrified of the power through which you ruled them all.

The shaking of the earth stopped. The warped trees stilled, their limbs now black and twisted as they reached for the sky. Inside my gut, the draining sensation faded away, leaving me trembling like a leaf in the breeze. My body felt ephemeral, like a ghost that would melt into nothing at the first flash of sunrise.

I stalked forward, my legs quivering beneath me, and rounded on Alaric, making no effort to hide my fury this time.

But shock made me pause. He looked winded. *Exhausted*, possibly even more than me.

My fangs slipped out as my muscles bunched. Now was my chance. I'd kill him and finally be free.

His metal teeth flashed in the moonlight. "Careful now."

The collared feeling inside me spasmed tighter, making me wince.

His grin broadened. "You're my creature, pet. You'll be dead before you cross the distance between us."

Rage shuddered through me, but I didn't move. "What now?" I bit out.

He turned his attention to the orcs. They were staring at him, not attacking despite how every story of their kind said they should be. Instead, they merely waited for his command.

"Now, we gather the rest. All who were awakened by my power."

His power. Not mine. Not something he'd dragged from me because I had no choice.

There would be no end to the ways I would kill him, the moment I had the chance.

But like the arrogant fool he was, he ignored me entirely. "And once my army is ready, we shred the world."

17
GWYNEIRA

Consciousness returned slowly, like snow melting from my eyes.

But something was wrong.

Alarm spread through me, clamoring like a bell through my veins while my heart thudded faster and faster. I didn't know what had happened or why I *knew* something was off, but it didn't matter.

This was what I'd feared. I'd wake up and something—*anything*—would have gone wrong.

But... what?

Blinking hard to clear my blurred vision, I let my eyes dart around. The ceiling above me was ornate. Rich wood carved with scenes of leaping deer and tangled forests. Golden firelight played across it, making the creatures seem to move in the shifting light and shadow. But the air was stale, as if it had been undisturbed for a long while, and to the right of the coffin's edge, I caught a glimpse of a red brocade bed curtain, its surface gray with dust and overlaid by a gossamer of cobwebs.

"Dex?" I whispered. "Byron?"

"You're safe." The voice was low and utterly self-assured.

I didn't recognize it at all.

Fear surged higher in me, and my teeth felt strange for the heartbeat it took for my fangs to descend. In an instant, my hands gripped the sides of the coffin and pulled me to sit upright so swiftly the air warped around me.

A man sat on a carved wooden chair several feet away from me, his elbows on his knees and his hands clasped in front of him. That he was breathtaking was an understatement. Something in me stuttered distantly at the sight of him, like a thread in my chest twinged for no reason I could ascertain. His expression was thoughtful but arrogant, as if he was simultaneously intrigued and yet certain he could get any answer he required. His skin was dark and unlined, and his features were sharp, from his harsh cheekbones down to the razor line of his jaw. He wore a shirt of black silk and pants to match, and his hair was long in a hundred tightly woven braids that hung around his face and down to his chest. Tiny gold bands glinted at intervals along the braids, catching the firelight like yellow stars. He appeared to be only a few years older than me, maybe half a decade at the most.

But his eyes belied that impression. Despite the handsomeness and relative youth of his face, they were... old. *Wrong.* And they sent shivers through me that I struggled to hide.

I ripped my gaze from him, scanning the rest of the ornate room swiftly, finding dust and cobwebs and no one else but the two of us.

"Where are they?" I demanded. "The men who were with me. What have you done with them?"

He regarded me for a moment, his dark eyes tracing my face like he was mapping it. "What's your name?"

I trembled, fury mounting to subsume my rising fear. "Princess Gwyneira of Aneira. Where the *hell* are my men?"

He hadn't stopped staring at me. "You are so... *alive*. How long has it been since you were turned?"

Ice rushed through me. How could he know...

I shoved the thought aside. "Answer me now." A thrill of energy carried through my voice, and tucked beneath my blouse and vest, the diamond pendant thrummed against my chest. "Where are they?"

His eyes narrowed and he straightened. "Witch."

I could have been a fool and still picked up on the hate in his voice when he spoke that word.

Not to mention the threat.

Pushing away from the coffin's sides, I rose to my feet and stepped away from the glass. Whether any magic I possessed would aid me, I didn't know, but my veins rushed with adrenaline and my heart raced as I braced myself to fight as Dex had taught me.

The man didn't move, though his gaze flicked to my neck and lingered there. I suddenly had the feeling he was watching the pulse throbbing in my throat, and the anger on his face drained, turning to something darker. Hungrier.

My fingers curled into fists. "If you harmed them, I will kill you."

"Your men are safe." He returned his gaze to my eyes with a deliberateness that made me think he was dragging it away. "I captured them, nothing more."

"Let me see them."

He tensed, a strange look flashing over his face, there and then gone so quickly, I couldn't catch it. "In time."

Like hell.

My eyes flashed across the room again, noting the door, the windows, every possible way out. Everything around me was caked by dust that muted the rich colors of the cushions and curtains, turning them gray. Cobwebs hung from the chandelier overhead, motionless in the quiet.

Utterly motionless.

Alarm prickled through me, and my eyes snapped back to the man. I couldn't see him breathing. Couldn't hear his heartbeat either. Besides the crackling flames and the rapid sounds of my furious breaths, the world around us was as still as a grave.

Oh gods.

"What are you?" I demanded.

His brow twitched up slightly, some trace of faint amusement crossing his face. "Young, but not so inexperienced then." His dark eyes flicked to my throat a second time, the amusement fading, and then he rose, turning away and pacing deeper into the room.

Confused curiosity flickered through me. Wait, was he putting distance between us?

"I am what you are," he continued. "At least in part. The whys and the hows are complicated. Suffice it to say you're not in danger." He paused briefly. "I have need of your help."

I watched him cautiously. His poise was effortless, his words smooth and charming, like someone accustomed to the dance of polite society. But everything Rufinia and the other witches had told me played back through my mind, along with what I'd seen of Eliasora. He was behaving like a gentleman, but with a vampire, that couldn't be more than a ruse.

Only with giant blood could we stay sane. Stay *human*.

Cold horror rushed through me. Giant blood...

"Have you fed from them?" I demanded.

He looked back at me. "No. Have you?"

My rage returned at his careless tone, never mind how I didn't trust the words. *Couldn't*. Not when it was my giants' lives at stake. "Then why capture me and the others? Why separate us? If they're not in danger—"

"I didn't say that. But I swear you are no captive."

"So we can leave, then?"

Tension flashed across his face again. "I'd rather you didn't. Not until you hear me out."

I didn't respond. My eyes swept the room while my ears strained for sounds of my giants anywhere nearby. But there was nothing. Beyond the door at the other end of the space, I couldn't detect a whisper of servants or other inhabitants, and past the windows, the night was still.

My men couldn't be dead. *Wouldn't* be. But the silence still sent cold terror boiling in my veins, making the vampire side of me threaten to break free. If it did, I wasn't sure what I'd do.

But this man wouldn't survive it. That much I could swear beyond any shadow of a doubt.

I strode toward the door.

He was between me and the exit in less time than it took to blink.

I slammed to a halt. On my chest, the diamond pendant thrummed harder against my skin, while my lips pulled back from my fangs.

"I *must* speak with you." He paused. "Please."

My muscles quivered. I could tear into him. Unleash my vampire side and the magic within me alike.

And what if he had allies holding my men hostage, knives at their throats waiting only for his word to strike?

I drew a slow breath. My political training pressed at me, whispering of strategies to get an enemy to act as you wished.

A bargaining chip, then. "Let me see them first. Do that and I'll listen to you."

His full lips thinned with a flicker of consternation. "For their sake and yours, I would ask you to reconsider that order of events."

"Why?"

"Because they are Erenlian. It has taken everything I have not to kill them already."

"What's that supposed to mean?"

He closed his eyes briefly. "Perhaps we could start over. Introductions first, yes? And an explanation. And if you wish to deny me help at that time..." His jaw muscles flexed like he was forcing himself to continue. "I will abide by your decision."

I studied him, weighing whether to trust his words.

"I *swear* your men are alive," he said. "A few more minutes will change nothing except to help you understand why I brought you here—and why they need to stay elsewhere, at least for now." He met my gaze firmly. "I know the power of those men's blood, Princess. If you wish to leave after you hear what I have to say, I give you my word I will do all I can to make sure you *and* they stay safe."

My caution had only grown, but in spite of everything, curiosity was still there too. "Very well."

His relief was palpable. "Thank you." He gestured toward the chair he'd vacated, his brow rising.

Not taking my eyes from him, I went. The aging wood creaked as I sat down.

"I am Casimir," he said. "Prince..." A quiet scoff escaped him. "*King* of Zenirya."

I knew my shock was written on my face. I couldn't help it. "Zenirya?"

He nodded once.

"Zenirya was lost. Destroyed in the Witch War."

He paused. "Is that what they call it now? The 'Witch War'?"

"What?" At his silence, I struggled to regroup. "It's what they call it, yes."

"Then yes, Zenirya was lost in the Witch War." His brow rose and fell. "*We* were, down to the last man, woman, and child."

"But you're..." My hand twitched toward where he stood.

"Surely you wouldn't count me among the living?"

At the cold irony in his voice, discomfort swirled in my gut like a wretched soup. While I knew I'd died from what Melisandre had done, I wanted to believe I was alive again. In my own unique way, yes, but living nonetheless.

Remorse crossed his face as if he'd detected something of my reaction. "My apologies. It is... *difficult* to feel alive when one has been alone for so long."

The silence stretched, and beneath my fingertips, the arms of the wooden chair were gritty with dust. "How long?"

He hesitated. "When did this 'Witch War' begin?"

"You don't know?"

167

He looked away, his eyes locking on the night beyond the grimy windowpane. "Time is strange here, as I'm certain your men will tell you when you speak to them. It doesn't always flow as it should."

I swallowed hard, worried for the giants all over again. "About thirty years ago," I made myself say. "Give or take a year."

He nodded carefully, still regarding the view past the window. "Indeed. That long, then."

I blinked, looking around. "But..." A breath escaped me, stirring the cobwebs on the bedpost nearby. "*How*? You..."

I couldn't fathom it. When I woke as a vampire, I'd been starving. Even now, I could feel how that hunger would return if I didn't feed again soon.

"And *this* is where my explanation comes in," he said when I didn't continue.

I waited, barely breathing.

"When the Kingdom of Zenirya still stood, I was Crown Prince. My father and mother ruled peacefully, and our people prospered. I hope this is the story the nations beyond the mountains still tell of us, and not... what came after."

He glanced in my direction but didn't seem to want confirmation, given how his gaze returned to the window a moment later.

"I was twenty-three years old when the fighting between the witches began. At first, we thought it wouldn't concern us. Our border patrols reported rumors of a power struggle, and my father ordered a host of our sorcerers to travel to the border and strengthen our defenses, just in case. But we trusted the Jeweled Coven to get matters in hand."

He scoffed softly. "The first blast wave took out our

western cities. The next hit the capital itself. I remember the night sky burning, not with fire but with magic, while the air rang with the screams of our people dying in the city beyond our walls. Our sorcerers fell one after the other, giving their lives to hold the shields they erected around the castle itself, but by the time dawn arrived... Zenirya as I knew it was gone."

"I'm sorry," I whispered.

A fleeting smile of gratitude passed over his face, changing his visage if only for a moment. He looked younger. Kinder, and it made me wonder who he'd been before magic destroyed his home.

But then the expression faded. "Those of us who survived gathered whoever was still alive in the city, treating the wounded and making ready to flee. It was as swift an evacuation effort as anyone could have managed with so many wounded and so much destruction all around." He shifted his shoulders. "But it wasn't enough. The forests had turned wild with magic. The trees moved and all we heard were the screams of those who'd entered the woods, cutting off with such horrid finality. There was no way out. And when night fell again, the vampire witch came."

I kept myself from fidgeting uncomfortably in the wooden chair.

"She never told us her name. She barely even spoke a word. But she had a hundred vampire servants with her, many of them dressed like they'd been our people only a short time before. Her vampires made quick work of our soldiers—or so I gathered from seeing the bodies later. Our royal servants fell next, and the survivors from the city too. I fought with all I had to protect my parents and my people."

He shook his head, old irony in the motion. "I died with her fangs in my throat."

He fell silent for a moment, and I couldn't bring myself to speak.

But then, what could I say to that horror?

"I suspect the king and queen would have been of no use to her. Their stances on political matters were already well known, and thus turning them and using them as puppets would not have convinced anyone. But I was another story. As yet untested in ruling the nation, known only for parties and random diplomatic functions, I was a tool she could twist as she saw fit." He shrugged. "At least, this is my theory."

Casimir turned to face me again. "There was a legend in the royal family, one I always believed was merely propaganda. It claimed our ancestors were celestial beings. *Angels.* That they descended from their home in another plane of existence and came here, falling in love with humans and eventually having children with them. And from those unions, came us. I always thought it was only a foolish story those of royal blood sometimes use to substantiate their claim to a throne, but after that night..."

He shook his head. "I have no other explanation for how the person I was survived, because when I awoke after she turned me..." Old pain passed over his face. "I suspect you know the hunger that gripped me. The ravenous thirst for blood that drives you near to madness until you can slake it. I think she'd planned it as an amusement for herself, watching me feed on my own people without care or control. The first victim she offered me was nothing more than a child, and I could tell from how she reacted that she'd expected me to slaughter that innocent boy like he was nothing. But when I cursed and fought and tried to get him away instead, she had me dragged to a dungeon cell and chained there, bound by magic so that I could not escape—but not before I saw people I'd known my whole life tearing into the survivors like a plague of locusts hungry for the feast. It didn't matter who their victims were. Who *they'd* been. Spouses... children... Her new vampire servants fed on them all and laughed at their cries."

The pain on his face grew. "We were good people once." His gaze turned to the window, staring through the glass like he wasn't really seeing whatever lay beyond. "So many good people."

The silence stretched for a time before I could find my voice. "How did you get free?"

He straightened a bit as if pulling himself from the memories. "Zeniryans were never like some of our fellow nations. We embraced magic, and since I was a child, I had tutors to help me develop any trace of magical gift I possessed. After she left me in that cell, that horrible craving tearing into my every thought, I worked to use any shred of magic I had to ease the hunger and escape the spells she'd placed on my shackles. It felt like an eternity, but eventually, I found a way to slip past them. She hadn't bothered to enchant anything else, likely never anticipating I'd break free at all, which left the castle open to me once I fled the dungeon."

I glanced around at the dusty room. "Had the vampires all left?"

"No."

I waited, confused.

He looked back at me. "I killed them."

I swallowed dryly. His eyes tracked the motion of my throat, and then he turned to the window again.

"Without the shackles binding me, the magic I possessed came back to the fore. Paired with the power I now had as a vampire and my rage at what they'd done... I was capable of more than I'd ever known. The vampires in the castle fell, as did those out in the forest feasting on the survivors who'd attempted to flee. I learned then that feeding from vampires was not only *possible* for us, but strengthening as well. Conversely, feeding on humans—while apparently enjoyable, if the looks on the faces of the creatures I killed was any indication—is less so. It can sustain us, but it doesn't provide the same strength. And if we leave the human victim alive, they become nothing more than a thrall begging for us to bite them again."

Unease prickled through me.

"So I drank the blood of vampires in order to stop myself from becoming a ravenous beast like the others were, and I tracked those creatures down until every last one had been eliminated. If their victims had any free will left at all, they fled from me, but the hungry forest was waiting. The rest... I tried to save them, but they were so far gone that in the end, I could only put them out of their misery. The vampire witch tried to stop me." His jaw muscles jumped. "She did not survive."

I barely breathed. "And now? If you've been here for thirty *years*..."

"Indeed." He dropped his gaze to the floor. "I've studied every book our sorcerers left behind. Every scroll and treatise on magic I could find in these walls. I am more skilled now than I likely ever would have been if I'd been able to live my natural life, and that magic has helped me.

Sustained me. Kept me from needing to feed for what was apparently three decades, though it has felt like many more." His eyes slipped back to me. "But it cannot last forever."

My fingers were curled around the ends of the chair's arms. My feet were pressing to the floor, ready to propel me away. I didn't breathe, waiting for whatever move he would make.

"I have spent every moment since Zenirya fell trying to mitigate the destructive magic that ravaged my nation. The trees no longer kill, though they love to torment anyone who enters the woods with visions of all those who died before. I've never been able to stop the warping of time, but I've done what I could to keep it from plunging travelers into eternal night. I know it's not enough to make Zenirya safe again. Perhaps nothing ever will be. And after this many years, when my hunger grows so strong that my magic finally fails to control it..." His brow rose and fell. "I cannot allow myself to become more of a monster than I am already. Before that happens, I *had* planned to find a way to destroy myself, but when one of my magic mirrors detected you and your men in the forest today..."

I watched him warily. "What are you asking of me?"

His eyes met mine. "Blood."

My back bumped into the chair and I realized I'd recoiled.

"It wouldn't need to be much. And I will be careful, I swear to you. I—"

"That's why you brought me here? To..." My gut twisted at the words. "To *bite* me?"

He hesitated and then tilted his head briefly in a nod. "Magic cannot sustain me indefinitely. But with a little vampire blood, I might make it another thirty years. Perhaps longer."

A ragged breath left me. I pushed away from the chair, retreating farther though there wasn't anywhere to go. The coffin lay near the foot of the bed, but on this side of the room there was only a solid wall. Casimir was between me and the door, and I could scarcely imagine it would go well if I tried to make a run for it.

Except...

I looked back at the coffin again, suddenly confused. "But you didn't. Before, I mean." I turned to him. "I was lying there and you could have easily..."

He didn't take his gaze from the window, his bearing stiff. "I may be a vampire, but I am not a *leech*, Princess. I will not take your blood without your consent."

I stared at him. At his rigid stance and how he wouldn't look at me. His body was a picture of restraint and control that *had* to be underlaid with fear. And why wouldn't it be? If anything he said was true—and I wasn't certain why anyone would tell such an elaborate lie—then he'd been starving for *thirty years*. Maybe more, if time moved as strangely in this place as he said. He'd stretched himself with magic nearly to the point of death, and when I'd been lying there, unable to defend myself...

My eyes tracked across the profile of his features as if seeing him for the first time. Could I have exercised such restraint in his place? To have the answer to my problems right in front of me... and then give that person the opportunity to deny me anyway?

I wanted to believe I was a good person, but if our places had been reversed, I honestly couldn't be sure I would have been able to resist.

He closed his eyes, turning away as if taking my silence as rejection.

"What will you do then?" I asked, my voice faint. "If... if I agree to help you?"

He was motionless for a moment, and then he turned back, surprise flashing through his dark eyes. His shoulders twitched in an infinitesimal shrug. "Continue as I have been, working to unravel what magic I can in the hope that someday Zenirya will be safe for the living again."

The thought hurt on some level, though I couldn't define why. It was his business, and a noble cause if the forest was even half as bad as he said. But what he asked...

"Let me see my men. Let me know they're safe. If they are..." I swallowed hard as my heart pounded. "Then, yes. I'll do it."

18
GWYNEIRA

My answer hung in the air between us like a snowflake frozen in time. For a moment, Casimir made no move in response, as if the reality of my words had paralyzed him. But his expression faltered.

For the first time, I saw hope in his eyes.

His head twitched in a small nod. "Thank you."

I smiled in return.

He hesitated a moment longer, as if the fact he'd soon have what he needed had shaken him, but then he turned and headed toward the door.

Warily, I followed.

"I must warn you," he said without looking back at me. "While I did not lie when I said I am alone here, the nuance of that is... complicated."

My feet slowed. "What does that mean?"

He cast a brief glance over his shoulder, a hint of uncertainty in his gaze. "I swear they won't harm you."

Wariness prickled through me.

He opened the door.

I gasped. Wolves made of black smoke regarded us both, their bodies so large they filled the hall. There were at least four of them. Maybe more, though it was hard to tell where one ended and the others began. They were as tall as me, and their eyes gleamed with brilliant green light that rose like glowing mist to join the black smoke of the rest of their forms. Fangs stretched from their mouths, each easily longer than my hand.

"What..." I whispered, afraid to move for fear they would lunge at me. "What are..."

"Magic. Summoned from the ether or the gods know where. They simply arrived here several years after Zenirya fell, and somehow they help hold the power of the forest at bay so that the castle stays safe." Casimir came up beside the nearest wolf, and it nuzzled at his chest like a loyal dog. Gently, he stroked the smoke as if it was fur while a smile crossed his face, caring and sad. "They don't speak, of course, but they do understand me, even if they don't always stay where I can see them. But it's better than being truly alone."

He glanced over at me and extended his other hand. "Would you like to meet them?"

I blinked, torn between the urge to retreat and the fear it would only make these strange creatures chase me. But at the same time, I doubted Casimir would invite me closer if he had any concern the wolves would harm me. After all, he said he wouldn't take my blood without my consent. My death at the teeth of his wolves likely fell into that category.

Fighting to keep my legs from shaking, I walked closer. The nearest wolf huffed at me, making my steps falter, but Casimir merely took my hand.

His fingers were like ice.

I tightened my grip, determined to give no sign of how very cold he was compared even to me. I'd been so self-conscious of my cold skin when I touched Niko. I suddenly didn't want Casimir to feel the same way.

It wasn't his fault he was a vampire any more than it was mine.

"D-do they have names?" I attempted to hold my voice steady, though I suspected I only barely sounded calm.

"I have a theory that they have names for each other, though I've never determined what they might be. I call this one Ruhl."

He drew me closer to the enormous creature, and I knew he could probably feel my body trembling. The wolf sniffed at me, a great inhalation that brought its teeth closer to my throat. I stayed still, not even daring to breathe.

In a flash, its tongue lapped my cheek.

I let out a thoroughly undignified squeak.

The wolf huffed again, and I had the strangest impression it was amused by me. Turning, it paced back into the smoky throng of its brethren filling the hall.

"He likes you."

I glanced to Casimir, and from the glint in his eyes, I was certain he found my reaction humorous too. With as much dignity as I could muster, I drew myself up. "My men?"

He bowed his head slightly in acknowledgement, his expression unchanged. Attempting to appear in control of myself, I walked with him into the hall.

The creatures fell in around us, a churning mass of black smoke with fangs and claws that shifted in and out of wolf form like storm clouds taking shape in the sky. I couldn't pick Ruhl out from among them, nor tell where one ended and the others began.

But the rest of the corridor felt like a grave.

I took it in with quick glances at first, but when the wolves continued *not* attacking, my attention started to linger on the hallway. Cobwebs dangled like gray gossamer from the chandeliers, and in the silver glow of my night vision, dust glittered in the air like stars. But among it all, ornate paintings hung on the walls. Some depicted what could only be the royal family, their subjects staring down at us beneath a layer of dust like silent ghosts witnessing our passage. Others showed scenes of life in Zenirya—markets and streets filled with people and holiday feasts that radiated joy.

But shattered mirrors hung between them.

And Casimir never looked up at them at all.

"There was a time I wanted to burn the paintings," he said suddenly, his quiet voice breaking the silence. "But it would only give the gods or the witch who turned me what they wanted. I didn't need to help them erase us fully."

He never took his eyes from the hall ahead.

"You could have covered them up?" I offered.

A rueful smile crossed his face and he shook his head. "It wouldn't spare me their judgment."

I bit my lip, unsure if there was a thing on earth I could say back to that.

The corridor twisted and turned, delivering us after a time to a broad stairway that wound through more levels, each as still and untouched as a mausoleum. But for occasional stray beams of moonlight coming through distant windows, nothing but darkness surrounded us, and if not for my night vision, I would have been utterly blind.

"Did you ever think about leaving?" I asked carefully, curiosity finally getting the better of me.

He glanced at me. "And go where?"

"I don't know. Someplace else?"

Casimir stopped and I did too, the wolves flowing all around us like a ring of black clouds. "Why would you ask that?"

I searched inside myself for a polite answer, but in the end, it felt more respectful to tell the truth than to attempt half a lie. "Because this place feels like a graveyard."

He blinked, clearly taken aback, and then his expression closed down. "Fitting for the dead then, isn't it?"

Without another word, he started off again.

"You're not."

He stopped. His face was cold when he looked over his shoulder at me.

I walked closer. "You're *not* dead. And neither am I. We died, yes, but..." I drew a breath and pressed onward. "We're alive now, even if it's a different kind of life than what we had before."

"Said with all the optimism of one so recently turned."

My temper flared. "That's not it."

He was silent.

"If you truly want to think that of yourself, fine. It's not my business. But you don't speak for me, and I—" Doubt tried to rear its head. I bashed it back, pressing onward. "I am *not dead*. Not while I can still walk this earth and do something to help the people here. And frankly, since that seems to be what you've been trying to do too, I would conclude that means you're not dead either." I met his eyes. "The living don't deserve to condemn themselves to a graveyard."

He was still, but his brow twitched down, his eyes on my face with something that almost looked like wonder, as if he'd never seen anything like me before.

With the faintest flinch of muscle, he bowed his head in acknowledgment and then gestured for me to continue with him.

I did as he asked, unsure if my words had accomplished much. Maybe nothing could.

But I couldn't abide the thought I'd lost my life completely. That I was doomed to end up in a graveyard too. Somehow, it was equally awful to think of this man here, alone, lurking in halls full of invisible ghosts.

All because he thought he was one of them.

The corridor turned again, and a heavy door stood at the end the hall, its sides reinforced by metal bolts and bars, while its center held a massive vault wheel like my father used to have on the room that held the castle coffers. The spokes were as thick as my arm. It would likely take several grown men all their strength to turn them.

Casimir came to stop before it, and I blinked, suddenly realizing where we had to be.

"You locked them in a *vault*?"

He gave a small wince. "Not exactly, though I understand how it looks—and likely what your men think."

"Then what the hell is this?"

"A safe room. The door is reinforced enough to slow down even the most determined monster, and the lock can only be disengaged by a spell. The spell in question will only respond if I am in my right mind. If I'm not—if I'm overwhelmed by hunger instead—not only will the door remain locked, but the spell will trigger a secret passage to open inside that room, allowing the occupants to escape."

I stared at him.

A wry look crossed his face, making him look simultaneously older and younger in the strangest way. "I've been here a *very* long time, Princess. I've had ample opportunity to plan for assorted eventualities."

I didn't know what to say to that, but thankfully, he didn't seem to need a response. Placing his palm to the center of the dial, he murmured words that sent a prickle of electricity over my skin.

Magic.

The unmarked metal at the center suddenly flared to life with glowing blue symbols that chased themselves across the flat surface like lightning rolling out from where his hand rested. The vault wheel turned on its own, and within the heavy door, a clank followed as the locks disengaged.

Casimir stepped back as the door began to swing ponderously open, the slab of reinforced metal moving slowly like it was as thick as a fortress wall and just as heavy.

Arguing voices I recognized reached my ears for the first time, slipping past the slowly widening gap, and my heart leapt. Lantern light gleamed through the opening, seeming so bright in the dark hall.

At my side, Casimir grunted.

I glanced at him, confused.

He'd squeezed his eyes shut. Shaking his head hard, his jaw muscles flexed as if he was clenching his teeth.

And suddenly, I understood.

He could hear their hearts beating. Maybe even hear the whispers of their blood flowing in their veins.

And he was starving.

"Casimir?" I prompted warily.

A shudder rolled through him, like he was fighting back something. "There is a study," he gritted out, his tone polite but tense. "Just down the hall. Third door on the left. If you need somewhere to talk. Rooms upstairs too. For rest."

He backed away. The door was almost open enough for the men to get through, and I heard them shoving at the other side, cursing its weight.

I moved between the gap and Casimir, my heart pounding—and I knew he could hear it. His eyes snapped up to mine, wild.

But then they lingered on my face. The feral light in his eyes faded. An odd sort of confusion came into his expression, like he'd suddenly thought of a question but didn't understand why he was asking it. His hand rose, his fingers hovering just beyond my cheek.

"You..." His brow twitched down, the questioning look growing stronger.

More frustrated grunts came from behind me. The men were still shoving on the door.

Another shudder rolled through Casimir, and he recoiled. "When you're ready, come find me. The wolves will lead the way." His fangs glinted in my night vision. "Please don't take too long."

He burst into smoke and shadow and raced away down the hall.

※

"Princess?" Niko shoved past the massive vault door.

Others followed, escaping the opening the moment the gap was wide enough for them to do so. Lars and Byron held lanterns, possibly taken from the bags still on their backs, while the others gripped weapons, clearly ready for a fight. Shock filled their faces when they saw me, turning to horror at the sight of the smoke wolves.

"Get the fuck away from her," Roan snarled at them.

Lars raised a hand. Heat radiated from his palm as he extended it toward the creatures.

"No, it's okay!" I cried, moving between him and the wolves.

Lars dropped his hand immediately, as if to stop himself from hurting me.

"They're…" I faltered. I couldn't say the wolves weren't a threat. They could become one in a heartbeat. But they also weren't attacking, and the last thing we needed was to provoke them into doing so.

"I'm safe," I amended. "It's okay." I glanced at the creatures behind me, praying they would listen and understand me as well as they understood Casimir. "It's okay," I repeated to them.

A heartbeat passed, and then the wolves pulled back, leaving only one of them close to me, and somehow, I suspected it was Ruhl. I swore the creature looked amused again. With a deliberate motion, the wolf stepped away too.

I turned back just in time for Dex to pull me into his arms. He squeezed me tightly, and then Clay and Lars were there, doing the same. When they released me, Niko took my hands, his gaze searching my face as if to be certain I was okay.

Which was what I *should* have been asking them. "Are you hurt?"

The men hesitated.

My heart beat faster. "*Are* you?"

"Bruises," Dex said. "No broken bones. We've had worse."

I remembered how to breathe. "What happened?"

"Those *things* and their master attacked us," Clay spat. "They knocked your coffin away from us. Swallowed it up, and we couldn't get to you." He glared at the wolves briefly before looking back at me, hints of worry leaking into his blue eyes. "We didn't know whether you were alive or dead, baby."

The traces of lingering fear in his voice made my heart ache, and I reached out, squeezing his hand.

"How did you get away?" Lars asked.

I shook my head. "It isn't like that. He... he had a question for me. It's hard to explain."

Clay scoffed. "Well, I would like to explain a few things to that fucker about asking nicely, then. And not fucking locking us up."

"It..." I searched for words. "He was protecting you."

I might as well have told them Casimir had three heads from the incredulous looks they gave me.

Niko recovered first, though disbelief still threaded through his kind tone. "How was this *protecting* us?"

I glanced around, uncomfortable with the wolves being here. Who knew how much the creatures understood or what might set them off? "May we talk about this elsewhere?"

Dex eyed the wolves as if weighing the best strategy for fighting them again. "Good idea. Where is the exit?"

"Yeah," Clay agreed. "Let's get the hell out of here."

I winced. "We can't go yet."

Every shred of their incredulity returned, tenfold.

"I promise, I'll explain. Just... please may we talk somewhere more private?"

Praying they'd follow, I started off in the direction where Casimir said the study would be. The wolves melted from my path, their green eyes watching me.

Murmurs passed among the men, wordless sounds of distrust and surprise.

But their footsteps followed a moment later.

The study was only slightly larger than the bedroom where I'd woken up, but unlike the dust that coated everywhere else, this room looked as if it had been in use recently. Books were everywhere, lying open on tables or dotted with bookmarks or scraps of paper sticking from between their pages as if to denote important sections. Candles covered in drips of wax stood near them all, unlit. Perhaps it was easier to read with light than with night vision.

I stared around at the towers of books stacked before the full bookshelves. How long must he spend in this place?

But then, thirty years was plenty of time to study.

Lanternlight poured into the room as the others followed me inside, and Byron made an impressed noise at the sight of the books. While Dex surveyed the room and Ozias prowled around checking every inch for threats, Roan retreated to watch everything from a shadowed corner, never meeting anyone's eyes. Ignoring them all, Byron made a beeline for the nearest stack of books, leaning over the open pages without touching them.

"Books on sorcery." He said it as if he was confirming something. His brow twitched up. "Formidable ones."

Clay muttered a curse under his breath, and even Lars looked grim.

"Who the hell is this guy?" Roan snarled from the shadows.

Even if the wolves had remained outside the study, I marveled that he wasn't concerned another one might still be hiding there.

But then, he looked as if he was seething with anger. Maybe he was hoping for a fight.

"What did he say?" Dex asked me, a tone in his voice like he was already formulating strategies and wanted my information to include in his plans.

"Or at least *claim*?" Roan added darkly.

Dex's mouth tightened, but he didn't take his eyes from me, waiting for my answer.

"His name is Casimir," I said. "He's the ruler of Zenirya. And as far as he knows, he's also the only one of its people left."

Clay scoffed wryly. "Easy to claim you're in charge, then."

"What else did you learn, Princess?" Byron asked, a look in his green eyes like he was recording every detail and comparing it to a list of facts in his mind.

I took a steadying breath and relayed the rest of what I'd learned.

"He wants *what*?" Clay demanded when I finished.

Byron's brow was nearly to his hairline. "And you agreed to that?"

I winced.

Niko gave me a concerned look. "Why would you agree, Princess?"

My discomfort grew worse, and I shrugged as I tried to find a way to explain. "Casimir could have just taken what he needed from me while I was unconscious. He didn't. And he swore that even if I said no, he would honor that and do his best to let us all go freely." I gestured toward the castle beyond the study door. "He's been here alone for thirty years. He's starving. But he won't let himself become a monster like the other vampires we've seen. Before he saw us in his magic mirror, his plan was to destroy himself before the hunger grew beyond his ability to control it." I shifted my weight uncomfortably. "I'd rather not force him do that."

I couldn't read the glance that passed among the others, but then Roan broke the moment with a disgusted noise. "Maybe that's just what he told you to guilt you into helping him."

I hesitated. "Or it was the truth."

Roan sneered, turning away.

Frustration pushed at me. "Casimir said he locked you up to protect you. The door was sealed by magic that wouldn't allow it to open if he wasn't in his right mind." I scanned their faces, seeing doubt everywhere I looked. "I *know* this could be some elaborate setup. I do. But I think he's telling the truth."

Niko opened his mouth, closed it again, and then seemed to finally figure out whatever he was trying to say. "I don't know what it was like for you, Princess, but..." He didn't quite glance at the others, seeming embarrassed to be discussing this in front of them. "Being fed from feels very... intimate. To have someone holding your life in their, well, *fangs* is..." He wetted his lips. "There aren't a lot of things I can think of that are more intense to share with someone."

My cheeks heated, and my gaze skirted away from the men. "I-I'll be okay."

"So you're attracted to him, then." Roan tossed out the

words coldly. "That's what this is about. You'd like a little *intimate* moment with him."

The others tensed.

I blinked, flustered. "I didn't say that. I barely even know him."

"You barely know *us,* but that didn't stop you."

"Roan," Dex cut in. "Enough."

I stared at Roan, horrified. "Is *that* what you think of me? That I just throw myself at the nearest man I see?"

"Well, explain why the hell you're willing to risk yourself for some stranger, then," he demanded. "Is it because he's a fellow vampire? Because you think he'll understand what you're going through?" A cold sound left him. "That vampire *stole* you from us, Princess. He took you even though you're *ours*. And instead of getting the hell out of here with us, you're offering him the chance to drain you dry." He stalked toward me, his voice dropping low and cruel. "He's not your savior. He's never going to make what happened to you better. And letting him even *touch* you when every inch of you belongs to us is—"

"*Roan!*" Dex barked.

Slamming to a stop, Roan's gaze snapped over to Dex, his eerie black eyes blazing with fury.

Chills rolled through me. The look on his face was inhuman and wild, with more of that *otherness* staring out than I'd ever seen before.

And the vampire side of me wanted to lash out at it, take him to the ground, and challenge him to do something about every word he'd just said. Tingling rushed through my body and my fingers curled, my nails feeling sharper than normal as they dug into my palm. Pinpricks of pain touched my lower lip as my fangs slid into place.

"Enough," Dex said, still watching Roan. "Calm down."

Roan was shaking. His knuckles were bloodlessly white as his hands squeezed into fists.

Around the room, the air began to feel charged. I couldn't tell which of the men it was coming from.

Maybe all of them.

Snarling a curse, Roan whipped around and stormed from the study, slamming the door behind him.

No one said a word.

Quivers ran through me as the vampire side of me receded and my fangs slid away again, all while something deep in my belly quivered with incongruous heat at the possessive things he'd said. But I knew Roan didn't actually want me. He'd avoided me, sneered at me with disgust and contempt at every opportunity, and made the fact I shouldn't come near him more than clear.

But perhaps what he just said had been on behalf of his friends. Perhaps he was being protective of them.

Perhaps... something.

But what was he going to do now? Go attack Casimir?

Cold fear suddenly prickled through me, but a heartbeat later it sparked with guilt. Why was Casimir my immediate concern? Yes, it was... well, *maybe* it was logical to be worried after the way Roan acted. But I'd just watched one of the giants storm out of the room, and instead of worrying about *him* or what might happen to my men if he angered Casimir, my first thought was for the safety of a stranger.

Was I truly putting a fellow vampire ahead of them?

I turned to the others, finding grim and discomfited expressions on their faces, and my heart sank. Gods, did they all think I was doing that?

"That was uncalled for," Byron murmured, but his green eyes wouldn't quite look at me.

"You okay, Princess?" Niko asked carefully.

I didn't know how to respond. He cared so much about my safety, and yet here I was, *not* getting the hell out of here with them but instead risking the gods knew what possibilities, all to help someone I just met.

"Was any of that true?" Dex's voice was quiet. "Are you helping Casimir for other reasons?"

My mouth moved. I wanted to deny it. Gods, I wanted to say no right away, but... "I-I don't know." Silence greeted my answer, and it burned too, making words spill from me. "I'd never choose anyone over you. Any of you. Please, *please* know that. I never could. You all..." My hand fluttered to my chest. "You're my heart. I feel that. I *know* it. That hasn't changed, I swear."

No one spoke and it made horror crush down on my lungs, stealing my ability to breathe. Had I ruined everything?

Gods help me, I should walk away from this place. I should leave right now in case that salvaged something I'd unintentionally damaged.

And if I did, I was sentencing a man to death.

"But you *are* drawn to him," Lars said quietly, watching me.

I trembled, wanting to say no, but the word suddenly felt wrong.

"And if he's lying?" Clay added.

My hands twitched in a helpless gesture. Roan wasn't mistaken. I'd just met Casimir, and yet I was risking everything to help him. It made no sense.

The memory of the pain that tinged Casimir's eyes when

he spoke of his past flickered through my mind. The struggle as he made himself promise he wouldn't hurt us, no matter what I decided. The way he held himself back, when every heartbeat he heard must have been driving the vampire inside of him mad. He'd lost everything and now he was left here alone, a sorrowful man who thought himself only a ghost, surrounded by memories of the dead and trying to use whatever remained of his existence to help the living.

And yet he still restrained himself. Still wanted to give me a choice, no matter what. He could be laying a trap for me.

Or I could be his last hope.

Byron sighed, and the sound pulled me from my thoughts. "I felt the spells surrounding that room," he said to the others. "They were strange. As focused outward as they were within." His head bobbed thoughtfully. "It is possible he is telling the truth."

Clay shifted his weight, looking away, while in the corner, Ozias crossed his arms and wouldn't meet anyone's gaze.

"He could have killed us," Niko said into the silence. "You all know that. Those creatures of his..." He shook his head. "Our magic couldn't touch them. Our weapons only slowed them down. He took the princess but he didn't hurt her, and while yeah, he locked us up, if he'd only wanted a snack..." Niko's mouth thinned. "Why tell her we were alive? Why bring her here? Why leave us alive now?"

"Leverage to manipulate her into doing what he wants?" Sarcasm was thick in Clay's voice as he jerked his head toward me.

"Possible," Dex allowed, his eyes skimming over the

carpet thoughtfully like the former soldier was running scenarios in his mind. "Or it's exactly what he said."

Clay grimaced.

My eyes flew across them. Were they truly arguing that I might be right?

I wetted my lips, weighing my words as carefully as I could. "I just know that I can help him. I... I can imagine how he feels. How much it hurts, being here. Starving. Losing your life and your home to a vampire." I swallowed hard. "I believe him."

"And if he wants more than your blood?" Lars asked, his blue eyes trained on me. "If it turns out you both do?"

"Then it's our treluria's decision," Dex interrupted before I could speak, finality in his voice. "And we abide by it."

I faltered, thrown. But at his words, only reluctant acknowledgement took up residence on Clay's face, while more firm agreement showed from Byron, Niko, and Lars.

Near the window at the far end of the room, Ozias remained silent. I couldn't tell anything from his expression, but even now he wouldn't look at me.

"I don't want to do anything that will hurt you all, though," I said, half-watching him as I addressed them all. "Nothing is worth that. That any of you would be willing to share as you have is a miracle to me. No one from my people would ever do such a thing. I can't ask you now to—"

"It's not sharing that's causing us to worry," Dex interrupted gently.

I floundered with disbelief, and my eyes darted toward the door where Roan had disappeared. "But—"

"If this man hurts you, it hurts us."

193

Byron nodded, his freckled face solemn. "That, I think, is what we *all* fear."

The others made noises of agreement.

"None of us want you harmed, *ever*," the scholar continued. "But if Casimir is the man you think he is, and if he's told you the truth as you believe... then that is not a concern."

A breath left me. The relief inside me felt unsure if it was in the right place. Could this really be okay with them?

My eyes slipped over to Ozias again.

Dex seemed to see the question I couldn't bring myself to ask. "Ozias?" he prompted.

With his scarred and bearded face nearly lost in the shadows, Ozias looked away from the ground. "She's not mine." His voice was detached, barely more than a cold grunt. "Makes no difference to me."

I blinked. It wasn't just his tone or how, from him, the words sounded like I was nothing but an object. His scent on his blanket had surrounded me while I slept. I'd seen him watching Niko have sex with me, in addition to how he'd reacted in the forest after.

A sick feeling swirled in my gut. I'd wondered if the former had been meaningless, and if the latter had only been arousal for the erotic show.

I supposed there was my answer.

With a lurch, Ozias rocked away from where he leaned on the windowsill and strode from the room.

Niko came closer, taking my hand and holding it in both of his own. "You're *ours*," he murmured. "Remember? You belong to us and we belong to you."

I ripped my gaze from the door, trying not to breathe in

too deeply for fear of smelling traces of Ozias's scent on my body even now.

Maybe Casimir would allow me time to take a bath after he finished with me, if only to wash any trace of that away.

Niko squeezed my hand. With effort, I dragged my attention back to the present and managed to nod.

He smiled, glancing at the other men still left in the room as if to include them in his words. "Sharing your heart doesn't change that you've given it to us, Princess. This isn't us letting you go. But life brings us where we go for a reason." He brushed a strand of my hair back from my face. "Maybe nothing happens between you and this man. Maybe that's okay." A smile crossed his face. "Or maybe there's something for you here too."

I looked at them all, somehow still so baffled they could accept any of this. In Aneira, such a thing would *never* happen. Exactly the opposite. My people thought such relationships were immoral and abhorrent—and that didn't even bring into it everything I'd done or said or wanted when I was with these men.

My own people would never have understood any of this.

"Just be careful," Lars said, giving me a caring smile as he ran a hand down my arm as if to soothe me. "That's all we ask."

Clay grinned. "And come back so we can fuck you senseless when the vampire's done."

I laughed.

19
ROAN

Cold night air bit at my face. All around me, silence reigned supreme. Beneath the silver moonlight, the cursed forest tangled between the icy mountain slopes, and the stone terrace on which I stood gave me a godlike view.

Not that I saw any of it.

The demon rampaged beneath my skin. It was awake, and gods, it was *furious*. Raging because my princess had been taken from me. Losing her in the forest snapped every shred of my hard-won control. It was a miracle I'd been able to keep my monster hidden from the others, to say nothing of stopping it from burning everything in sight until she returned.

And now that she was back...

The monster snarled within me, the noise coming out as a choked groan as I fought to hold it inside. She wanted another. And not just *any* other, but the very man who had captured us. A man who set every instinct I had on edge, as if everything about him was wrong, wrong, *wrong*. He had stolen her away, taking her from me as if she was *his* to claim, not mine, and I...

I had done nothing. For fear of killing my friends. For fear of killing her.

I'd. Done. *Nothing.*

Another surge of rage rolled through me, hot as fire and just as deadly, and I caught myself on the stone banister as my body quaked. Patches of my skin turned gray, burning while my fingertips crushed into the granite.

My thoughts blurred, lost between the *me* I knew and the me that was something else entirely. The demon was coming, and when that monster arrived, Gwyneira would finally understand. She would see that she was mine. *Ours.* No one else could have her but those *we* chose to share her with. She belonged to us, and when I finally showed myself to her, she...

Would die.

The last shreds of my sanity flung up an image of Gwyneira's face. Her horror. Her pain. Her precious skin blistering and turning to ash while she screamed. And I knew that was the truth. The real result of showing my other self to her. After all, I'd seen it before.

The last time I murdered those I loved.

In my mind, the demon howled in pain at the sight, the cry tearing through me with enough force to send me crumbling to my knees, and my grip took a chunk of the granite banister with me as I fell. Curling in on myself, I pleaded with the monster to go back to sleep. To stop. To understand what it would be doing if it showed the truth to her. We wouldn't just lose her to a vampire. We'd lose her forever. No claiming her. No protecting her. Nothing but her horror and pain, and gods, if we caused that, then we would truly want to die.

The creature's rage dimmed. We'd already hurt her. Those things I'd said. The possessive rage that had poured like acid from my mouth. I'd cut her with my words, given her contempt instead of love. We wouldn't do worse.

But for her own sake, I prayed she hated me now.

The demon moaned.

I closed my eyes, desperately struggling to regain control. She *couldn't* be ours. That could never be my reality.

The monster slunk back into the shadows of my mind, aching from our shame.

Because we'd already lost her.

20
GWYNEIRA

Time truly was strange in this place.
My eyes traced the mountains beyond the window at the end of the corridor. The slopes looked entirely different from those near the Jeweled Coven, as if the giants had crossed more miles than should have been possible. To hear them tell it, they'd only traveled a day, but one that felt like it had lasted for weeks.

And now the night lingered like a guest who wouldn't leave, waiting for me to follow through on the agreement I'd made.

I turned away from the grimy glass. From the corners of my eyes, glowing emerald gazes watched me from the shadows, vanishing whenever I looked toward them fully. Doors lined the hall in which I stood, most of them closed, though Dex still leaned against the frame of one, watching me. The bedrooms were right where Casimir had indicated, and though they were as dusty as everything else, the men hadn't seemed to care. Not when no one could say how long it had *actually* been since they'd slept, given how the forest had been playing tricks on them.

Of Casimir himself, I'd seen no sign.

Dex shrugged away from the door frame of one of the bedrooms as I walked toward him. Most of the men had dragged mattresses and cushions into the large bedroom behind him, none of them willing to trust Casimir, the wolves, or the castle itself enough to sleep separately.

Safety in numbers, Clay had said, his wry tone unable to fully hide the distrust in his eyes.

I missed his lighter humor. I'd only seen flashes of it since we left the Jeweled Coven, and I hoped when this was done—when we escaped the forest and made it back to Aneira—maybe it would come back to stay.

"Are you sure you don't want us to accompany you?" Dex asked in a low voice.

I shook my head immediately, discomfort surging to the fore. "No, I... I'm okay."

He didn't look convinced.

"You need to rest," I pressed. "I'll be fine."

Silently, I prayed he would agree. I knew he was being protective as always, but allowing myself to be bitten was awkward enough without an audience.

"Take care of yourself first and foremost," Dex said, the order in his voice more than clear. "And if anything seems off to you, get out of there."

My head moved in a nervous nod. "Yes, sir."

His lip twitched, but then he stepped closer, the amusement fading as he took my cheek. Bending lower, he drew me to him.

The castle melted away as his lips met mine. His other hand gripped me, pulling me up to him while he plundered my mouth with an intensity like he never wanted to let me go.

But time was slipping past, and at last, he drew back. "If he hurts you, no magic will save him."

Gratitude and love warmed me at the unequivocal promise in his eyes.

He placed a small kiss on my forehead and then released me. "See you soon."

"Soon," I echoed.

Turning, I walked carefully down the hall. I could feel his eyes on me, tracking me as I went.

But not *just* his.

I glanced at a brilliant emerald gleam in the shadows, my heart skipping. "Ruhl?"

A wolf rose from the darkness as if it had only been lounging there, the dark clouds of its form swirling up into a creature as tall as me.

I swallowed hard. "Take me to him?"

A wry look gleamed in the creature's glowing green eyes. With paws larger than my head, it turned and paced down the hall, leading the way.

I looked over my shoulder.

Dex hadn't moved.

Giving him an awkward smile, I trailed the wolf around the turn and up a spiral stairway of stone steps and unlit candles set in alcoves along the walls. Any trace of moonlight faded as we left the level where my giants rested. Darkness encased me, though it was cast with silver by the night vision I was growing more grateful for by the moment.

The wolf never looked back.

At long last, Ruhl turned and started off down another hall. Narrow windows lined one side of the corridor, and

201

ratty curtains of faded red fabric hung over them, peppered with holes from being eaten by moths and mice.

My eyes tracked across them. How did Casimir stay safe from the sun with such paltry coverings?

Unless he never left his room during the day.

The wolf huffed at me, and my attention snapped back to the matter at hand. Ruhl had come to a stop at a pair of ornate double doors at the end of the corridor, and its shining green eyes regarded me flatly.

It seemed we'd arrived.

Unsure what to do, I lifted a hand to knock, but Ruhl simply turned and poured through the seams around the double doors like smoke.

Indeed.

I bit my lip. It was still likely rude to simply stand here.

My knuckles rapped a hesitant rhythm on the carved wood door.

Seconds slid past, my nervousness growing with every one. Gods, what had I gotten myself into? This was madness. My whole *life* was madness. Roan was right; I didn't know this man. What if Casimir was downstairs right now, proving me wrong about him by attacking my men, and all of this was just a ruse to—

The door opened.

A tiny breath left me. Casimir stood there, still dressed in the black silk shirt and slacks from before, the glow from a fireplace silhouetting him and tracing his dark skin with gold. "Princess. I wasn't sure you'd come."

I drew myself up, trying to give no sign of nerves. "I promised."

He stepped aside. "Enter?"

I nodded briefly in thanks and walked past him, my eyes

darting over the space as I came inside. Wherever the wolf had gone, it was invisible now. But like the study, there were books everywhere in the room. Notes, too, stacked neatly across every surface. A chair sat by the fireplace, and after the darkness of the halls, I blinked a bit as my eyes adjusted to the light of the flames. A desk stood near the window, papers stacked atop it, and through a doorway to my right, a bed waited, large enough that I could lie in the middle and stretch out my arms but never reach the sides.

I bit my lip nervously. What did one do when they'd just agreed to be bitten by a vampire? Was standing here appropriate? Should I take the chair? The bed?

My cheeks flushed. I probably shouldn't think about the bed.

The click of the door latch behind me made me turn. His back to the door, Casimir stood watching me.

Self-consciousness washed through me. What was he seeing? A meal, perhaps? A stranger who had agreed to give him what he needed to survive?

Gods, the intensity of his focus held me like a fly in honey. But somehow I still trusted that if I told him I'd changed my mind, he wouldn't force anything.

It was the strangest feeling.

"Do you need anything before we begin?" he asked.

My head shook. "I'm fine."

"And your men? They gave you no trouble over coming here tonight?"

I hesitated. "They understand."

He made a thoughtful sound. Pushing away from the door, he walked toward me.

A tremble radiated from my core. His movements were liquid and graceful as a wild animal, much more so than I'd noticed prior to now, and a tangled, churning sensation started up inside me, one that felt so much more complicated than fear.

Like I was predator and prey at the same time, waiting for the crack of the whip to start me running.

Except I wasn't sure I wanted to give in to the impulse to bolt.

He came to a stop only inches from me, his dark eyes staring down into mine. He wasn't as tall as my giants—more the size of a tall human—and he was leaner too. The black silk of his shirt gave the impression of strong muscles beneath, while a hint of spicy scent surrounded him, unidentifiable but intoxicating nonetheless. The gold bands in his braids glinted in the firelight, and around his fathomless eyes, he had such thick lashes.

Strange how I'd never noticed those until now.

I dropped my gaze away, my cheeks burning hotter. Gods, my thoughts were running for shelter in random observations rather than facing what I was about to let this man do.

His hand came up, hovering for a heartbeat before gently coming to rest on my cheek. His skin was cold as ice, but I didn't recoil. I wouldn't, because I knew what the other side of this was like. How it felt to know that anyone you touched would be aware in an instant that you weren't human anymore.

My eyes rose back to his.

"Are you still okay with this?" he asked softly.

"Yes," I whispered.

A small smile crossed his face, and I swore I saw relief in the expression.

"Choose a word," he said. "If you wish me to stop at any point, you only have to say that and I will. Understood?"

I nodded. My thoughts raced for a moment, every word escaping me, before I spoke the first one that came to mind. "Apple."

"Apple," he said as if confirming it.

He drew closer. My heart pounded like a drum in my chest. The air stirred as his hand slid down to my neck. A shiver ran through me when his fingers brushed my skin as he gently drew my hair aside. Silk whispered as he bent closer.

"Don't be afraid," he murmured, his voice only inches from my ear.

I didn't breathe.

His fangs sank into my neck.

My mouth fell open in a silent gasp, and my eyes flew wide. There was no pain. Only the brief pinch of the bite.

And then heat and need were flooding me like I'd been swallowed by the tide.

My body went liquid, melting into his, and only his arms holding me to him kept me upright. His heart surged to life in his chest, the pounding reaching me from where I was pressed to him, and his breath moved against my throat as he drank me down. Hot craving tangled within my core, becoming a rush of desire that made the flesh between my legs throb. In an instant, I was as turned on as I'd ever been, my pussy aching with the need to be filled and my body tingling with the compulsion to let him be the one to do it.

Gods, Niko hadn't said anything about feeding being like *this*.

My breasts ached, my nipples hardening in silent plea for Casimir's touch. My legs moved wider, my clit grinding on his thigh as his length pressed into my belly, so hard and ready beneath his pants. Utterly on instinct, I leaned my head farther to the side, baring more of my neck as his lips moved against my throat.

A groan left him, and then the world shifted. My back hit the ground, and then his weight was on top of me, his lips never leaving my throat.

I moaned and writhed beneath him, my body on fire from the sensation of him feeding from me. I ground my hips up against him, the delicious friction only stoking my need higher.

Because this was heaven. Pure ecstasy. I could almost feel myself rushing into him, being taken into him in service of his need to survive. It was erotic as hell to serve him like this, and gods help me if my body didn't scream for more.

"Take me," I gasped. "Oh, gods, Casimir, take me."

A hungry noise escaped him, and then he pulled back. His tongue lashed a hot line over the bite wound, and my skin tingled faintly there, but I scarcely noticed.

"You want..." His voice was a growl, ragged with need. "You want me to..."

I nodded frantically.

In an instant, he'd yanked my blouse off, taking the vest with it. My pants and boots were next, tugged away from me with dizzying speed. And then I was bare beneath him, my back on the hardwood floor and his body above me with only the diamond pendant resting between my breasts.

His eyes lingered on the jewel, a sudden tension on his face like it reminded him of something. Witches, perhaps.

Gods, I didn't care about that right now.

I yanked the pendant over my head and let it fall to the side.

Gratitude flickered through his expression. Swiftly, he shed his clothes, revealing carved lines of muscle beneath smooth dark skin, traced with veins down to his hard, ready cock. He positioned himself over me, his eyes burning into mine.

"Yes," I answered the question in his gaze. "Please, y—"

His cock impaled me in a single thrust.

I cried out, my pussy stretching and rippling around him in relief at finally having what I needed. My hips jolted upward in a frantic desire to take all of him.

"I never... knew..." he grunted, driving himself into me. "Feeding could feel... like this."

I could only nod. "Drink," I begged him. "Drink more from me. Please. I need you to drink from—"

His fangs struck my neck and I came. The blast of my orgasm washed away my view of the room, leaving only the sheer pleasure of his cock thrusting into me as he drank me.

My skin stung again as he licked the wound sealed a second time. "I have wanted you since I first saw you," he growled in my ear, still driving himself into me as I came back down. "Since you lay there before me, so beautiful. So perfect. I wanted to take you on that bed and everywhere else, until there wasn't a place in this castle where you hadn't come around my cock."

I gasped, clawing at his back as another orgasm built hot and tingling inside my core. "Casimir... oh gods..."

He yanked me up, shifting me around until I was straddling his hips as he sat on the ground, still thrusting up into me. "You like feeding me your precious blood, Princess? You like giving yourself to me?"

I nodded breathlessly.

"Will you allow me to drink from you a different way?"

A thrill of fear shot through me, but exhilaration and need were there too.

I nodded again.

A dark chuckle left him. He hoisted me higher and then a bite of pain whipped around my nipple. I looked down.

He held a short blade. The gods knew where he'd found it. But he'd cut a razor thin circle on my left breast, and all of it was dripping blood down my chest.

My pussy spasmed.

"Did you enjoy that, Princess?"

My core clenched. Gods, I did, even if I couldn't explain why, and all I could manage to do was nod.

He chuckled again, sinful promise in the sound, and then he lifted me. His lips locked around my breast, sucking it into his mouth and taking the wound with it.

Holy gods. My eyes went wide as my back arched, thrusting my breast toward him. His tongue played over my nipple as he drank from the wound before it sealed.

"Yes," I gasped. "Oh, gods, yes."

His mouth released my breast in time for him to drop me onto his cock again. I threw my head back, rocking against him in desperate need.

I'd never imagined being turned on by anything like this. Somewhere inside, I was shocked at myself. But other parts of me, the wild and new side I could only think of as *vampire*... oh, gods, it loved what he was doing.

And it just wanted more.

"You like this?" I could hear the smile in his voice. "You like being my little toy to drink? My bloody girl to fuck?"

My core throbbed at his filthy words, and my mouth moved for a moment before I could speak, nonsensical pleading pouring from me. "Yes. I'll be your toy. Just fuck me, oh my *gods*, please..."

He growled, yanking me up again. A lash of pain whipped over my other breast, and then that wound was in his mouth too, pulsing my blood into him as I moaned.

Whether I'd ever imagined being turned on by something like this was irrelevant. *Everything* was. Maybe I wasn't who I used to be, and maybe the vampire made me crave this.

Or maybe I was just discovering something about myself I never would have learned in Aneira. Because *gods*, I loved bleeding for him. Feeding him. Being his in this overwhelming way.

And he wasn't done. Again and again, he dropped me onto his cock, fucking me until my body hovered at the brink of coming, only for him to pull me up again, stealing me away from the edge of my orgasm as his mouth sealed over another narrow wound he'd slashed into my skin.

My awareness became a blur of craving. I couldn't see the room anymore. Couldn't think. Drips of drying blood were scattered across my chest and arms, fragmented trails left from wounds long since sealed. My core was soaked, and every slap of my skin against his sounded profane and yet it was never enough. My body quivered, reduced to nothing but a mass of need like putty in his hands. "Please, sir," I whimpered. "Please let me come. Please..."

He dropped me back onto his cock, and my words disintegrated. His fingers dug into my ass, holding me to him so hard it was painful, and suddenly, he was driving himself into me with so much force, it was like he'd die if he didn't fill me with his seed now. "Come for me, Princess," he grunted. "Come now like my good little fucktoy to drink—"

My orgasm exploded through me as if obedient to his command. I gushed around his cock, my release rolling over me like a wave, and only his rough grip on my back kept me from collapsing as I came and came.

A satisfied sound left him only to cut short as his movements sped up, his cock thrusting up into me with desperate speed until at last, he roared out his release.

I sagged against him as his cum dripped from inside me.

"Good little fucktoy," he murmured.

My body thrummed at his words.

His grip moved, and then the world shifted again as he lifted me. My brow furrowed, but I didn't have long to be confused. Air caressed my skin as he carried me across the room and then gently laid me down on the bed.

A blanket rustled as he draped it over my body, and then his footsteps moved away.

I bit my lip. I'd heard of men who simply left after sex, but thus far I hadn't experienced it. And maybe I shouldn't have expected anything more, but—

His footsteps returned. I lifted my head from the pillow to see him setting my clothing on a chair in one corner before he returned to the bedside.

The diamond pendant was in his hand.

"In case you wanted this," he murmured.

I bit my lip, unsure how to explain that it wasn't mine. I didn't even know how to use it, not really. But at my silence, he simply looped the chain over my head.

"May I join you?" he asked.

I nodded, speechless.

He slipped between the blankets, and nervously, I nestled in beside him, resting my cheek on his chest. The pendant slipped down between us, warm against my skin, but he didn't seem to mind. His arms wrapped around me, holding me close despite the jewel between us and the lingering remnants of blood on my skin from his knife play.

Seconds slipped by.

"Thank you for sharing that with me," he murmured.

I nodded.

His hand stroked my hair. "You surprise me."

I glanced up, confused.

"You wanted that. What I did. What I said." He paused, looking down at me. "At least, you seemed to. Was I mistaken?"

I shook my head. "No. I... I did." Embarrassment tangled with remembered arousal in my gut, but I made myself continue. "I liked it."

A soft sound of amazement left him. "You're incredible."

I blushed.

"That embarrasses you?"

I shrugged. "Where I come from, it wouldn't be acceptable for me to say that. Or want it."

He nodded thoughtfully. "Aneira."

I made a noise of confirmation.

"Nor for you to have gathered... what would be an appropriate word? A harem?"

I choked on a laugh. He grinned at me, and a warm feeling radiated through me at the sight.

Sighing, he pulled me closer. "Would that I could be among them."

I froze. It took me a moment to find my voice. "You'd want that?" I looked up at him. "Even if I'm... you know, part witch?"

He was quiet for a moment. "We're all part something, Princess. But in the hall earlier..." His brow rose and fell. "I only had to look at you, and the hunger's grip abated. Whenever I'm around you, it's the same. My thoughts are clearer. Calmer. I don't think I realized how much of a hold the craving for blood has been gaining on me these past few years. But when you're here, it's better." A soft sound of wonder left him. "With you, I feel alive."

My heart ached for him. "You don't have to stay here."

He rested his cheek against the top of my head. "I doubt your men would be comfortable with me or my desire for you."

I bit my lip briefly. "They're okay with it."

I could feel the way he stopped breathing for a moment.

"We discussed it. The... the ones I'm with, anyway." I pushed back my continued confusion over Roan's reaction and the ache of how uncaringly Ozias behaved. "They don't mind sharing with you."

He was silent for a moment. "And what do you think?"

I hesitated, and then I shifted around, lying on my stomach so that I could look up at him more easily. "I don't want to leave you here."

Cold dignity touched his face, as if I'd insulted him. "Pity, then? Is that what this is?"

I shook my head. "Empathy."

He paused, the coldness fading.

"I couldn't have held onto who I am without those men downstairs sacrificing their blood for me. But I still know how hard it is. To be... this. Not what you were. Even with my will intact, I don't know if I could have survived the pain of losing my old life if I hadn't had those men with me. Yet... you did." I put a hand to his chest. His heart beat steadily beneath my palm. "But that doesn't mean you have to keep going that way. Not if you don't want to. There's a whole world out there, and I think..." I wetted my lips, trying to find the right words. "I think I would be sad to go on and know you weren't part of it."

He was quiet for a long moment, his eyes drifting over the room around us like he could see past it to the entire castle. "To leave here..." he murmured, shaking his head.

My heart sank.

But then his eyes dropped to mine. "I would have conditions."

I blinked. "Conditions?"

A cocky smile pulled at his lips. He moved me on top of him, and my legs parted, straddling one of his while his hands strayed down my sides.

"I will share you with those men." His grip slid down farther, cupping my ass and pressing my pussy to his leg. "They may fuck you and feed you, as I want you healthy, happy, and ready for me at all times." His fangs slipped into place. "But every drop of your blood belongs to me."

I gasped as he pulled me harder against him.

"Do you agree, Princess?" His brow arched, a wicked light in his eyes. "Will you serve me in this way?"

My core throbbed. "Yes, sir."

He grinned. "Good little fucktoy."

21

OZIAS

"We shouldn't have let her go alone," Clay said for the hundredth time.

Seated by the door of the large bedroom suite we'd turned into a makeshift camp, I didn't respond. Sleep had come in fits and starts throughout the long night, interspersed by horrific dreams that sent me jolting awake and searching for Gwyneira in the darkness. I had no illusions she would attempt to wake me when she returned from her time with the vampire. Hell, I had no illusions she'd ever want to speak to me again after how I'd rejected her.

But now sunrise was coming.

And she still wasn't back.

"Should we go look for her?" Niko asked.

Closing my eyes, I tuned out the rest of their murmurs while my beast paced an endless loop through my mind. The other men had been circling the carcass of this argument for the better part of an hour, with no more progress to show for it than when they'd begun. But I'd already determined that the moment the first trace of sunlight began to lighten the night sky, I would go find her. I could track her scent anywhere—and that was before I'd caved to the impulses of my beast and put my own scent on her with that blanket. No vampire would be able to hide her from me, and thus there was nothing to be gained by debating until then.

But logic did nothing for the worry boiling inside me, nor did it calm the beast keening in my mind out of fear for the one it thought was my mate. The wilder part of me hadn't stopped straining at my skin since I'd spoken to her so harshly in the study—when I'd done the only thing I could to give her what she needed and keep myself safe at the same time.

Reject her. Tell her she wasn't mine, when every part of me howled that was a lie. But to say anything else meant the possibility she'd think there could be anything more between us. Better she believe I didn't want her, because then she'd never be exposed to the violent, despicable creature who would only break her in the end.

My beast glowered at me from the depths of my mind. And being with a vampire was so different?

I gritted my teeth. Of course it was. The vampire would simply bite her. It was hardly the same.

A whisper of sound came from the hall.

I was on my feet immediately, yanking open the door. The others fell silent in surprise at my actions and then scrambled to follow when they realized what must be happening. But I paid them no attention, my eyes already raking the shadows and the moonlit extent of the hall, seeking the mate I could never have.

Gwyneira descended the steps and emerged into the corridor, Casimir at her side. Her vest was loose, the ribbons gone, and her shirt beneath it was missing a button. The vampire held her hand and had his other arm around her as if to steady her, and while she smiled prettily at him, I didn't miss how she was paler than before.

My nostrils flared when the two of them came closer. The scent of blood clung to her, as was to be expected. But my own scent was nearly gone. And that was hardly all.

She smelled of sex. They both did. Soap too, as if she'd tried to scrub it all away, and I doubted anyone else would detect much past that.

I was not anyone else.

"Princess," Dex said from behind me. "Are you all right?"

She nodded. "I'm fine." A tiny smile flitted over her face as she glanced again at Casimir, though it couldn't hide how exhausted she was. How drained. "It was just... a lot."

My lips twitched toward a snarl, my skin burning with the urge to change. I was going to kill him.

Damn me, I wished I *was* him.

Seething at myself as much as the vampire, I forced myself to hang back as the others strode past me to be closer to her. I couldn't give her a reason to believe I cared. I still had to think of her safety.

My eyes caught on Roan lurking in the shadows even farther down the hall than where I stood, his arms hugging his middle. I'd only seen him stand like that rarely prior to Gwyneira's arrival in our lives. Like he was holding himself inside with sheer muscle and will. His focus was locked on the princess, a ravenous intensity to his gaze, and not for the first time, I wondered exactly what thoughts were playing out behind those pitch-black eyes. There'd been times over the years when his body language and reactions seemed *wrong* somehow. Not quite like any other Erenlian or human I'd ever seen. But the difference was slight, and at the time, I'd thought perhaps I was misreading it. Regardless, it had never been enough for me to doubt his loyalty to our group or question whether he was who he seemed.

But then Gwyneira had entered our lives, and ever since, I could no longer convince myself I'd been mistaken.

Something was different about him.

My beast didn't know what to make of the change. Roan wasn't the same type of creature as me. I would have known that right away. But he was *something*. His scent had gone strange when the woods tried to drive us mad, and it'd gotten worse the entire time we'd been trapped in that vault. It was as if his normal scent had been subsumed beneath burnt wood and smoking ash. Since the princess returned, the new scent had lessened, but it hadn't entirely gone away.

Likewise, his behavior had been unusual for him. He'd always been anxious, with a tendency to turn surly when his worries became too much. But these past few weeks he'd been almost as antisocial as *me*. He'd stayed away from the others, barely acknowledged Gwyneira was there, and snapped at her whenever he was forced to speak. When faced with the prospect of her being with someone outside our group, he'd become downright *cruel*, to the point my beast wanted to attack him if only to protect my mate. The entire time, that unusual scent had spiked wildly out of control.

Yet to see him right now I'd swear he wanted her as much as I did.

And he was hiding it too.

He spotted me watching him and distrust flashed over

his face. Still clutching his arms to his middle, he disappeared back into the bedroom.

"Come *with* us?" Dex stated behind me as if repeating something.

I spun back, alarmed.

Gwyneira was nodding. "He can help us."

"I've been working to mitigate the magic in these woods for what has been apparently thirty years," Casimir said. "Though in this place, it felt more like a hundred. But I can help push back the magic trying to trap you all and teach your scholar how to do it as well." He nodded respectfully toward Byron. "The more people who can keep the princess safe, the better, I believe."

Glances passed between the other men, and I could read their body language even though their backs were to me. The vampire was saying the right things. Gwyneira appeared to trust him too.

Bastard.

Grinding my teeth, I turned away, my beast keening louder inside me. My gaze came to rest on the window.

The sky was growing brighter.

Dammit.

"The sun," I said, speaking over the continued explanation the vampire was giving. At my words, he cut off, and several of the others gave a brief glance at the window as well.

Clay scoffed. "Daybreak's always such a party crasher."

Gwyneira looked away from the window, stress flickering over her face. "How do we travel? There's only the one... you know, box."

Casimir gave her a reassuring smile. "My wolves can protect me. They could shield you as well, if you wish?"

My beast snarled. I clenched my teeth to keep from making a sound.

Trepidation flashed over Gwyneira's face.

"Perhaps rest, though," Casimir continued seamlessly.

She bit her lip nervously, those pretty little white teeth of hers pinching her red flesh. My cock ached.

"Let's get out of the way of the windows, if nothing else," Dex said.

I moved aside as the others retreated to the bedroom. From the corner, Roan glowered at us like a snake sulking in a cave, clearly irritated we'd invaded his hiding space.

At the sight of the mattresses scattered over the floor, a wry expression crossed Casimir's face. "I take it you didn't trust me."

No one replied.

I watched the shadows as the planning continued, my eyes tracking over the patches of darkness around the room. Those wolves were here. I could feel them. And when Gwyneira and the others finally concluded their planning, the creatures flowed away from the room with only the tiniest shift of darkness denoting they'd left.

My beast grumbled and paced within me while I trailed the others through the castle. That side of me did not want those *things* accompanying us. They were a potential threat to our mate.

Pushing the beast down, I glowered at the hall. She *couldn't* be my mate.

The others came to a stop. From the snippets of conversation I'd heard, this was where Casimir had taken her glass box after he stole her from us.

I went still.

A bedroom.

"Presumptuous bastard," Roan muttered behind me so low the other men couldn't hear. But Casimir cast a brief look over his shoulder, while Gwyneira blinked and dropped her gaze away.

Vampire hearing, my beast noted with approval for its mate. One more way she was like me.

I shoved the observation aside.

"You would have preferred I place her elsewhere while I waited for her to wake?" Casimir asked Roan. "In a kitchen perhaps? Or a dining room?"

Roan took a step forward while my beast snarled in my mind.

"Stop." Gwyneira gave Casimir an incredulous look, like she couldn't believe he'd said that.

A hint of chagrin flashed over his face as he turned back to the room. "The wolves can carry the box. Their shadow forms are quite versatile. But I cannot bring them all with me when we go. Some will be needed here to keep the castle protected against the magic on these mountains."

"We'll carry it." Dex nodded to the twins and Niko, who moved immediately to grab the box from the ground. "Byron, check it over."

The red-haired man followed the others immediately. An amused glint in his eyes, Casimir said nothing.

"One thing?" Gwyneira spoke up before they could lift the box.

The others paused.

"I... I won't need a blanket on the bottom. I think it'd be better if... whoever owns it took it instead."

My beast went still. A cold ache started in my gut, like the time I'd been stabbed by shepherds who thought they were attacking the thing responsible for killing their sheep.

Gwyneira never looked at me. Never even turned my way. And yet her body language was clear.

She knew the blanket was mine.

She didn't want it anywhere near her.

"Are you sure, Princess?" Niko asked, glancing between her and me. "It might be uncomfortable without anything there."

A tight nod was her only response.

With an awkward glance at the rest of us, he retrieved the blanket and bundled it up. Distant gratitude flickered through me for how he didn't move to hand it back, even if Casimir was likely the only one who didn't know it was mine.

It was a kindness.

It did nothing for how I felt like something inside me had died.

The others picked up the coffin, Clay and Lars and several of the others casting distrustful glances at Casimir as they went. Gwyneira moved immediately to follow them, never looking at me once.

I drew a breath, keeping my face still despite how the ache inside my gut was unchanged. But I deserved this. I knew I did. I'd hurt her with my words and my actions, and I was a fool for not anticipating that she wouldn't want anything connected to me near her.

I trailed the others as they wound their way through the castle, until at last we reached the exit. The door was formed of ornate carved wood turned gray by dust, while cobwebs dangled from the chandelier overhead.

"Are you going to be okay staying awake all day?" Gwyneira asked Casimir while the others laid the coffin carefully on the marble floor.

Casimir nodded. "With what you've given me, I could go for a hundred days."

She blushed, though the color was faint against her pale cheeks. She would need to feed again soon.

But it wouldn't be from me.

I said nothing while the twins helped her into the cold, hard coffin, both of them murmuring their goodbyes and promising to be there when she woke this time. It killed me how I wanted to be there for her too. *Comfort* her too. It wasn't right, any of this. Sure, it was better that she wasn't dead than what could have been the alternative.

But she should have had the life she wanted, not this half-life that had been thrust upon her by her damned stepmother.

The beast inside me whimpered how, in that case, I never would have met her.

I pushed the observation away. Maybe it would have been better for both of us that way.

Dex lowered the lid over her, and Byron checked the seals one more time. In the shadows, Roan watched, his dark eyes locked on her, unblinking.

I returned my focus to the wolves. They rose from the darkness like creatures from a nether realm, pouring up into the form of massive animals nearly the size of horses. But Casimir merely put a hand to one of their muzzles as if the creature was a beloved lapdog.

"Thank you," he murmured softly.

The creature bowed its head as if it understood him. My beast growled in response.

One of the wolves' heads whipped around, pinning me with its glowing green eyes.

Alarm shot through me. Surely it couldn't have detected my beast's reaction.

Slowly, the wolf's head twisted to the side like a curious predator trying to assess the enemy in front of it.

Did that thing know what I was? What I hid from the eyes of sentient beings everywhere?

My beast growled louder.

Swiftly, I pushed the creature within me down even as I held my body still, not twitching a single muscle. I didn't wish to inspire that shadow wolf to attack, no matter how the creature inside of me wanted to lash out. Not when the princess or the others might be hurt in the fight.

I'd swear to the gods I didn't even believe in that the shadow wolf *smirked* at me before turning its attention back to Casimir.

I glanced at the others, checking if anyone else had noticed what just happened.

No one was paying me the least attention.

I breathed a shade easier.

As the twins, Niko, and Dex hefted the coffin between them, I studied the others more closely, silently reading their body language to ascertain their thoughts. They were taking up the same positions as before, so I strode past them to where Casimir had assumed the lead in our little caravan. My sense of the earth had been disrupted by the magic here, but it would still aid me.

Like hell I would let this vampire guide us into a trap.

Casimir smiled beneath his cloak. "Shall we go?"

He didn't wait for an answer as he lifted a hand to the door ahead of us. Blue light flared around the edges of the door, and then the lock clicked back and the handle turned.

The wolf with him turned to smoke, flowing around his body like water to swirl up in a defensive shield of darkness.

The door opened, pouring morning sunlight into the hall.

At the rear of our group, I heard Roan mutter something about bad ideas.

Agreeing wholeheartedly, I started out into the daylight.

❋

The forest didn't like Casimir any more than I did.

I scowled as the earth shifted infinitesimally beneath my feet again. The changes were subtle. Tremors through the underbrush that scarcely disturbed the snow on the branches. Quivers in the trees barely stronger than a breeze stirring the spruce needles.

But wrong. All of it wrong. But other than Niko and Byron, I wasn't sure the others could tell what was happening.

And those two weren't saying a word.

I cast another dark glance at the Zeniryan ruler and then back at my younger friends. Sweat dripped down Niko's olive skin. His eyes darted around like he was searching for the threat, uncertain from which direction it would come. Byron was muttering under his breath so softly that only fragments of the old tongue reached my ears.

I respected the younger men's powers. I knew they would do whatever they could to protect us.

And protect the princess.

But the forest had just been toying with us before.

Now it was angry.

Byron's green eyes met mine, shared understanding

passing between us. The Zeniryan had been "mitigating" the power of this place for decades. His wolves had been too, so he claimed.

But his wolves were back at the palace, save one, and the Zeniryan was out in broad daylight, certainly the most vulnerable time for a vampire—if they could even survive it.

If I hadn't been concerned about the danger, I would have demanded that we wait for nightfall to make our way through the woods.

But even I didn't want to risk traveling through this hellscape forest in the dark.

Another shiver coursed through the earth, stronger than before, and in a way even I couldn't define, I could feel the rage of the rock and soil beneath me. The forest hated Casimir. Blamed him. Wanted to destroy that Zeniryan vampire.

And us with him.

I returned my attention to the path ahead, such as it was, my power flowing out through the soles of my feet into the earth below, fighting it, ordering it to stay stable. Stay sane in spite of this force that wanted to convince it to destroy us. But the wild magic of the forest could tell that Casimir was leaving, and while a rational mind would be happy, this one saw only opportunity, like a cold-blooded predator driven so mad by hunger that it cared nothing for tomorrow, only what it could achieve today.

"To the left," Niko murmured.

I glanced where he'd indicated. Vines were twisting between the trees, their thorns bending and snapping like the fangs of snakes. Around the princess's coffin, the others shifted enough to allow Niko to extend a hand, his power stretching out to hold back the vicious vines.

"I thought you were supposed to be helping," Dex ground out at Casimir.

"Would you care for me to show you what it would be like if I wasn't?" the Zeniryan replied from within his veil of the shadow wolf, strain in his voice. "It's never fought me like this before."

"Think it's more of the disruptions?" Clay asked, a thread of nervousness in his mildly joking tone.

"What disruptions?" Casimir asked.

Silence hung for a moment as if the others were debating whether to tell him.

But there was nothing to be gained by silence. Not likely, anyway.

At Dex's nod, Byron asked, "What do you know of ley lines?"

A pause. "I've read of them," came the cautious answer from beneath the swirling black clouds.

Byron relayed what we had learned from the witches in the Jeweled Coven.

When he finished, Casimir was silent for a long moment. "That would explain some things."

"What do you mean?" Byron replied.

"This. And the way that my own strength was failing until the princess came."

My beast grumbled at the reminder of what she had shared with him.

I shoved it back down. It wasn't helpful here. If he was a threat to her, we would have the opportunity to address it. But the forest's magic had to be our primary concern. It was only waiting for an opening to tear into us.

We had to put up with him, at least for now.

Another quiver passed beneath my feet. To my right,

Casimir gave a low huff of frustration. My eyes darted toward his smoky veil and then back to the forest. We were nearing a mountain slope again, the path ahead slowly constricting between a sheer cliff to our left and a drop-off several yards to the right.

The quivering grew worse.

"Something else is here." Roan's voice carried from the back of the group.

I looked back at him in surprise, as much for him speaking up as what he said, even as I sent my power out into the earth, searching for what he might mean. That he could have felt something in the earth—or even on it—that I could not seemed unlikely.

But he also wasn't acting like himself, and that was enough to make me wary.

I stretched deeper into the ground, tracing the fault lines, finding nothing.

A quiver came from deep beneath the mountain to our left. I turned my attention to it, spreading my awareness out even farther, trying to locate the fault line or damage that was causing the quivering so far inside the—

Alarm shot through me.

Roan wasn't wrong.

It wasn't a fault line. Not a volcano either. *Something* was buried in the mountain, far inside the rock.

And it felt... alive.

My heart drummed. Whatever this was, it was bigger than the entirety of the Jeweled Coven's hideout. Bigger than anything I'd felt walk the earth. Old too.

And waking.

Fuck.

The ground shook, hard.

I hurled my power into the ground, fighting to stabilize the rocky terrain around us, but this wasn't just an earthquake. I couldn't force the rock to stay together or break in different places than where we stood. The presence in the mountain was fighting back against me, shoving through the rock around it.

Rising.

The cliff beside us cracked.

"Byron!" Dex yelled.

I threw a look over my shoulder to see the scholar raise his hands, frantically forming a shield above the coffin, protecting it as rocks rained down.

The ground shook worse.

I dropped to my knees. My palms slammed down onto the rock, the contact strengthening my control as I poured everything I had into the earth.

This would not kill us. Or kill *her*. Not as long as I had breath in my lungs.

A rumbling sound carried through the rock beneath me. On either side of our stretch of path, chunks of the trail crumbled away. Stumbling, the men desperately tried to keep the coffin from falling.

Whatever was within the earth started coming this way.

A snarl left me as I fought to hold the space around us together. But what was coming was more powerful than all of us. It wouldn't be stopped.

Beneath Byron, the path cracked, sending him staggering and making his shield flicker.

Her coffin tipped. Dex and the others cried out as they struggled hold onto it, but stones shot past Byron's barrier.

The rocks struck. Fractures raced through the glass, spreading fast like fissures in ice.

"Guard her!" Casimir yelled.

The shadow wolf poured away from him to wrap itself around the coffin. Swiftly, Casimir pulled his hood over his shoulders, shielding himself from the sun.

A roar shook the world. I looked up.

A snarling creature burst from the earth. Emerald scales flashed in the sunlight. Wings spread wide, beating the air so hard it sent us stumbling. A long muzzle full of fangs roared in the sunlight and sent a gout of flame whipping across the sky.

Oh gods.

I scrambled to my feet as the dragon kicked higher in the air, its head swiveling back and forth to scan the earth. My hand gripped my axe, instinct having brought it into my grip, though what good it would do me against a beast that size, I had no idea.

The dragon wheeled to the left and beat the air again, taking off across the forest and then disappearing behind the mountains.

No one moved.

"That..." Clay's voice was breathless with shock. "They don't..."

"They were extinct," Niko whispered. "They've been extinct for centuries."

I looked back at Roan. He wouldn't meet anyone's eyes, his gaze locked on the ground. With his face bloodless, he had his back pressed to the cliffside. His fingers dug into the rocks with a white-knuckled grip, as if he'd been hanging onto the stones for dear life and couldn't be convinced to let go yet.

But... he'd known of that thing even before I did.

How?

No one else seemed inclined to question. A shudder passed among them as they turned their attention to the coffin. The shadow wolf engulfed it fully, but Dex still looked to Casimir. "Is she okay in there? Can you tell?"

The vampire nodded, the motion more a bobbing of his hood than any discernible movement of his head. Every inch of skin was covered, from his black gloves up to the oversized covering that shadowed his face. "Ruhl got to her in time."

He sounded stunned.

"Everyone else good?" Dex continued.

Murmurs of confirmation came from the men. By the cliff wall, Roan pushed away from the rock, every line of his bearing held with rigid control.

"Did you know that thing was there?" Lars asked the Zeniryan.

Casimir shook his head. "No. And I have no idea what woke it."

A look passed between all of us. The answer seemed clear. "Whatever is happening with the magic," Byron said.

Casimir nodded at the statement.

The sun peeked through the trees, playing across Casimir's black leather hood. He flinched back.

Clay gave him a cautious look. "You going to be okay in that, buddy?"

"Yes."

I wondered if anyone else could hear the thread of worry in the vampire's tone.

Dex just nodded. "We have to get her somewhere safe. Now." His gaze flicked over to Casimir. "Both of you. I don't want us anywhere near this place if that thing comes back again."

22
GWYNEIRA

The looks of relief when I opened my eyes instantly filled me with alarm.

I sat up. "What happened? Is everyone okay?"

Hesitancy took the place of their relief, and several of them shared a silent look. I caught sight of Casimir, his cloak hanging around him though his hood was down. Ruhl wasn't with him, however. The massive shadow wolf was curled up near the coffin, watching me with his tongue lolling out between fangs longer than my hand.

He looked quite satisfied with himself—and also like a lap dog from hell.

"What happened?" I repeated, looking back at the men. They all were here. I couldn't tell what had upset them.

But gods help me, this now made two times I'd woken only to find that something else had gone wrong.

And I couldn't have done anything about it to help them.

"There was a rockslide," Dex admitted. "The box was damaged. We're just glad you're okay."

"What?" I glanced down. Cracks ran through the glass on either side of me. Dozens of them.

My heart began pounding faster, though the beat was weak. I would need to feed soon. Already, I could feel quivers of hunger in my gut, reminding me I hadn't fed since Casimir bit me at the castle.

But gods, at least I was still alive. "The sun didn't get through?"

Dex nodded his head toward the wolf. "That thing stopped it."

Ruhl growled briefly as if displeased by the description. Dex's mouth thinned.

"Let's get you out of there, yeah?" Clay came over to me, taking my hands and then drawing me to my feet.

"Are you okay?" I asked Casimir as I stepped from the glass box. "How did you keep the sun from hurting you?"

"It wasn't a concern." He shrugged. "My cape was sufficient."

I caught the hesitancy that flashed over several of the others' faces. Somehow, I suspected it hadn't been that simple. "Where are we?"

Clay shrugged. "A cave Oz found." He nodded toward the front of the cave where Ozias, Roan, and Niko were seated, obviously keeping watch on the forest.

Only Niko gave me a smile.

"How are you feeling, Princess?" Clay continued.

I hesitated. "I'm okay."

"He's asking if you're hungry." Roan's voice was cold. "After having been drained and all."

Beside me, Ruhl growled.

Roan leveled a glare on the wolf.

The creature fell silent.

I blinked, glancing between the man and the massive magical wolf that was now avoiding his gaze like he wanted to pretend the exchange hadn't happened. What was that about?

And how the hell had Roan done that?

"If you're hungry, Princess, I'm sure we can help," Lars offered.

I froze, sudden discomfort warring with the way the vampire side of me wanted to take him up on the offer *right* now.

But what happened with Casimir flashed through my mind, not to mention what happened with Niko. And yes, I'd had sex with a number of the men here. I'd even had an audience, at least where Ozias was concerned.

But that was before he made it clear he didn't give a damn about me, he'd only been in it for the show. And I'd die if *Roan* watched me with the others.

That man already treated me contemptuously enough.

"How about a different way?" Dex offered.

I gave him a curious look.

He nodded to Lars, who removed a small cup from a bag. With a smile to me, Dex drew out the short blade strapped to his side and flicked the sharp edge briefly across his forearm.

My insides twisted with hunger as blood dripped from the wound into the bowl.

After a moment, he pulled his forearm away, taking a bandage that Lars offered him. Niko took up the cup next, doing the same as Dex and then bandaging his arm a moment later.

One by one, Clay, Byron, and Lars followed suit, cutting their arms and then dripping blood into the cup.

"You should let her seal those wounds," Casimir commented. "Safer against infection."

The others paused.

"It's okay," Niko said. "There are some ointments in the bags that should do the same."

Relief rippled through me. I couldn't think about just closing wounds now. Not when I was about ready to lunge across the space between me and the bowl if only to get to it faster.

Gods, how had I never understood how *good* blood smelled?

Casimir bowed his head slightly in acknowledgment of the logic of what Niko said.

Clay offered me the bowl.

"Thank you," I murmured, managing to keep from grabbing it if only to prevent any of the blood from spilling.

He smiled.

My eyes fluttered closed as I swallowed the contents down, even as discomfort still twisted somewhere inside me. This shouldn't be as euphoric an experience as it was. I should have been repulsed by what I was doing.

But I couldn't be. Hunger took precedence, and the rush of air into my lungs was too wonderful, the steady drum of my heart too much of a relief.

Never mind that it tasted *amazing*.

Swallowing the last of the blood down, I wiped my mouth with the back of my fingers as delicately as I could and then handed the cup back to Clay. None of the men seemed bothered—well, none of the five who'd fed me their blood, anyway. Roan and Ozias were both watching the forest like none of us existed. But I couldn't really imagine how anyone could be so comfortable with what I'd just done, even after how I'd let Casimir drink from *me*, not simply a cup.

The memory made a blush begin to burn my cheeks, and I ducked my face away, covering the reddening of my cheeks by pretending to wipe more blood away. The guys gave no sign of noticing, though. Lars and Clay simply began gathering supplies for their own dinner while Dex and Byron went to lay out blankets for beds, none of them pressuring me to seal their wounds beneath the bandages or to do much of anything at all. For his part, Casimir settled into a spot by the far wall, drawing his cloak around him and watching them all with a bemused expression.

Ruhl nudged my hand, and I glanced over at him, finding an oddly expectant look in his green eyes. "What?" I whispered.

He nudged my hand again and my brow twitched up. I'd seen dogs at the palace do this.

Cautiously, I sank down next to him and ran my hand along his fur. It was strange beneath my touch, simultaneously soft and dense like real fur and yet twisting around my fingers like smoke.

The wolf let out a sigh as if I'd given him what he wanted.

I bit my lip, continuing to pet him as I watched the men get their meal ready, all of them moving so seamlessly, it was obvious they'd done this for years. And it didn't matter that now we were in a cave in the Wild Lands or that they had two vampires and a shadow wolf in their midst.

There was a togetherness to everything they did, and with every smile Dex or the twins flashed at me, it was obvious I was included in that too.

Tears prickled in my eyes. Had I ever felt this much like I

just... *belonged*? Like I wasn't royalty someone had to defer to or a chess piece to be moved by a politician who only wanted favor? My father never made me feel like an outsider, no, but he had also been king. Moments with him had been few and far between, and we'd often only shared dinners during political functions. Otherwise, he was off waging a war or making an alliance.

But here in the middle of this cursed land, I was just me, these men were just themselves, and for this one moment, everything was okay.

Could it last?

I dropped my gaze to Ruhl's smoky fur, trying to hide the discomfort I knew had to be on my face. The Aneirans would never accept us. Not really. Even if I set aside the question of being a vampire or the issue of how I'd been accused of murdering my father, I wasn't so naive as to expect that simply taking my throne back and issuing some decree would be the end of the pushback we'd receive for wanting to be together. Being royalty came with expectations—thousands of them. I existed to serve my country, not my heart.

Even if the mere thought of losing these men felt like it would kill me.

To say nothing of what would happen to my vampire side.

Ruhl sighed and laid his massive head against my leg. Even though he was made of nothing but smoke and shadow, the weight of him was real. His fur felt warm against me, and the strangest sense of comfort radiated from him.

Like maybe even the wolf wanted to let me know it could be okay.

I swallowed hard, sinking my fingers deeper into his fur. I couldn't let go of them. Any of them.

But when we made it back to Aneira, everything of my previous life would try to make me do exactly that.

※

The men gradually fell asleep one by one until only Ozias, Roan, and Casimir remained awake with me.

Though only one of that trio deigned to acknowledge my presence.

I glanced at Casimir where he sat with his back to the wall beside me. I'd joined him here at the rear of the cave while the others fell asleep, and for the past hour, we'd sat in silence together. Ruhl lay between us, still in wolf form but flopped on the ground like he too was resting. I supposed even shadow creatures might need sleep.

But so did vampires. "Are you okay?" I asked Casimir softly.

"Of course. You?"

"I'm fine." I hesitated. "You're not tired?"

He shrugged, returning his attention to the cave. He'd been studying the others this entire time, a look on his face I couldn't hope to read. "I'll sleep soon. I just..." He chuckled softly. "I haven't been around this many people in decades."

I wasn't sure what to say. Did he want to leave? Or was it something else?

"Are you..." I searched for a way to ask, suddenly painfully aware of Roan and Ozias several yards away. We were speaking quietly enough, they shouldn't be able to hear. But it still left me uncomfortable. "Do you need more...

you know?" I twitched my head in a vague gesture toward myself.

He shook his head with a smile. "It's not that—though I'd never pass up the opportunity to share that with you again." His expression took on a devilish edge. "Both to bite you and let you do the same to me this time."

Heat flooded my cheeks and my core alike at the thought.

Ozias shifted position on the rough cave floor.

Quickly, I ducked my face to the side. He couldn't have heard us, but if he glanced back here and spotted me blushing, surely he'd suspect why. And yes, he had no right to care nor judge.

It was still uncomfortable.

"I'm fine, Princess," Casimir said, innuendo fading from his tone. "It's just... different."

Reaching over, I took his hand, squeezing it gently. Smiling, he squeezed back.

On his blanket near the front of the cave, Dex murmured in his sleep. "Stop..."

My eyes snapped over to him. His voice was barely more than a mumble, but his brow was furrowed and he twitched as if trying to retreat from something.

I glanced at Roan and Ozias. They'd turned their heads as if listening, both of them, but they kept their attention on the forest.

"Don't do this." Dex squeezed his eyes shut tighter, a pained look on his face. A flush of sweat was breaking out over his light brown skin, but still he didn't wake. "Please, gods, don't..."

The two men on guard shared a glance, but neither of

them appeared alarmed. Instead, they seemed resigned, like they knew what this was and they hated to see it.

"Keep watch?" Roan murmured to Ozias. The other man nodded.

The dark-haired man rose to his feet.

I stood first. Roan had been such an asshole lately. Maybe he'd always been one, and I'd just overlooked it at first. But I didn't want him treating Dex rudely for what was obviously a horrible nightmare.

Roan froze when he saw me move. Something unreadable flickered over his face, cold but strange.

I headed for Dex, watching Roan as I moved.

Without a word, he sank back down beside Ozias.

Crouching next to Dex, I reached out, shaking his shoulder gently. "Hey. It's okay. Wake up."

He shook his head, still in the nightmare's grip.

"Dex." I nudged his shoulder again. "Wake up. It's—"

He lunged away from the rocky cave floor, his hand grabbing for his sword. I retreated fast, while Ruhl and Casimir shot to their feet behind me.

Dex froze. For a moment, he just stared at us, the unfocused look in his eyes of someone still trying to extract themselves from a dream. But then awareness returned, and with it came grim embarrassment, as if he realized what had happened. Scrubbing a hand over his short hair, he turned away.

Not quite taking my eyes from him, I motioned Casimir and Ruhl back. The wolf sank down to the ground again, and a moment passed before the vampire did the same.

"Are you all right?" I asked Dex carefully.

He nodded, but he wasn't looking at me. "Yeah. Sorry to wake you. And..." He grimaced. "Sorry."

"It's fine." I hesitated. "As long as you are, anyway."

"Yeah."

I bit my lip. I should probably give him space. Privacy too. But the thought of him hurting made me ache inside. "You were yelling for someone to stop."

He didn't respond.

"Do you want to talk about it?" I pressed softly, casting a brief glance to Ozias and Roan. Both of them had returned their attention to the forest, almost as if offering the privacy I was denying him.

"It's nothing. Just old bullshit."

I was silent.

His mouth tightened, and his eyes darted toward Casimir.

"The war," he admitted in a quiet voice.

My stomach sank. "Did the Aneirans hurt someone you cared about?"

"No."

Confusion flickered through me.

He closed his eyes briefly, as if resigning himself to something. "I was one of them."

I froze, lost for a moment. By the entrance of the cave, neither Roan nor Ozias moved. Maybe they'd already known this, but Casimir's brow twitched down like he was as baffled as me.

"One of..." I couldn't quite wrap my mind around it. "The *Aneiran* soldiers?"

He'd told me he'd been a soldier. I'd just assumed somehow it was for Erenelle.

"The Erenlians threw me out when I was a kid," Dex said. "I ended up staying in a town about twenty miles outside Lumilia, and when I was a teenager, I joined the army. Then the war came." His brow rose and fell, though he still wasn't meeting my eyes. "I believed your father when he said that the giants killed your mother. They would've killed me, so why not her? But the villages... the people... they weren't expecting an attack." He was silent for a moment. "It was horrible."

I shivered. "I'm so sorry."

He shook his head. "I should have tried to stop it. I just didn't trust that the Erenlian leaders hadn't made their villages into some sort of trap. But it's no excuse."

I wasn't sure how to respond, and after a moment, I reached out, taking his hand.

He glanced at me, a hint of surprise in his eyes that I didn't understand.

"What?" I asked.

"I guess I thought you would be disgusted by what I'd done." He paused. "Or *didn't* do."

I hesitated. "You forgave me for all I didn't do."

His brow drew down, confused.

"For not helping your people. For all those years I knew they were imprisoned, and I didn't even consider how awful and unjust that truly was." I shrugged, a twist of shame still burning in me for that. Making myself push past it, I continued. "And you saved me. You fought to help the witches when my stepmother attacked their hideout. I know you're a good person, Dex, even if you made mistakes."

For a long moment, he was silent, his dark eyes searching mine like he was reading something there and he couldn't quite fathom all he saw.

His hand came up, and he brushed his fingers along my cheek, sending shivers through my body. Gently, his thumb strayed along my lip and then moved down. His fingers encircled my throat, and the pad of his thumb tilted my chin so I had no choice but to look up at him.

Quivers radiated through my core, turning it molten.

"And what about you?" he asked softly.

"What about me?"

"Do you understand you're a good person too?"

My eyes darted around. Against the rear wall, Casimir was watching us, one eyebrow raised with an intrigued glint in his eyes. By the cave entrance, Ozias' head was half-turned toward us, while Roan was still as a statue with his gaze on the forest outside.

"Princess." Dex's fingers closed tighter, drawing my focus back to him. My core throbbed. "Do you understand?"

My head nodded slightly, as much as I was able. "Yes."

His brow twitched up.

"Yes, sir," I amended in a breathless whisper.

His lips curled. "Good girl." His fingers loosened, slipping back into my hair and bring me to him. His lips took mine, and he plundered my mouth for an eternity before drawing back again. "*Very* good girl."

I was wet and throbbing, and I desperately wanted to beg him to touch me more.

But the twins, Niko, and Byron were asleep around us, to say nothing of how Roan, Ozias, and Casimir were here too.

"If I may suggest..." Casimir began in a low voice.

I glanced over at him and Dex did the same.

The vampire met Dex's eyes. "The cave continues back that way for some distance." He tilted his head to one side, not breaking eye contact.

For a moment, Dex was silent. I knew what Casimir was implying, and gods, I thanked him for it. But given the way the two of them were pausing, there seemed to be something else to what he said.

But neither of them explained. Taking my hand without looking at me, Dex rose to his feet, bringing me with him. Carefully, we wove past the sleeping forms of the others and into the tunnel Casimir had indicated.

A whisper of sound came from behind me. I looked back to see the vampire following us.

Heat quivered between my legs. Was he going to watch?

Dex didn't pause, continuing until we were so deep in the tunnel that only the barest hint of firelight reached us and there was no chance the others would be able to hear us as long as we were careful. On either side, the walls were close, and stalactites hung from the ceiling like an upside-down forest.

But nothing stirred around us, and our breathing was the only sound. Whatever magic had twisted the Wild Lands outside this cave, here was nothing but stillness.

Suddenly, Dex pulled me around, whirling me to face him. His lips slammed into mine and his hand raked up through my hair, holding me to him and kissing me like he needed me to survive.

Too soon, though, he drew back, leaving me breathless with my heart racing.

He threw a look to Casimir, his hands still gripping me. "You good with sharing, then?" he asked, his voice rough.

Casimir paused. "Actually, I had something else in mind." He stepped closer, watching Dex like he was weighing every word and motion before he took it. "I'd very much enjoy feeling you take our princess."

Dex went still, his eyes locked on Casimir while his

hands stayed on me. My lips parted, but I couldn't make a sound.

I was too busy imagining what Casimir suggested.

"Have you ever had such an experience?" the vampire continued.

Slowly, Dex shook his head.

"Would you like to?"

Dex's grip tightened on my arms. The air sparked between the two men, a silent collision of two dominant forces evaluating more factors than I could name.

And then Dex's dark eyes slid to me, a question in his gaze.

My mouth moved. "If you..." Gods, my core throbbed at the idea. I'd never seen him express interest in any of the other men nor hint at desiring this sort of thing. But to see the two most commanding of all my men *together* as one of them fucked me...

If Dex wanted to that, I would be *more* than willing. "It's okay with me if it's okay with you."

A heartbeat passed, and I couldn't hope to catch whatever was racing behind Dex's eyes.

His head twitched in a slight nod.

Holy gods, I was so wet right now.

Casimir smiled. "Then let's begin."

23
GWYNEIRA

Moving like the predator he was, Casimir smoothly walked up next to Dex, his dark eyes tracing over me. Their forms were silhouetted in the barest traces of firelight that carried down the long tunnel to us, casting their faces in shadow while making the gold bands in the vampire's countless braids glint in the faint glow.

But even without my night vision, I would have felt their eyes on me. That my vampire abilities lined their faces with silver now, letting me see the way their gazes seared me and stripped me bare, only added to my need for them.

"Where should we have her, do you think?" Casimir asked Dex conversationally, never taking his gaze from me.

A hint of a smile lifted the corner of Dex's lips. Releasing one hand from me, he extended it palm down, toward the stone floor.

Energy tingled through the air. Breathless, I glanced back to see part of the ground rising up, the stone growing before my eyes.

Worry nibbled at the back of my mind. We were still in the Wild Lands. If he used magic here, could it go wrong or bring something to attack us?

But then, the cave had been still all night, and Dex was smart and cautious as hell. He knew what he was doing.

The stone stopped growing. A low slab of stone now stood at my back, smooth as marble, and a ledge ran along one side, as if to give someone a place to kneel.

My lips parted. If I lay on that... if he kneeled down to take me...

Casimir gave a low chuckle that made my pussy clench. "Perfect."

Dex's gaze returned to mine, molten with desire. In short, swift movements, he stripped me down, until I stood bare and on display before them both.

"On your back," Dex ordered. "Legs spread."

I clambered up onto the table and lay back as he told me, my heart pounding.

"Mmm," Casimir murmured, eyeing my wet center. "Our little fucktoy has the most delectable pussy, does she not?"

Dex nodded.

"Would you like to taste her before we begin?"

He nodded again. Moving into position with his knees on the ledge, he shifted me backward and then bent down, his dark eyes meeting mine for a moment with sinful promise.

His tongue traced up my slit.

My head fell back.

"Eyes on us, Princess," Casimir said.

I lifted my head with effort, my body shuddering as Dex's tongue circled my clit. His motions were sure and skilled, and the stubble on his cheeks created a heady mix of pinprick pain amid the pleasure.

Watching me, Casimir ran his hand up and down Dex's arm. "Good little fucktoy, Princess. Spread those legs for your giant."

I tried to move my legs apart farther, my pulse pounding at his words. Breaking away from me briefly, Dex whipped his sweater over his head and tossed it aside before diving back to my center. His breath was quick and hot against my wet core. He was turned on too, and I loved it.

"Mmm..." Casimir trailed a hand down Dex's spine. Still watching me, he leaned down by the other man's ear, the gold bands on his braids glinting in the distant firelight. "She looks so beautiful laid out there, her skin flushed and her nipples hard like little gemstones. Can you reach one of them? Pinch that pink nipple while you're tasting her?"

Never stopping his motions with his tongue, Dex slid a hand up my body, doing as Casimir said.

My hips bucked at the stronger bite of pain amid the pleasure.

Casimir chuckled. "So responsive."

Dex hummed in agreement, and I shivered at the vibration against my clit. His fingers tightened on my nipple and his tongue never let up, dipping into me and then returning to my clit in a dizzying rhythm.

Sweat broke out across my body. I fought to keep my hips in place despite how I wanted to press myself closer if only to get more of his intoxicating attention. My fingers curled against the smooth stone beneath me, and short, pleading sounds escaped me as the pleasure built higher in my core.

A strangled cry left me as the orgasm broke free and

rushed through my body. Shudders rolled through my muscles as my pussy spasmed, pleading for more, for them, for everything.

Dex straightened, a satisfied smile on his face. He glanced over at Casimir, his brow rising.

The vampire smiled back, but his expression took on a hungrier tinge when his eyes flicked down to the way my slick coated Dex's lips and chin.

Dex paused for a moment and then leaned over, brushing Casimir's lips with his own.

Gods, just when I thought I couldn't be more turned on.

A grin split the vampire's face, and he pulled Dex closer. Their kiss was like a war, each of them devouring the other, and when they broke apart, I couldn't hope to know who won.

Casimir traced his tongue around his lips and gave Dex a devious smile. "She tastes good on you."

Dex chuckled. His eyes slid back to me, the satisfied glint still in his gaze. Without looking away from me, he shed the rest of his clothes and then took my hips, pulling me closer to the edge of the stone slab.

"Are you still okay with this, little one?" he asked me.

I nodded, speechless, while Casimir shed his clothing too.

"Don't you just love how innocent she is?" the vampire commented as he came up next to Dex, sliding a hand along the man's back almost absently.

I swallowed hard, laid out like a display before them.

Dex made a noise of agreement, giving no sign he minded the other man's touch. "She was a virgin the first time I had her."

Casimir's brow twitched up. "And look what a good little fucktoy she's become."

My core pulsed at his words.

Dex smiled. Shifting to one side, he made space for Casimir as the vampire reached down, running his fingers through my folds, gathering my moisture. I twitched beneath his touch with a tiny gasp, and Casimir gave me a warning look. "Patience, Princess."

I tried to stay still.

"How you could go a single night without fucking that sweet pussy, I'll never know," Casimir mused as he spread my slick on his shaft.

"Oh, I didn't make it more than a few hours after meeting her before I had to," Dex replied.

Casimir chuckled, nodding briefly for Dex to move back toward me. "That makes two of us, then."

Dex shifted back between my legs and leaned forward, bracing one hand on either side of me on the stone. His knees were on the ledge, putting the tall man lower than he would have been otherwise, and my legs dangled on either side of him, my ass at the very edge of the smooth stone. His enormous cock hung between us, and I quivered with the urge to lift my hips toward him if only to put him inside me faster.

Casimir positioned himself behind Dex. "If you wish to stop," he said to Dex. "Simply give me a word and I will."

My heart tightened at the memory of his first time with me, when he'd offered the same. The vampire was like a devilish god when it came to sex, but it soothed me to know he never wanted to actually harm us.

"Forest," Dex said.

Casimir gave a soft laugh. "Fitting." He glanced down at me, his brow rising pointedly. "Remember yours?"

I nodded.

The vampire smiled. "Well then..."

A twitch went through Dex as the vampire began sliding his fingers in and out of Dex's rear entrance, preparing him.

I looked up at my giant. "Still okay?" I whispered.

He nodded, the barest hint of vulnerability showing past the dominance. "Just... different."

"Not bad?"

A shudder rolled through him and his eyes closed for a moment. But the corners of his mouth still curled up. "No."

I lifted my hand to his cheek, his stubble rough against my palm, and my throat closed against all the things I wanted to say. How much I loved this. Wanted this.

How much I loved him.

The thought was so huge, it filled my chest, leaving no room for anything but its weight. This amazing, powerful giant was my protector, my stabilizing force against the madness that had taken over my world. He made me feel like I could do anything.

And to share this with him...

A soft gasp left Dex as Casimir began to push inside him. His face tightened, his body tensing for a moment and then releasing like he was consciously making himself relax.

I bit my lip, watching as more tension eased from him and slowly, inexorably, need began to take its place as Casimir sank into him.

"Fuck..." Dex murmured.

"That's what this is, yes," Casimir replied with a grin as he eased backward.

"Smartass."

Casimir pushed into him again and he gave a small gasp.

"Take our princess, Dex," the vampire said. "Let her feel us both."

I lifted my hips, breathless. I was so wet, the stone beneath me felt slippery, and my body trembled with anticipation for what was to come.

Dex slid into me. I exhaled sharply. His cock was still as huge as ever, but I was so aroused, it only felt like a relief when my body stretched to accommodate his girth.

I craved this. Him. I'd swear my desire for his massive cock filling me was written into my very soul.

"Good girl," Dex murmured.

My inner muscles clenched around him.

He rocked back, and Casimir went with him. A shudder passed through Dex, but he only paused for a heartbeat, the head of his cock hovering at my entrance, teasing me with sensation. Casimir slid his dark hands along Dex's lighter brown shoulders, and then he thrust forward and Dex did the same, driving deep into me.

I bit back a moan, moving with them as they gradually took up a punishing rhythm, pounding into me faster and faster until I had to grip the edge of the smooth slab to keep from being driven back across the stone.

Dex's hand took my breast, squeezing down, and I bucked beneath him. "Do you want to know what it feels like," he whispered. "Fucking your little wet pussy while he's in me?"

Oh gods, I nearly came on the spot.

"How it's as if we're both pounding into your sweet hole?"

I wasn't going to last.

Casimir drove himself harder in time to Dex's movements, and gripping me, Dex gave a choked sound on the verge of becoming a moan. "How much I'm going to pump you full of my cum when I... when he..."

I gasped as a ragged sound escaped him, and at his back, Casimir groaned, pleasure tightening his face.

"Come, Princess," Dex gritted out. "Come like our good little—"

My orgasm didn't wait for more. Pleasure roared up through me like a flood breaking past a dam, rushing over me so fast it swept away my view of the tunnel. I was nothing but this moment. Nothing but the feeling of Dex pounding against my flesh, his cock pulsing his seed into me. I was theirs, and I never wanted this to end.

Slowly, the tide of my orgasm ebbed, drawing back until the tunnel returned and I lay limp on the stone table, boneless and sated. Distantly, I felt Dex slide from within me. Heard him murmur to Casimir and the vampire say something in response. I opened my eyes long enough to see them share a kiss, gentler this time. Like a thank-you that ended with a smile from both men.

Blissful exhaustion sank over me, dragging at my eyelids.

A cloak draped over me like a blanket, and then hands scooped me up.

I opened my eyes again. Casimir cradled me as gently as if I was a prized treasure. He was clothed again, and Dex was too.

The vampire looked down at me, a softness in his dark eyes. "Rest, my princess. Our good little fucktoy deserves to relax after what she gave us tonight."

I blushed, nestling closer to him. But then a shiver

coursed over me, like something light and soft tracing across all of my skin.

My heart sank. I recognized that feeling.

The sun was coming up.

Casimir sighed, setting me down again. "This gods-forsaken magic scarcely allows us a moment before cutting the night short, doesn't it?"

At Dex's questioning look, he explained, and the giant grimaced ruefully. It'd only been a few hours since nightfall, at most. Yet already the Wild Lands were making the sun come up again.

Was it taunting us? Trying to steal this moment, same as we'd stolen a bit of peace just now?

I cast a worried look to the men as I pulled my clothes on. "Will you be all right today? You barely got any sleep, either of you."

Dex brushed my hair back from my face. "We'll manage. And I couldn't have imagined a better way to spend these hours."

Casimir bent slightly, kissing my forehead. "Come now, Princess. Surely you don't think a little lack of sleep will give this place a chance against us?"

I managed a smile as the two of them led me back down the tunnel. I didn't doubt their skill, nor the fact they could keep going despite exhaustion.

But these were the Wild Lands, and the magic here had already tried to kill us.

I only prayed I'd open my eyes to see my men all safe this coming night.

24
LARS

It didn't take a genius to tell something had happened in the night. Between the way Ozias seemed strangely distracted and the way Roan glowered even more viciously at Casimir, I could guess *something* had gone on.

Plus Dex was walking a little stiffly, which was definitely odd.

None of the men explained, however, and I wasn't sure how to ask, so after we said goodbye to the princess and settled her into the coffin, we set off into the forest with silence unequivocally reigning between us all.

And gods, was it awkward. It wasn't even like we were a chatty group to begin with. Besides Clay, most of us worked in silence even in the mines. But this was different.

I just couldn't get a read on why.

As time dragged on, I distracted myself by falling back on the habit I'd developed of silently listing the positive developments we encountered in this gods-forsaken forest. For one, we were likely at lower elevations than we'd been before. The trees were changing, turning to what Niko called deciduous as opposed to the evergreens and spruce of higher elevations. For another, the snow was lessening, giving way to dirt and underbrush that made it less likely we'd slip and fall on the ice. Casimir's shortcut was working, finally enabling us to escape this place.

Oh, and we weren't dead yet.

There were good signs all around us, really. Yes, I'd been carrying this coffin for so long, it felt like a groove was starting to wear in my shoulder where the box rested. But we hadn't run out of supplies even though it felt like we'd been walking for weeks, and barring the rockslide that had cracked the princess's coffin, we'd mostly been able to keep her safe.

So why did I still feel like half our group was about to explode?

Behind his veil of the shadow wolf, Casimir yawned.

"You okay there, buddy?" Clay called.

"Just a little fatigued."

The smile in the vampire's voice was more than clear, and from the way my brother's head cocked to the side, I could tell he heard it too.

Ozias shifted his shoulders and started walking faster.

Clay sped up, and the rest of us did the same, trying to keep pace with him. "Something wrong, Oz?"

"No."

A soft scoff left my twin. "Uh-huh."

Clearly I wasn't the only one who noticed this.

Dex didn't press him for more, though, which also surprised me. Normally, the man defaulted to acting like our leader, and he definitely would have spoken up in the interest of keeping cohesion in our group.

Yeah, awkward didn't cover it.

This was just strange.

"Um..." I tried to think of the best way to ask. "Did something happen last night we should be aware of?"

Ozias flinched. Roan made a scathing noise. And Casimir merely looked back at Dex.

They weren't honestly going to pretend everything was normal, were they?

"Come on, guys," Clay pressed, obviously coming to the same conclusion.

"Casimir and I shared some time with the princess," Dex said finally. "And each other."

My brow climbed. Oh.

"So..." Niko prompted, sounding confused. "What's wrong with that?"

Byron spoke up from the far side of our group, his tone cautious. "Was the princess upset?"

Casimir chuckled. "Oh, not at all. She seemed to quite enjoy it."

Now I was really lost. If the princess was fine with it, what had Ozias so distracted and Roan even more surly than he'd been lately? They weren't interested in Gwyneira—or Dex, as far as I knew. And the gods knew they'd not shown the least desire for anything to do with Casimir, so...

Wait. Surely not.

Clay blurted out what I'd been carefully trying to determine how to ask—as usual. "*Tell* me you two aren't mad Dex and the vampire fucked."

I swore it was a fluke of nature that I was more closely tied to fire when he was as impulsive as a hungry blaze. But then, tidal waves weren't exactly known for their restraint either.

At the statement, Ozias tensed like he'd bolt into the

woods if he could, but Roan reacted with enough rage to make me think *he* was the one with the affinity to fire. "Why the hell would you think I cared about that?" he demanded.

I threw a look over my shoulder at him, incredulous.

My brother scoffed. "Because you seem mad enough to spit flames, man!"

Roan stopped walking, everything about him going still.

I made a noise and the others holding the coffin came to a halt. Carefully, I lowered the box in sync with them and turned my attention on Roan.

He hadn't moved a muscle and his expression had gone as blank as stone.

"You both just seem upset," I said, trying for the reasonable tone my twin had failed to find. "We can't afford to become distracted in this place, so if there's something bothering you—"

"There's not." Roan's voice was like ice.

I didn't buy that for a second, but I glanced at Ozias all the same, waiting for his response even though, given how little he normally spoke, I wasn't sure I'd get one.

But the bearded man only looked lost. "She's just... I..." Ozias blinked, clearly searching for words. "She's... more adventurous than I expected."

Casimir chuckled. "You have *no* idea."

Ozias turned away quickly, but not before I saw his face going red around his beard.

I stared at him. *That* was why he'd been distracted? Because...

Clay turned to me. My twin's face was always somewhat a mirror of mine, even if his personality always showed through, but now his blue eyes held the exact same question that I knew had to be in my own.

Was Ozias actually *interested* in the princess?

"We should go," the large man grunted out, starting to walk without looking back.

Eyes wide, my brother gave me another glance, but for once, he didn't say anything. With the others, we hefted the coffin again, starting after our friend.

But I threw a look over my shoulder when I didn't hear Roan follow. "Are you coming?"

The man didn't move. His eyes were locked on Gwyneira. I couldn't even see him breathing.

And for a moment, I could have sworn he was about to say no.

His head jerked in a short, swift nod. He started walking again.

I let out a breath, hit by an unexpected wave of relief. We were a group. Practically a family, in our way.

To lose one of them...

I shoved the worry down hard as I continued on with the others, ordering myself to focus on the positive. We were alive. We were moving forward. No, I didn't have a clue what was going on with Roan right now, but dammit, that wasn't what mattered.

This was. Our family and the fact we were still together.

We only had to hang on until everything else worked out.

25
CLAY

We were fucked.

Well, not like *fucked*, fucked. But gods, if even Ozias was starting to crack and Roan was about ready to lose it over something as simple as Dex and Gwyneira spending a night with that vampire...

Yeah, things weren't exactly great.

I gripped the sides of the princess's box, wondering how many upsides to this situation my brother was probably trying to list behind me. He'd always been the optimistic one, and when we were kids and shit got rough, that was his fallback.

Focus on the positive, he'd say.

I was positively sure I'd ask him to burn this place down if we had to stay here much longer. And I was also positively sure most of the guys around me would support that.

My lips twitched. See, I was focusing on the upside already.

Ahead, Byron suddenly made a warning noise. I could

barely see him around the edge of the coffin, but I caught enough to see him look back at us in alarm.

"What's wrong?" Dex asked.

In a rush, a chill swept over my skin like I'd passed through a fine mist and a cool breeze all at once. "What the hell?" I demanded, glancing around in case some new nightmare was waiting for us.

"I think..." Byron allowed carefully. "That was the border to the Wild Lands."

Casimir gave a brief look to the shadow creature drifting around him and then nodded at the rest of us. "I believe the scholar is correct, yes."

"Hold up," Dex ordered.

We stopped, and when he began lowering the box, we did the same.

"What makes you say that?" he asked the vampire.

"Ruhl appears less stressed. I would assume this is because we are in less danger."

My brow twitched up. How the hell he could tell a smoky shadow thing was "less stressed," I had no idea.

But whatever. "Well, uh, where the hell are we, then?"

Byron unfurled the map. "I think..." He turned a slow circle, evaluating the position of the sun in the sky and the mountains around us. "If the sun is now where it's meant to be..." His brow twitched down. "We're only a day's walk from the border of Aneira."

His green eyes were wide when he looked up at us again, and I understood why. We could have come out of the Wild Lands anywhere. It wasn't like that place was exactly trustworthy when it came to a path. And while, yeah, Aneira was its own problem—to put it mildly—at least there we wouldn't be facing magical terrain with a murder fetish.

"Once we reach the Aneiran border," Casimir started. "The plan is... what exactly?"

Lars glanced at the rest of us. "Well, with her stepmother gone, Gwyneira's people may be back to their right minds. They could want her back on the throne."

"And if they're not? If they've taken this opportunity to claim power for themselves?"

"First we need to evaluate the situation at the border," Dex replied. "Then we'll have a better idea how to proceed. Until we have that information, our contingencies are only theories."

Casimir regarded him for a moment. "But if they are hostile?" His brow rose. "Hope is an asset, my friend. It is not a strategy."

"So you just assume we don't know what we're doing, is that it?" Roan spoke up from the back of our group.

"*If* they're hostile," Dex interrupted before the vampire could reply. "We could do everything from fall back to caves that Ozias would locate, to tear the ground out from under them as a method of attack. We have Lars' fire, Byron's magic, as well as Niko's ability to mobilize any plant as a weapon in *easily* a hundred-yard radius, and that's before we get into Clay's powers, Roan's, or my own. The seven of us lived in the mountains beyond Lumilia for half a decade, scouting countless tunnels and hideouts in that time, and before that, we snuck past that entire nation without being spotted—and that was on the heels of a war against our kind." He gave Casimir a pointed look. "But until we see the situation at the border and find out if the Warden Wall guarding Aneira still stands, choosing which of those plans to implement is nothing but a mental exercise."

I couldn't help but smirk. "Bit more than *hope*, eh?"

Casimir's gaze flicked to me before returning to Dex, respect obvious in his eyes. "Indeed."

Dex nodded briefly in acknowledgment.

"May I ask, though," the vampire continued. "What is this 'Warden Wall'?"

I tensed, glancing at my brother. Both he and I bore scars from a baby version of the magical barrier that surrounded Aneira, one we'd encountered when we'd tried and failed to save some of our people from a prison camp during the war. Even thinking about it made me itch.

Not to mention it brought back memories of how every other "true" giant with us had died bloody when they touched the thing.

"A vicious creation of magic," Byron said, "designed to slaughter any of our kind who come in contact with it. The Warden Wall surrounds Aneira, while smaller versions have been used to shield other locations. It was crafted by the vampire queen who turned Gwyneira."

Casimir's brow arched, a cold look on his face. "Was it now?" His eyes rested on the princess's coffin for a moment before returning to us. "Very well, how do we destroy it?"

A chuckle escaped me. The vampire really wasn't half bad. I may not have liked him initially—locking us up and kidnapping the princess had that effect on me—but I sure as hell could appreciate the desire to fuck shit up on Gwyneira's behalf.

"That, we have not determined," Byron said.

Casimir's mouth tightened. "Tabling that issue for the moment, then... What is the plan for getting past it? Will it leave you unharmed since you don't appear like the rest of your kind?"

I scoffed. His expression turned curious.

"It doesn't work like that," Byron explained. "The seven of us were simply fortunate before. A section of the barrier dropped for a contingent of soldiers to pass through at night, and we were able to shadow them across the border. We look enough like humans to pass from a distance, and as long as we stayed clear of any soldiers who knew Dex, that strategy worked. But we still know it will harm us, even if we're not like... other giants."

Lars rolled up his sleeve, showing the vampire the gnarled scar that wrapped his wrist. Grudgingly, I tugged up the hem of my coat and sweater, revealing the tangled rope of tissue that coiled down my side.

Far be it from me to leave my brother looking like he'd been the only one damn near eaten by that magic.

"It only tries to kill us slower," Lars said as he tugged his sleeve back into place. I yanked my sweater down, eager to forget about what that barrier had done.

The vampire appeared taken aback. "I understand."

"I doubt that," Roan muttered behind me.

Casimir's mouth tightened, but he ignored him. "Assuming there is a way to deal with this Warden Wall, I suppose the only other consideration will be convincing the Aneirans not to be alarmed at the sight of their princess in a coffin—and not to kill her by opening it in the sun."

A breath left Dex. "We're still working on that one."

"Actually..." Byron glanced around at us all, appearing oddly hesitant. "I have an idea about that."

26
GWYNEIRA

I opened my eyes to nervous faces looking down at me.

"Oh, gods," I groaned. "What's happened now?"

Dex threw a glance at the others, jerking his head at them to back away. "Nothing." He extended a hand to me, drawing me out of the coffin. "We've just had a possible breakthrough."

I gave them all a confused look. The twins, Niko, and Dex were close by, while Byron hovered near the bags, fidgeting with the tie of one of them like he didn't know what to do with his hands. Casimir watched him and me equally, Ruhl hovering like a low-lying storm cloud around his feet. Even Roan and Ozias were here, watching me from the far end of the cave and the entrance respectively.

To a man, they all looked too cautious and cagey for a breakthrough.

At least, not the good kind.

"And that is?" I prompted, still wary.

"Well," Dex admitted. "Byron hasn't gone into detail on it yet, but..." He gave an expectant look to the scholar.

"He thinks he has a way to stop the sun from burning you."

"One that doesn't involve a box," Lars added.

"Or you sleeping all day long," Clay chimed in.

Elation made my heart race. "How? Could we do it now? What do you need from me?"

Clay chuckled. "I'd say she's on board."

A grin tugged at my lips, but it couldn't last long against my worry. Because Byron wasn't speaking up. Wasn't even looking at me. And the others still looked edgy. "So what's wrong?"

Byron shifted his weight uncomfortably. "It could be risky."

"So is traveling in a glass box," I replied, adrenaline making my tone shorter than it would ordinarily have been.

But gods help me, if there was a way I could travel in the daytime... help them when they were in danger...

Stand in the sunlight again...

"What is risky about it?" I amended, trying to remind myself that, if he was concerned, he probably had a good reason.

Byron grimaced. "It will require me weaving magic from several of us together and then applying that to you. With luck, it will work. With more, it will last. I think I can manipulate the spell so that it will be self-sustaining. I just... I will need to check it frequently, and if it should start to fail..."

"Ruhl and I will be ready," Casimir spoke up.

Byron cast a glance back at him, barely seeming mollified.

"Man, we've already told you," Clay said, "whoever you need help from, sign us up."

"Good. Because it's your power I need. Lars' too."

Clay blinked, glancing around. "Wait. Just us?"

He suddenly didn't look so certain.

"The sun is a ball of flame, yes? And if Gwyneira steps into its light, she'll burn. But Lars' power is tied to fire, while you are his opposite, linked to water that quenches flames."

Clay appeared baffled. "So you're going to... soak her with water?"

Irritation crossed Byron's face. "Of course not."

"But—"

"It's *energy*," Byron cut in. "I believe I can use it and Gwyneira's own magical energy to insulate and counteract the effects of sunlight on her." He hesitated. "Hopefully."

The men fell silent, and I swallowed hard, not sure what to say. I wanted it to work. Gods, I'd give almost anything for it to let me stand in the sunlight again.

But this was asking me to risk a great deal.

For a "hopefully."

"I would like to assist," Casimir said into the silence.

Byron gave him a confused look. "You're a vampire. I don't see how that could help offset—"

"I'm more than that." His jaw muscles jumped. "My ancestors claimed to be descendants of angels."

Roan scoffed in the shadows. "Of course they did."

Casimir ignored him. "I remained sane after I was turned. I survived thirty years without blood, using only magic to sustain myself. And though it is still dangerous to me, I can withstand traces of sunlight for short periods of time. Do you know any other vampire capable of this?"

Silence reigned.

"I have studied magic for decades," he continued to Byron. "I am no stranger to spellwork or the manipulation of my own energies to various ends. Thus, if my gifts can aid the princess, consider them at your disposal."

A warm feeling spread through my chest at his words, and I dipped my face away as my cheeks heated in turn.

"All right," Byron conceded. "The four of us, then. And the princess." He nodded to himself. "It should work."

I wished he could sound more confident about that.

"And what about Casimir?" I asked. "If this works, could you do it for him too?"

At the slightly surprised smile Casimir gave me, I shrugged. "In case Ruhl needs a rest."

His smile spread. Around his feet, green eyes glowed to life amid the smoke, watching me for a moment before fading back to darkness.

"We could try, yes," Byron agreed.

Roan shrugged away from the wall and walked farther into the shadows as if entirely done with all of us.

I watched him go, something in me hurting, even if it was absurd. I couldn't make him get along with the others any more than I could make him explain why he was always so surly and angry. And maybe it was foolish, wishing all the men around me could share some kind of camaraderie.

But would it be too much to ask for them to stop arguing all the time?

I pushed the thoughts aside. Roan's problems were his own, and if he chose to act this way, it was on him.

"What do we need to do for this spell, then?" I asked.

"As we are out of the Wild Lands," Byron said, "it would be best to undertake this in a more open space. The magic could be volatile. Enclosed spaces could send it ricocheting in unexpected ways. And only those involved in the spell should be present, lest anyone else's magic interfere with what we are about to attempt."

"You need someone keeping watch," Dex countered immediately. "Preferably several someones. Your attention needs to stay on the spell, and if a threat shows up..." His brow rose and fell.

Byron hesitated.

"That's not a request." Dex gave him a pointed look.

The red-haired man frowned, but after a moment, he nodded. "As long as you stay at least fifty feet away... *preferably* more."

Dex tilted his head in brief agreement.

I let out a breath as Byron bent to grab his bag and Dex set to telling Ozias and Niko what he wanted them to do in standing guard around us.

Roan never left the shadows.

I turned away, pushing him from my mind. All that mattered now was this spell and the chance—the blessed, amazing chance—that I truly could travel with them in the sunlight again.

Shivers rolled through me at the mere idea.

"Ready, Princess?" Dex called.

Nodding fast, I hurried after him, clinging to the hope that somehow, this would work and everything would be all right.

27
BYRON

Oh gods have mercy and let this work. Gripping my bag, I led the way through the forest, mentally rehearsing the spellwork that I'd been trying to create ever since we left the Jeweled Coven's hideout. It would have been too dangerous to attempt it in the Wild Lands. I knew that. The erratic magic there could have easily infiltrated the spell. It could have made me blind to errors or convinced me all was well.

Right up until the moment my princess burst into flame.

A grimace twisted my face. Not *my* princess. Theirs.

Slip-ups like that were exactly the distraction I could not afford right now. Not if I wanted to make sure she survived the sunrise.

The trees parted ahead, opening into a clearing that shone beneath the moonlight in patches of dirt and dead grass like an erratic quilt. Most of the trees had lost their leaves, while the evergreens stood like shadowy monoliths against the night sky. The stars shone amid a blanket of black that was interrupted only by the glow of the full moon.

It was objectively quite beautiful here.

I didn't trust that.

While Dex, Niko, and Ozias spread out through the forest, I extended my hands toward the clearing, feeling for the energy there. Most people were unaware of the ebb and flow of power that surrounded them at all times. And on some level, I understood why the witches gravitated towards the peaks of mountains, seeking distance and objectivity above the sea of energy that was the rest of the world. But in this clearing, the power from the earth was stable, the wildlife had fled from us minutes before we even arrived, and the trees were not too close for their energy to interfere with my work.

I lowered my hands.

"So..." Clay prompted behind me. "We good?"

"Yes." Not looking back, I strode farther into the clearing. "Princess, if you would stand in the center, please."

She nodded. I could see the nervousness on her face. It only worsened the dread wrapping cold fingers around my heart.

Gods, please...

I shoved the reaction down. I knew what I was doing. "Clay, Lars, Your Highness. If you would take positions around her?"

The men moved into position without a word.

"Excellent. Now..." From my bag, I withdrew the few crystals I'd brought from my mentor's library at the Jeweled Coven. I hadn't been able to carry much. Despite being a giant, lugging rocks down the mountain was not something

I particularly enjoyed. I only carried enough to serve as a protection in case of emergency.

And now to help with this.

Keeping my face calm, I strode around the circle, placing the crystals at intervals.

"What are those for?" Gwyneira asked, a sort of polite interest in her tone that I suspected was covering up for her nervousness, though I didn't look at her to check.

The others could reassure her. I needed to focus.

"Decoration," Clay joked.

My fingers tightened around the last of the crystals. "They are meant to contain the energy we are about to summon."

"I was just teasing, man."

"Now is not the time. You need to focus." My eyes darted to Gwyneira before I could stop them, and I yanked them away again. "For her sake."

A flicker of remorse crossed Clay's face.

Good.

Letting out a breath, I put the last stone in the dead grass and then straightened again, shaking out my hands a bit as I drew slow, steady breaths, centering myself. Already, I could feel the effects of the crystals on the clearing, the way the energy shifted to concentrate here rather than flowing out into the surrounding forest.

This would work. It had to. The princess would not be forced to spend her days locked in a glass box, her body drained of color and her skin cold as ice.

A shudder went through me. I shouldn't be thinking like that. Not now. Yes, something in my chest ached for her. Something made me call her my treluria. But I could control that pain, that longing. My mind was more powerful than my body, and it always would be. That was the way of the Order of Berinlian, and I would maintain it.

Especially when her life was in my hands.

My stomach twisted. Best not to think about that either.

"Now..." I turned back to the other men, keeping my attention on them and not the beautiful woman at the center of their rough triangle. "If you would allow your power to extend beyond your form." I glanced at Casimir. "Your Highness, if that isn't clear —"

A prickling sensation coursed over my skin, like a wave of a thousand bright and shining needles sweeping across me. My gut clenched as the power of it rolled out over the clearing.

Never mind. Apparently, he understood.

Dear *gods*.

Impulsive as ever, Clay's power rushed out immediately to join it, while Lars' gift spread more slowly, controlled and careful. After all these years of living with the twins, their powers were as familiar to me as my own gift—and telling them apart was easy too. Clay's was a summer storm surging from out of nowhere and a rioting river sweeping around everything in its path. Lars' was a controlled burn, like a candle flame in a lantern. It held the potential to erupt into an inferno and burn down everything in its path, but like the man who wielded it, right now it was cautious, concerned with protecting everyone around him.

Sometimes, I wondered if the six giants with me felt each other's power the way I did. After all, I didn't have an elemental gift. Not exactly, anyway. Part of the reason I'd been so suited to the life of a monk was that my power was more... general. Energy itself came to me. The monks believed I was more closely aligned to the stars themselves than any earthly power. A unifying force, in a way, tied to the nature of energy itself and able to manipulate it.

Which meant, of us all, I was the one who would be able to do this for her.

The coincidence of that registered in the back of my mind, the analytical part of my brain acknowledging how intriguing it was that each man in Gwyneira's life was so uniquely suited to helping her.

Almost as if we'd been chosen somehow.

I pushed the thought aside, forcing my mind into the patterns of focus that I had practiced ever since I was a child. Reaching out with my own energies, I wrapped my power around that of the vampire king and the twins, drawing them together as I paced a circle just inside the perimeter of the crystals. The stones would serve as a balance, holding back the energy outside our circle while helping to concentrate that within.

Everything in balance...

Casimir had not lied when he said he was something more than just a vampire, though. The longer I was exposed to it, the more his power felt like a golden glow I could see behind my eyes, even though nothing changed in the night around us. With such strength, it surprised me that he hadn't already tried a spell such as this, though perhaps his angelic ancestry was distant enough that what protection he had from the sun already was the most he could gain without assistance.

And of course, such assistance was nonexistent when you'd been a veritable recluse for the better part of three decades.

Like a monk.

I shoved the observation away, gritting my teeth in an effort to concentrate against how my thoughts wanted to wander like rabbits in the underbrush of my mind.

Carefully, I wove his energy in between, around, and through the water and the fire of my friends' gifts. My own power twisted around them all, serving as a guide and a focusing force to keep the disparate energies unified.

Around... and around... and around...

My awareness of the forest faded. Any sense of the night sky too. Over and over I walked around them, until the threads of magic were woven so thick, it was a miracle they weren't glowing in the air.

And now...

I turned towards the princess, extending a hand toward her and pushing down the flutter of trepidation that twisted deep inside. She was watching me with such trust.

Gods, let this work...

I sent the energy coursing toward her.

She gasped, her back arching as the power poured into her, rushing across her body, coating her skin, and then sinking into it. My awareness followed, tracking it over every part of her.

Every soft curve. Every tender spot. Every inch, as if my fingers were teasing across her form to ensure the magic shielded it all.

Focus. Gods, I had to focus. This was her life at stake, fool.

Yet... how much easier would the spell be, how much *safer*, if she was truly beneath my hands? If I could *actually* touch every part of her, feel every curve and ensure my magic was there?

The need was unbearable.

I trembled with the effort of holding myself still, even as both my hands rose, my fingers weaving intricate motions through the air, guiding the magic.

Her breath hitched as my power twisted around her waist and hips, down her legs.

And between them, across her soft, wet folds.

I shuddered. She was reacting to this. To my touch. Every little twitch of her muscles, every flutter between her legs was clear to me, and even as I watched, her lips parted, a faint gasp slipping from her. My cock ached in response, hard as stone and weeping with need. I had only to cross the distance between us for her to be in my hands, and *gods* have mercy, I knew it would be ecstasy.

But would that make the spell fail?

I closed my eyes, clinging desperately to my training. I couldn't move toward her. I wouldn't. The spell was all that mattered, and so I had to focus.

For her.

Always for her.

The diamond glint of her power danced in my mind's eye. The witches at the Jeweled Coven had been right. If she'd been allowed to grow up as the witch she was born to be, Gwyneira's affinity undoubtedly would have been to diamonds as her mother's had been.

But I could feel the cold black coal of her vampire self in there too. The darkness was bonded to every inch of the crystalline light that had been her human self, inseparable.

A light like the stars themselves...

Shivers rolled over my skin, my aching need for her growing worse, as if her natural element called to mine. Like we'd been made for one another, right from the start.

Oh, how the gods must have laughed to see me dream of becoming a scholar when they made someone like her...

Sweat prickled my brow. I wouldn't fail her. I would focus the way I'd trained and guide this power with careful precision so that nothing would ever harm her again.

Gold glints of Casimir's energy, bright as the sun... the cool rush of Clay's, soothing it... the heat of Lars' gift blazing like a firing kiln, hardening the magic into a shield to guard her...

And my gift holding it all.

My heart raced, my breaths coming short. Sweat dripped down my temples despite the wintry cold.

The last of the magic twisted into her, tying off and linking with the first threads of my spell to form an endless loop, spinning eternally through every part of her and yet invisible to the naked eye.

And gods, it was beautiful.

Carefully, I let the spell go, watching the energies with my mind's eye.

They persisted, unaffected by my gentle release.

Safe. Secure. Holding just as I had prayed they would.

"It's done." I cleared my throat, glancing at my friends and the vampire king. Their eyes were wide. Even Casimir seemed taken aback.

"Holy shit, man." Clay sounded breathless. "That was... awesome."

Lars nodded. "I had no idea you could do something like that."

The vampire king straightened slightly, shaking his head as if in wonder. "Impressive. Truly."

I turned away, mopping the sweat from my brow. "Are you okay, Princess?"

She was silent for a moment. I couldn't bring myself to look at her.

"Yes," she finally said, her voice winded. "Do you think it worked?"

"If anything was going to work," Casimir replied, respect in his voice. "I suspect it would be that."

"We should be careful at sunrise," I countered quickly. "Just in case."

Clay walked up to her. "You sure you're all right, baby?" He took her hand while Lars came up beside her, putting an arm around her as if reassuring himself she was okay.

I looked away.

She gave a breathless chuckle. "It was rather... *intense.*"

I glanced back immediately. Had my spell hurt her after all?

Her eyes were locked on me, her lips parted ever so slightly, a flush of pink to her cheeks.

My face heated, and I made myself turn away a second time, unable to bear her gaze.

Or how much I wanted to feel her again.

"You sure you're okay?" Clay asked her.

I didn't look back while she murmured a response, locking my attention instead on checking the crystals around the circle, making sure they were still intact. But desperate need still clamored within me, my thoughts betraying me at every turn. I'd trained my mind for years to record every detail of information I observed. My mind saw books like a picture, remembering every word on the page.

And now, it could only remember every soft curve and line of her beautiful body.

I shuddered, closing my eyes tightly for a moment. I knew how to purge unwelcome thoughts. How to focus against distractions. I'd studied for years despite all manner of discomforts.

But I could not bring myself to push this away.

"So... for Casimir," she started.

Discomfort shot through me. I didn't care that he and Dex had spent a night together. But I didn't have the same draw to the vampire that I felt for the princess, which would make this awkward to say the very—

"Actually, I believe I was able to track what happened with the spell," Casimir said. "If Clay and Lars are willing to allow me to draw on their power, I would like to attempt to reproduce it myself."

Relief rolled through me, but I only confined my response to a nod, not wishing to insult someone who'd done nothing but help me.

He nodded in return. "It was an ingenious bit of spell craft, truly." His brow twitched up. "Were you a member of the Order of... what was it called?"

I froze. "Berinlian. Yes."

"I thought I recognized the technique. One of my childhood tutors was of your Order. When we have a moment, I'd love to discuss that energetic weaving pattern you used. It was—" A bit of amusement tinged his expression. "—impressively thorough."

Indignation rose in me before common sense doused it. I didn't protest that it had been important to be "thorough," as he called it. That Gwyneira's life had been on the line— and may still be if my spell failed.

No, I said nothing of the sort, because to do so would draw attention to the fact I'd touched damn near every inch of her with my energy.

Though the redness I could feel like fire in my cheeks was probably drawing attention, regardless.

Locking my eyes back on the bag, I held my voice calm and steady as I said, "Of course."

The others began walking back toward the camp, discussing whether to rest before Casimir tried the spell on himself.

It took me a moment before I started after them.

Truth was, I'd likely overstepped with the spell. Been more "thorough" than was required. And for that, I should apologize, because it may have made the princess believe something that couldn't be true.

I would never be able to feel her softness around me. Never slide into the wet folds I'd felt between her legs, nor fill her soft pussy as she writhed and moaned. I couldn't give her pleasure because every vow I held sacred stood between us.

And perhaps the torture of that fact was my penance for giving in even for a moment to this desire I couldn't seem to escape.

That I didn't *want* to escape.

I glanced up, seeking her in the darkness. Up ahead, Clay had his arm around her. Lars and Casimir were at her side, while Dex and the others were moving through the forest to join them.

Shudders rolled through me, driven by heartache. The greater truth was, however she'd reacted to the spell, she didn't need me. Not like that. Perhaps, now that the magic and the moment had passed, she would even realize she *didn't* want me that way, and my maelstrom of desire and doubt would be for nothing.

She had them. I had my calling. Whatever the gods had schemed by making my magic fit so seamlessly with hers, it could never amount to anything. Thus I could only go on, keeping my vows intact, protecting her from a distance.

No matter how it left me aching inside.

28
GWYNEIRA

I was still trembling from Byron's spell.

Or, really, from how it felt to be touched by it.

I chuckled at something Clay said and I reassured Lars when he checked again that I was okay, but all I wanted to do was turn around and ask the scholar if he'd felt what I felt.

If it had been intentional.

My body still burned from the caress of his magic. I was still wet from the feel of his power moving over me. As we all walked back to the cave, I tried to give no sign, but gods, his touch had been everywhere.

And now I just wanted *him* everywhere.

I snuck a glance back at him. He trailed us all, his arms clutching his bag of ore and his eyes on the ground.

Really, he'd been avoiding my gaze this entire time.

I bit my lip as I looked ahead again. This wasn't how a person acted if they *meant* to arouse someone. Therefore it was likely he'd intended nothing of the kind.

And thus knowing how I'd responded was making him uncomfortable.

I gave Clay another smile, guilt nibbling at me for how distracted I was about what the twins were saying. I couldn't help how my body had reacted to Byron's magic, nor what I secretly wished he'd do about it. But even though he'd said I was his treluria, back before I was turned, I needed to respect the fact he didn't seem to want to act on that.

With effort, I tried to push away my craving and the way my pussy wept to be touched and filled. It was only an unfortunate side effect of that magic.

It would pass.

Roan was waiting for us when we reached the cave. "Well?" His gaze swept all of us.

"It may have worked," Byron replied. "We will know when the sun rises."

Roan's dark eyes landed on me. Worry flashed across his face, startling me.

He spun and strode into the cave. "Fine."

I exhaled, not sure what to make of that.

But maybe even Roan didn't want to see me go up in flames.

I swallowed hard. The thought of what could happen if this went wrong sent anxiety spinning up in my stomach.

"How long till sunrise, do you think?" Clay asked while we made our way into the cave again.

I glanced at Casimir. "Few hours," I said.

Casimir nodded. "Enough that most of us could get sleep, then, I imagine."

The others hesitated, a look passing between them all.

"What?" I asked.

"If this doesn't work..." Lars started, clearly uncomfortable.

The bees spun faster as I understood. If the spell went wrong... if the sun burned me...

This could be our last night together.

The thought was unbearable. "It'll work. You'll see. Byron's spell, your magic." I forced a confident smile. "I couldn't hope to be in better hands."

At their silence, I turned the smile on all of them. "Get rest, please. The gods only know how long you've actually been traveling or what could lie ahead once we reach Aneira. We all need to keep up our strength."

"Will you come rest with us, then, Princess?" Dex asked quietly.

My heart twisted strangely in my chest, aching and yet warmed by the sight of my powerful, commanding giant giving me such a gentle look.

"*When* this works," he continued, "you'll be traveling with us too. No more of this lying around all day."

I chuckled and nodded.

Curled in Dex's arms with the rest of my men around me, I never wanted the night to end. I wasn't sure how many of us slept. As the hours passed, every time I woke from a doze one of them would be there with a calming touch and a kind smile, softly urging me to go back to sleep.

It was perfect.

But I could feel the sunrise coming, like a feather brushing stronger and stronger across my skin.

"Not long now," Casimir whispered to me in the darkness.

Tucking my cheek tighter against Dex's chest, I smiled,

trying to look confident. The vampire lay on the other side of Dex, the smoky form of Ruhl nowhere to be seen.

My night vision traced silver across his face. "Can you feel the spell on you?" I whispered back.

He shook his head. In the short while leading up to sleep, he'd pulled the twins aside. Together, they'd tested out his theory that he could recreate Byron's spell.

I just prayed he was right.

The feather sensation on my skin grew stronger.

Casimir reached over, squeezing my hand gently. "It's going to be fine, Princess. You'll see. Your scholar's spell will work, as will mine."

I nodded, hanging onto the words.

At the entrance to the cave, Ozias rose to his feet. His eyes landed on me for a moment, but I couldn't hope to read his expression.

He crossed to the others and nudged Clay with his boot. "Wake up. Now."

"Gods, man," Clay griped. "I'm up, I'm up."

Ozias walked back to the cave entrance while all around me, the other men stirred. Dex kissed my cheek while Niko murmured good morning to me and smiled. Combing my fingers through my tangled hair, I sat up, watching as they rekindled the fire at the center of the cave and got out food for breakfast.

Shivers rolled over my skin.

"Come on, Princess," Casimir said. He drew me to my feet. In the corner of the cave, green eyes flared to life. The shadows swirled into smoke, transforming a moment later into Ruhl.

I gave the wolf a nervous smile, grateful that he'd be here.

Praying he'd be able to act in time if anything went awry.

Casimir and I walked to the cave entrance. Behind us, the others stilled.

"How long?" Dex asked.

"Minutes," Casimir replied.

I exhaled slowly, glancing at where Ozias leaned on the edge of the cave opening, his arms crossed and no expression discernible beneath the thick mass of his beard.

Beyond the treetops, the dark sky began to take on a blue hue.

"Take her hand, scholar," Casimir said, wrapping his fingers around mine. "In case more magic is needed to intervene."

Coming up beside me, Byron grasped my hand. I swallowed hard and kept myself from looking at him.

The sky grew brighter, gaining a hint of pale gold, purple, and pink.

Light pierced the forest.

I tensed, fighting not to crush Byron's hand with my grip.

And then the glow of sunrise touched my skin.

Tingling coursed through my body, cold and yet hot in the strangest way. A gold shimmer ghosted over me, shimmering wherever the sun touched like I had gold dust in my skin. My breath caught and my teeth clenched against the fear that at any second, my body would burst into flames. From the corner of my eye, I threw a terrified look at Casimir out of fear he'd be burning too.

His fingers tightened on mine, but his face was solemn. "Breathe, Princess."

I struggled to do what he said as the tingling all over my

body grew stronger, turning painful. A panicked noise left me. "It hurts."

"Breathe," was all he said.

A short gasp of air entered my lungs, followed by another. And suddenly, the pain began to fade, taking the golden shimmer with it.

Leaving only me.

In sunlight.

Alive.

My mouth moved, but for a moment, my shock was so great, I couldn't make another sound.

"It worked," Byron murmured.

I spun toward him, grinning, and the relief on his face was so strong, I wanted nothing more than to throw my arms around him.

But then discomfort flashed across his face. Nodding to me, he took a step back, releasing my hand.

Disappointment flickered through me, but I struggled to set it aside. I wouldn't push him, no matter how much I wished something more could happen. "Thank you," I said instead. "Truly."

"Always," he replied.

I smiled, turning as the others came up to me, hugging me and grinning their relief. Ignoring us, Byron returned to his bag, clearly interested in getting ready to go.

"Thank you," I told Clay and Lars. "I..." A laugh escaped me. "I don't even know what else to say."

"Nothing needed, baby," Clay said, squeezing my hand.

"We're just so glad it worked," Lars agreed.

Niko and Dex nodded emphatically at the words.

I smiled, glancing over at Casimir while the others went

to gather their things. I reached out, putting my other hand into his. "And thank you for getting me through that."

Casimir mirrored my expression. "Of course. I never wish to see you in pain, Princess." He bent closer, his lips by my ear. "Not unless it's in fair trade for making you come."

My core tightened at his words, and my eyes darted around to see if any of the others had heard. No one was close enough anymore, and only Ozias was watching us, his face so expressionless, I could have more easily determined the thoughts of a stone.

But then, that likely had more to do with his general disinterest in me than any chance he could have heard Casimir's whisper.

Ozias looked away the moment my gaze came to rest on him.

"Ready?" Dex asked, coming up to us with no sign he'd heard a word Casimir said.

I nodded, my cheeks heating up, and I ducked my face away.

"Absolutely." Casimir gestured for the other man to lead the way, and as Dex walked onward, Casimir flashed me a grin with a hint of fangs.

My cheeks grew warmer. Avoiding everyone else's gaze, I followed as the others headed out.

29
MELISANDRE

Over the years, plenty of fools had called me a monster. I'd heard the word gasped or sobbed, screamed or whimpered.

It was nonsense. A term the weak applied to those they couldn't defeat.

But now, I wasn't certain what other word to use for the menagerie Alaric had unearthed.

An entourage followed us now. Beings with tentacles. Others with barbed tails. Still more with horns or scales... or both. They trailed after Alaric like the very army he claimed them to be, with more of them appearing behind us every few miles. Where they came from, I had no idea. The insufferable man wouldn't answer, and the creatures never spoke.

But I hadn't failed to notice how, as the monsters deferred to him, they did the same to me.

Not as much as to Alaric, obviously. None were coming within a dozen feet of him. But they kept their distance from me and skirted wider away when I happened to come close.

It was interesting.

Like the orcs, most of the monsters here had been lost to myths and fairytales over the past few centuries. Even the Jeweled Coven had only spoken of them as if there was an equal likelihood they'd never existed as that they had ever walked the earth.

Yet each of the creatures seemed to sense what I was.

And they feared me.

A smile pulled at my lips as we walked across the open field beneath the starry sky and the moonlight. The mountains were behind us now—a jagged force of stone and snow rising against the night sky at our backs—and Aneira lay only a few more miles ahead. The brittle grass crunched beneath the feet of the army of monsters, creating a susurrus like a rushing river bearing down toward the boundary of the nation that was mine, no matter what Gwyneira believed.

Though, that assumed she'd even survived after I was ripped away into the void. I still could feel nothing of her. Nothing of my other vampire creations either, though I scarcely cared if they lived. I could always make more.

But Gwyneira was witchblood. She'd managed to reclaim her will, thanks to those damned giants. And if any of them survived, I knew she'd be on her way back to Aneira as well.

I'd gut her before I let her take my throne.

"Your thoughts are tumultuous," Alaric commented.

My gaze snapped over to find him smirking at me.

"Perchance you're scheming to break yourself free of me?"

Typical man, assuming all my thoughts centered only on

him. "What are your plans for Aneira?" I asked rather than respond.

He chuckled. "Your vision is so limited, pet. One paltry nation is nothing compared to what I intend."

"Yet you tell me nothing of what that is."

His eyebrow rose as if my impertinence entertained him. "Perhaps I should show you instead."

He stopped walking, and all around us, the monsters did as well.

My teeth grated as my feet came to a halt too, stopping because he willed them to do so. But I would break free of this leash. I swore it.

Extending his hands toward the field before us, Alaric paused a moment as if for dramatic effect, a smirk still hovering around his lips.

I hated him more with every passing second.

A feeling of pure *wrongness* emanated from his outstretched palms, chilling with its intensity. My skin crawled at the sensation, as if everything in me that still could be considered living wanted to flee.

My body wouldn't move a muscle, and though a murmur of muted growls ran through the monsters around us, none of the creatures retreated either.

A tremor ran through the ground beneath us.

My attention snapped to the open field. At first, the earth only quivered, as if shivering against how Alaric reached toward it. But the sense of *wrongness* that emanated from his hands only grew stronger.

Pure panic gripped my throat like a vise. I didn't need to breathe, but right now, I *couldn't*. My heart stuttered in my chest, fluttering with fear like I was a trapped rabbit facing a wolf the size of the mountains themselves.

Fissures opened in the terrain ahead. Great black chasms that split the earth like knife slices cutting flesh.

From the wounds, darkness poured.

I clamped my lips shut against a cry. I wouldn't give this bastard the satisfaction of hearing me whimper in fear.

But the darkness was coming.

And it was alive.

Metal teeth flashed in twists of shadow. Tentacles whipped through the air, moving like savage eels. Glowing eyes glinted like a thousand sparks of multicolored flames. The vicious black smoke lunged at the monsters around us, spearing their chests and backs, driving into their bodies like lances. The creatures howled, thrashing against the assault, but the smoke didn't stop. Pouring into them, it made their bodies spasm and flail as it gushed from the cracks in the earth straight into the beasts' bodies.

The skin-crawling sensation grew stronger, sinking into me like sludge from a swamp. But the feeling that came on its heels was even worse.

Nothing. Just pure, unadulterated nothing, the likes of which made me want to recoil and run screaming in terror, except there was nowhere to go.

I knew this. I'd felt it, decades ago on that fateful night my sister witches and I reached into the void and summoned the beings who lived there.

The empty realms were here.

Even that small realization stabilized me, though. What had I to fear? I'd faced these creatures once and they made me a vampire. I'd faced them again and ended up tethered to this bastard Alaric.

This bastard with hints of strain showing on his face.

My gaze flashed over him, taking in every twitch, every

hint of a crinkle around his eyes and mouth, while inside myself, I felt for the connection between us. The tether had been latched onto me so tightly, it was hard at times to remember where I ended and it began.

But I was not his beast. I was not his ferry to carry him around this world, either. I'd slip free of this leash.

The link between us flinched as I focused harder on it, as if Alaric was straining even more than I knew. But it wasn't quite the uniform binding I'd believed. Not now.

Now it was woven of a thousand strands of darkness, like a braid of hair.

And some of those strands were on the verge of breaking.

Around us, more tentacles poured up from the gashes in the ground. I ignored them, more of my focus coming to bear on the bond between us. It was strange. Like magic but not, and if I just focused on it a *little* more...

On the field around us, the beasts stilled. The rumbles from the earth raced onward, the cracks tearing past the horizon and taking the roiling darkness with them.

And inside my chest, Alaric's hold tightened on me once more, every trace of weakness in it gone.

My teeth ground, but I willed myself to still. I wouldn't give him the satisfaction of seeing my frustration.

Except... he didn't seem to notice what I'd just done. His eyes were locked on the monsters, satisfaction radiating from him like the glow of a dark sun.

Had he truly missed how close I'd come to breaking his hold?

Wary, I followed his gaze, scanning the creatures all around. Wild eyes now glinted with a malicious light, hinting at the colors I'd seen in the twists of smoke before they dove into the monsters' flesh.

The Voidborn were inside those creatures now.

One of the orcs nearest to us made a hissing-click sound. Alaric grinned and responded in kind.

A whisper of meaning ghosted through my mind, like a thought I couldn't quite catch. A greeting. That's what the sound had been.

How could I know that?

Alaric turned to me, that damned smirk returning to his lips. What did he expect? That I would now cower in terror because he'd brought his fellow Voidborn out to possess monsters?

He hadn't possessed *me*. I was not his puppet, no matter what he called me or how he behaved.

Still, he gave no indication he'd noticed my attempted escape.

A thrill threatened to bubble up inside me, but I battened it down quickly. Coolly arching an eyebrow at him, I lifted my chin, giving him a disdainful look. "Am I meant to be impressed?"

Was that surprise that flashed through his gaze faster than a lightning bolt?

Arrogant bastard. He'd truly expected me to cower.

"You're scared, pet. I know it. It's hardly worth pretending otherwise."

I was nothing of the kind. Not fully.

He was struggling to read me, and he didn't know it.

It was hard to keep my exhilaration from my face. "What was this meant to prove? Is this your plan, to take over every creature here?"

His smile broadened. "Hardly. This is only to give us a better foothold for the next step."

"And that is?"

Around us, the creatures started moving again as if on some unspoken signal, walking as one toward where the Aneiran border lay beyond the horizon.

"You'll see."

Irritation boiled up in me at his non-answer.

"Come, pet."

On command, my feet followed when he began walking.

Rage seethed in me, but it was tempered by something else. A boiling feeling of its own, underneath the anger and apparently beyond where he could now see.

Hope.

Because next time he slipped up, next time he drew on his power, I would slip this leash.

And I'd erase him from existence.

30
GWYNEIRA

I'd never seen a more beautiful sunrise.

And I truly hadn't fathomed how much I missed the light.

No matter how long we walked, I couldn't stop smiling. Everything was beautiful. The trees. The creeks. Even the soggy riverbanks that caked the soles of my boots in mud. The puffs of our breaths on the air glistened in the sunlight, drifting up to the brilliant blue sky, and winter berries dotted the deep green trees with pinpricks of red.

There was *so* much color in the world, now that I could see with more than just the silver of my night vision. Relatively speaking, it had only been a short while since I'd been turned, yet every shade and hue felt like I hadn't seen it in an eternity.

Or maybe I'd only feared I'd never see it again.

I smiled as a sleek brown rabbit darted away into the underbrush, its white tail flashing before me for a moment and then gone. For the first time since we left the Jeweled Coven, I was starting to believe I truly could reclaim my life.

Gradually, the foliage grew thinner and the trees younger, with more slivers of sky visible between the branches overhead. The terrain flattened as we descended, until at long last, the forest fell away and revealed open fields, the grass yellow and chilled by the winter but free of snow.

And beyond the rolling grassland ahead, trails of smoke rose as if from chimneys.

"Well, there we go," Clay commented. "Civilization at last."

I bit my lip, trepidation suddenly swirling in me, stealing some of my joy. Yes, I could now stand in the sunlight. Yes, I had my giants to keep me stable and sane.

But I was still a vampire. Casimir was too, and the others were Erenlian.

My people were still unlikely to accept us.

"Do we head toward the village?" Niko asked.

Roan immediately began shaking his head, but it was Dex who said, "No, not unless we have to."

Relief stole some of my tension, though embarrassment followed on its heels. I needed to return to my people, and now I was grateful for the chance to avoid them?

Gods, how was I going to make this all work?

"Come on," Dex continued. "We'll circle wide of people for as long as we can. No sense letting anyone who might oppose the princess's return know she's here until we have to."

And then there was that.

The others started walking, forging a path through the dried yellow grass.

I didn't move. In the Wild Lands, the prospect of facing my people had been concerning, true. But now that I was here, on the verge of coming face to face with the reality of what they could do...

We weren't an army. We were nine misfits tied together by necessity and suffering and... me.

My eyes darted across the men ahead. Would Casimir want to stick around for a confrontation that was *decidedly* not his fight? Would Roan or Ozias stay to help when they could, at best, barely tolerate me? And what of the rest? Dex my fearless soldier. Brilliant Byron, gentle Niko, playful Clay, and steadfast Lars.

My hand pressed to my chest where the diamond pendant Rufinia had given me rested. I wasn't a witch. But I could still get these good men killed, and for what? A magical ley line situation I didn't have the *least* idea how to resolve and a throne I wasn't sure I could reclaim?

But if it freed the Erenlian people...

Fear ached in my gut. So many lives hung in the balance, and so many things had to go right in order for them to be saved.

"Princess."

I flinched. Ozias still stood to my left, lingering beneath the shade of one of the last trees by the field as if he was reluctant about returning to civilization too.

Discomfort made me smooth my coat, if only to avoid his gaze. "Yes?"

His eyes slid to where the others had paused several yards ahead and then returned to me. "You're not moving."

He was so blunt.

"Yes, well..." I took a step forward—and away from him. "I was simply thinking for a moment."

"Could I... That is..."

I glanced back at him, confused. "What?"

Again, he looked at the others and then back at me. In a low voice, I heard Dex tell them to keep going.

Like he was giving us space.

My confusion grew. "Ozias, what is it?"

He took a step toward me like he was forcing himself to move. "I made a mistake."

My gut twisted. Oh, gods, I hadn't been wrong. He'd realized what a mess this was, what it could cost him.

And he was going to leave.

"At the castle," he said like he was pulling the words from deep within himself. "And... before. This whole time. I assumed... things. And because of that, I said things I never—"

Beneath my feet, the ground quivered.

Ozias swore, his attention whipping to the west. For a heartbeat, he stared in horror at the mountains and the forest. "It's breaking."

I stared at him. "What's break—"

He lunged at me, but before he could reach me, the ground shook harder, sending us both staggering.

From the west, fissures ripped through the fields, cracking the earth open.

"What the fuck?" Clay cried.

"Run!" Dex yelled.

I scrambled to do just that, stumbling and shoving myself back to my feet as I tried to escape the cracks that were ripping across the countryside.

And gods, they were moving fast, zigzagging like a thing alive and racing through the ground like fissures cracking a shell of ice. The forest shook like each tree was a child's rattle, and avalanches of snow cascaded from the distant mountain peaks.

From the cracks, darkness rose. Billowing clouds of it, full of tentacles of shadow that whipped across the terrain, searching.

A herd of deer bolted from the forest.

They didn't make it twenty feet before the tentacles wrapped around them, and the animals screamed as their bodies turned to bone and ash.

"Princess!" Ozias raced at me, veering past cracks that were already sweeping toward us.

A fissure ripped through the ground directly beneath me. I gasped, trying to throw myself to the side away from it, but I wasn't fast enough.

Pure darkness rose from the opening, catching me in midair. It wrapped around me. Sank into me.

But I didn't die.

Color sapped from my hands, turning them white like the distant snow. My heart stopped with a suddenness that terrified me, but the fear was swiftly fleeing. Hunger rose in its place, savage and insatiable.

And different.

The darkness spread through me like it filled my veins. It whispered in my mind of empty places, *endless* places, and all the ways we could watch the world burn and die.

I hit the ground. Light flared in my mind from the pain of the impact.

And for a moment, I was myself again.

Casimir started toward me, moving as if to jump over the cracks.

"No!" I flung out a hand to stop him.

A thrum carried through my voice, same as it had when I first met the witches at the Jeweled Coven.

The power to command. A gift of the magic I could

suddenly feel burning inside me and in the diamond pendant on my chest alike, the power blazing like a dying star struggling against the endless night.

But the dark part of me was rising like a tide, and it could use that gift too.

To command the men to come to me.

To force them to let me feed until they died.

Casimir flinched back from my first command like he'd run into a wall, his eyes wide. "Princess..."

More darkness poured up between us in billowing clouds. Niko grabbed Casimir's arm, yanking him away from it while Dex shouted for the others to fall back and find some other way across.

Alone with me on this side of the widening fissures, Ozias stared at me.

Hunger surged higher inside me. My vision sharpened to the point it was painful, fastening on his every detail with such vivid relief it was overwhelming. His beard hiding his throat. His scarred face, and his unblinking eyes locked on me. I could hear his heart beating, the pace of someone preparing to attack or run.

My fangs punched out, and my fingers curled like claws. My eyes darted around, but we were sealed off by billows of darkness pouring up through the cracks. There was no way the others could reach him in time to stop me.

Flecks of light struggled to stay alive in my mind. If I attacked... I'd kill him.

I didn't care. I *couldn't* care, not when I was so hungry and all I needed to do was bite him.

But then he would be gone.

What did it matter? He cared nothing for me anyway.

Hell, he'd been about to leave. I didn't need him. I needed to feed.

Better him than one of the others, then.

The *delicious* others...

I stumbled back, conflicting signals reaching my brain as the earth stopped shaking. I didn't want to hurt Ozias.

I *desperately* wanted this.

Ozias started towards me. "Gwyneira..."

Had he ever spoken my name before? Shivers rushed over me to hear it on his tongue.

Would he moan it as he died?

He took another step closer. "Mate."

My brow twitched down in confusion.

Longing tinged his eyes. "Treluria."

Shock shot through me, bringing everything to a halt. Was this a trick? Why would he call me treluria? He didn't feel that way about me.

He pulled his sleeve up, baring his arm. His eyes burned into mine. "Take what you need."

My head shook and I choked on a cry. Didn't he understand? I couldn't do that. The others couldn't reach us to help him. The darkness was so thick, it was like we were the only two people in the world.

And I was losing this battle. Already, I could imagine the taste of his blood on my tongue, the memory so fresh given that he had offered it to me willingly when I'd first woken from being turned.

But this wasn't like that time.

This time, I would end him. This time, I would betray the impossible concern in his eyes and become exactly the monster that my stepmother had always intended me to be.

Terror battled against my hunger, and as Ozias took another step closer, terror won.

I whirled and fled into the dark forest, leaving all my men behind.

❄

Want to know what happens next for Gwyneira and all her men? Read the third book of the series: **Of Fate So Dark!**

TITLES BY SIERRA ROWAN

The Vampire Rebellion Series

Blood Pawn

Blood Captive

Blood Rebel

Blood Queen

Forever After: Crimson Snow

Of Snow So White

Of Blood So Red

Of Fate So Dark

Of Nine So Bold

ABOUT THE AUTHOR

Sierra Rowan is the USA Today bestselling author of action-packed reverse harem paranormal romance and urban fantasy novels. Sierra loves to write stories filled with steam, heart, and adventure where a happily-ever-after is guaranteed, even if it takes a few magical battles and wild escapes to get there.

Get updates about all of Sierra Rowan's books at sierrarowan.com.

- amazon.com/author/sierrarowan
- bookbub.com/authors/sierra-rowan
- goodreads.com/sierrarowan
- facebook.com/authorsierrarowan
- instagram.com/authorsierrarowan
- tiktok.com/@sierrarowanbooks
- x.com/SierraRowanBook

Made in the USA
Middletown, DE
04 March 2024

50816734R00184